I0621743

RICHARD STONE

the burn

First published in Great Britain in 2021

All characters and events in this publication, other than those clearly in the public domain, are fictitious and any resemblance to real persons, living or dead, is purely coincidental.

Design, typesetting and publishing by UK Book Publishing
www.ukbookpublishing.com
ISBN: 978-1-914195-49-5

PART ONE: PERUVIAN PORTENTS

CHAPTER ONE

Alex Morales got down from the minibus and stretched his limbs. Hours of bumping over dirt roads had left him stiff and weary. The mountains to the west were closer now, tree-clad slopes visible. To his left the land dropped away in fissures, with rows of spindly green bushes running down the slopes in cultivated lines. A track led through the bushes towards a pair of thatched huts.

Two peasant farmers, dressed in faded cotton work clothes and straw hats, stood twenty yards down the track, motionless, guarding their patch of land like scarecrows. Alex glanced back at the bus. Most of his escort team, which included an armed soldier, a doctor, and two officials from Lima, were still inside it, dozing or fiddling with paperwork. Marco, the local student who functioned as an interpreter between Quechua and Spanish, was already on his way down the track.

Bueno, Alex thought, shaking off his fatigue and setting off in pursuit; maybe he could get this one done without the guys from Lima messing it up. He stopped a pace short of the group and smiled at the farmers. Marco was giving them his spiel in Quechua. Their expressions, as they listened to Marco, remained detached, skeptical, but at last one of them turned towards Alex.

"*Vámonos*," he said, and led the way down the path.

When they arrived at the first of the carefully-tended bushes, Alex squatted down and examined the recent growth. *Erythroxylum coca* had become very familiar to him in the last couple of days. He detached a leaf, which was small and oval, and split it cleanly between his thumb and fingers; the sign, he had learned, of a healthy crop ready for harvesting.

He moved on to where Marco and the farmers had regrouped. "Ask them if they've noticed anything wrong with these trees," he said to Marco in Spanish.

"No," Marco said after a moment. "They've inspected a lot of trees, but they haven't found anything unusual in the way of insects or fungi. In fact, they're proud of their crop."

It was the answer he had come to expect. "And yet, when they chew it, they get this burning in the throat. *La Quemadura.*"

"*Sí, Sí, Sí,*" the farmers said, recognizing the word. "*La Quemadura.*" They held their throats and launched into explanations in Quechua. Marco summarized these, which included corroborating anecdotes from around the region.

Alex said to Marco, "Is there any difference between these new leaves and older stock?"

Marco put the question and reported: "They don't keep old stock. They sell what they produce."

Alex nodded. This was a plantation legally authorized by ENACO, the Peruvian government enterprise. ENACO claimed that their products, tea and toothpaste, had so far shown no sign of contamination: if true, this was one of the more interesting aspects of the puzzle. "How do they explain the fact that, when I chew coca from elsewhere, from the next valley even, I don't have any problem?"

When this was translated, both men looked at him with interest. Was this true?

"Yes," Alex said.

They looked doubtful. Obviously, they said through Marco, the

Americano was doing it wrong.

No, he'd used the approved method.

Would he try some of theirs?

It would be an honor.

One of the men went on down the path to a hut and came back carrying a bag of leaves and a small pouch. Alex smiled and bowed his head when some leaves were chosen from the bag. He put the leaves in his mouth and chewed gently and worked them around into a soft mass, conscious of the critical scrutiny of the farmers. They seemed satisfied with his efforts and the one with the pouch extracted some whitish powder and worked it into a ball. Alex put the ball in his mouth and began the difficult procedure of working the leaves around it and keeping the wad pressed against his gums or his cheek.

The farmers watched him even more closely now, as though some negative reaction must be imminent. In fact, the creeping numbness, the flavor of tea, as the *quinoa* released the active ingredients in the leaves, was not unpleasant; in a few minutes he would feel a mild, energizing buzz; but so far there was nothing that he could describe as toxic or disagreeable.

The farmers began talking to themselves in Quechua, their eyes constantly flickering in his direction. He had the feeling they would like to peer inside his mouth, make sure he had not employed some clever technique for keeping the ball of *quinoa* out of contact with the coca.

At last one of them took some leaves out of the bag and began the coca-chewing process for himself. Alex watched the expert contortions of his mouth as he tapped and softened the leaves with his teeth, added the *quinoa*, and maneuvered and shaped the plug. After a moment, Alex saw the frustration in his eyes, followed by anger. The farmer moved his head back as though trying to escape from something, then a spasm of pain tore across his face and he jerked forwards, spitting out the plug of leaves with a grunt of disgust.

Marco briefly put a hand on his arm. Both of the farmers seemed enraged, holding the bag of leaves up to the sky and showering curses on it.

Alex removed the leaves from his mouth and threw them aside and waited. In previous encounters, the peasants' innate suspicion of Americans, and also of the bureaucrats from Lima, had led to some difficult moments.

"Please say that I'm sorry I started this," Alex said to Marco, "but I'm very glad to see exactly what they're suffering. It helps me to understand the problem."

Marco took a while to make this point. The man who had taken the coca continued to cough and spit, but in the end neither of them seemed angry at Alex. They were raging at fate, at the system.

At last Alex risked another question. "Are they sure that here among their own community there are no others like me? People who don't get the burn?"

The two men took their time, talking between themselves. One finally spoke, staring directly at Alex.

"Yes," Marco said, "they've heard reports of one or two who seemed immune. But probably these people are like you, visitors or outsiders. People protected by different gods, different customs."

"So they still believe their coca has turned bad?"

Marco put the question and they both nodded.

"Then may I take samples?" Alex said.

"Of course."

Alex put on surgical gloves and extracted plastic bags from his pocket. He took leaves from several trees and one from the farmer's personal bag.

Marco gave them his usual pitch about the importance of blood samples, including Alex's offer of fifty dollars, American, to anyone volunteering. The coca-chewing farmer, his face still sour from pain, agreed to cooperate. Alex thanked him and waved at the soldier, one of his escort team, who had taken up a position on higher ground just above the minibus. The soldier sauntered down and knocked on the window of the bus. The officials began to appear at last. Ramon, the team doctor, trotted down the hill, clutching his medical bag.

Alex wrote out descriptions of the samples on his pad of labels, and a couple of minutes later there was another round of handshakes, and they were done.

***

In the evening, after supper at the family guesthouse where the team was lodged, Alex and Ramon held a clinic at the school and listened to more stories of the burn, translated by Marco. Afterwards, they walked through the empty streets to the bar Ramon had discovered to the south of the square. A full moon was shining from the west. In the square, the dark mass of the church was cast in shadow, the painted curbstones reduced to grey. It was quiet and cold. Alex had bought a thick pullover made from llama wool, and was wearing it on top of a heavy work shirt. The doctor, who was nearly a foot shorter than Alex, wore a quilted jacket with the collar turned up around his ears.

The *Bar Olímpico* was a place of utilitarian simplicity, except for some faded pictures of Peruvian football teams on the walls. An oil stove gave off a comfortable glow.

A couple of locals sat quietly at a table. The *dueño*, a thickset man wearing a cardigan striped in vivid colors, appeared from a door in the corner of the room. He half-raised an arm in a muted gesture of greeting and gestured at a table. Alex and Ramon sat down and Alex ordered a bottle of the best red wine. Ramon brightened up a little after he had taken the first sip.

"Are you married, Alex?"

Alex stiffened slightly. "Separated. And you?"

"I gave it a try. Twice, in fact. But I could never give my wife the attention she deserved." His expression turned quizzical. "Is it possible to be a good doctor, with a proper respect for your patients, and a bad husband?"

"Why not?"

"I hope so," Ramon continued, "because I think I'm a good doctor. And I was definitely a bad husband. I was born into the wrong class, Alex. The rich class. The entitled class. The arrogant class. Lima's finest, ha, ha. Even as a boy I despised them. But instead of escaping, pursuing my dream of equality, I took the easy way out, stayed with the life I knew. Married the people I knew. Result: disharmony; unhappiness; divorce."

Ramon paused. "And then there's this stuff." He raised his glass and looked fondly and sadly at the contents. "As a doctor, I should know better. But as a doctor, sometimes, I need it. More important, I like it. In the end I made a choice. I would be a good doctor, and I would drink when I felt like it, and I would discard the burden of making someone else unhappy."

As though to make the point, Ramon took a long draught of wine from his glass. Two men, dressed in bush coats and woolen hats, entered the bar and sat at a nearby table.

"So you're not a big user of coca tea," Alex said.

Ramon chuckled. "I'm afraid in my part of Lima no one is a big user of coca tea. Or coca toothpaste. Cocaine, of course, that's something else; but it's not my scene."

"So you're not aware of people getting the burn down in Lima?"

"I've never come across it."

"So what is it, Ramon? "Where's it coming from?"

The doctor took another sip of wine. "I have no good answers. Maybe it's one of those things that appears for a while and then disappears."

"That's unlikely, isn't it?"

Ramon gave him a probing look. "It's important to you, no?"

"It's important to a lot of people, surely. And to your country."

"I mean personally. It's important to you to find the answers, isn't that true? I can see it in your urgency, your impatience."

Alex tightened his hold on his wine glass. "Ramon, it isn't often a humble assistant professor like me gets a challenge like this, a challenge where the science is crucial, and where there's a lot riding on the solution. So yes, it's important to me. I want to make a success of it. The truth is..." He hesitated. "Back home in Rutgers, which is a great school, by the way, with a real orientation towards social issues, and it's a privilege to work there, but... it's easy to get bogged down in faculty politics. For me to be able to do something like this, back in the Hispanic world, well, it's exciting and liberating."

Ramon swirled the wine in his glass and nodded slowly. "I was idealistic once. I wanted to go and fight for your revolution, for the Sandinistas."

"So did I, even though I was just a little schoolboy in Managua. We thought that Ronald Reagan was the anti-Christ."

"Which he was, in a way. It was a good revolution."

"But you decided not to go?"

"It was a youthful dream. A romance. And I think I understood there was a problem."

"Which was?"

Ramon said with a hint of wistfulness, "I might be unlucky. I might get killed. There you are: on top of everything else, I was a coward."

One of the pair in woolen hats had got up and was standing by their table.

"Morales?" he said.

Alex looked up, mildly surprised. He nodded.

"You're the one who knows about the burn?" His Spanish was

halting but adequate.

"Yes. A little. That is, I'm collecting information."

He gestured at Ramon. "And this one?"

"Dr. Ramirez," Alex said. "A member of the study team."

"My boss wants you to come with us. He has some information for you."

Alex felt a sudden tension in the air. He glanced across at the *dueño*, who was busily polishing a glass.

"What kind of information?"

"People. People who suffer from this thing, the burn."

"And where is your boss?"

"Not far. About an hour."

Alex glanced at Ramon: he was hunched over his wine glass, a thin fatalistic smile on his face.

Alex turned back to the two men. "It sounds interesting. What about tomorrow? We have some time in the afternoon."

"No," the leader of the two said, "both of you should come now."

Alex turned again to Ramon. The half-smile was still there, and Alex was now able to interpret the look in his eyes. The truth was, they hadn't been paying attention. They were in a town which bordered on areas of cartel dominance. During the day, with a government escort, they were safe enough. But here in this bar, at this time of night, they were probably in territory where one or other of the drug producing and trafficking organizations would hold sway. Ramon was telling him, with his resigned and ironic expression, that these men beside their table were the law. Resistance was useless, and could only be counter-productive.

As though to emphasize the point, Ramon heaved himself to his feet. He picked up his medical bag and grabbed the wine bottle from the table. "Come on, Alex. It seems we have an emergency call."

CHAPTER TWO

Outside, the streets were deserted. The two in bush coats hustled Alex and Ramon into a six-seat pickup truck, Ramon in the back, and Alex in the front. The diesel engine fired at the first touch of the starter. They made noisy progress between the close-set buildings, and then emerged into the emptiness of the starlit altiplano.

Alex guessed they were heading south and east. The road got rougher. When there was a gap in the towering wall of the Andes, the moonlight showed dark masses of jungle foliage far below. They passed shacks, a couple with lights in the windows, and a rusty Coca-Cola sign picked out in the headlights of the truck. It seemed to Alex that a lot more than an hour had passed, but the driver gave no sign that they were approaching their destination.

Suddenly the driver stopped the truck and turned off the headlights. Alex thought he heard gunfire, angry pops in the distance. They proceeded slowly on down the road. He could see nothing. Then the truck skidded to a halt, there was the bang of something being thrown onto the floor of the truck at the back, a voice outside the truck shouting a few words. They drove on: the driver reached forward, and the headlights suddenly cut white tunnels into the gloom.

They passed a couple of makeshift barriers at the side of the road, and a parked jeep, and went over a low bridge. Alex stared at the shapes and shadows lingering threateningly at the roadside.

"What happened back there?" he said at last.

The driver took his time answering. "There was a checkpoint. We were being cautious."

A government checkpoint? Alex wondered. But that seemed unlikely. Down here, deep into coca cultivation territory, the checkpoints were probably manned by traffickers. For a moment, his thoughts ran wild: they were being abducted into a cartel stronghold; they would be interrogated, then killed; or trapped by gang-related violence. He watched the road obsessively, looking for the next sign of trouble, glancing occasionally at the driver. But the driver seemed calm, and their progress was now uneventful. At last he closed down his anxious thoughts. Half an hour later, he began to doze.

***

A change in the sound of the engine and the hum of the tires made him open his eyes. The headlights showed houses on both sides, some on two stories, and poles carrying wires. After a couple of minutes, the driver turned onto a track and drew up in front of two large buildings.

The driver said, "Morales. Come," and got out and started towards the second building. Light was visible from small high windows. Alex turned to look at Ramon: the doctor was just waking up and seemed dazed. Alex got out of the truck and followed the driver across the gravel. He could hear the hum of a generator. His night-adapted eyes could make out little except the outline of a patch of land, clear and flat beyond the buildings. An airstrip, he thought suddenly.

The driver had opened up a small door inset into a much larger pair of steel doors. They stepped through into a barn-like space. In front of them was a single-prop light aircraft, inspection lamps making it look like a museum object on display. Trucks and heavy equipment and bags of feed or chemicals on pallets loomed in the dark recesses.

The engine cowling of the aircraft had been removed and a man in a bush coat and green safety trousers was standing on a step ladder, working away with a wrench. When they reached the foot of the ladder he came down and stood squarely facing them, his eyes on Alex.

The bright inspection lights were behind and above him, so that his face was partly in shadow, but it was clear that he was a man in his fifties and a native of the region. Here that could mean ancestry stretching back to the Incas, and indeed the strong jaw and straight nose hinted at some trace of nobility. The eyes gleaming in their sockets were lively and intelligent.

His inspection of Alex complete, he picked up a cotton rag and wiped his hands, turning as he did so to the driver and asking a rapid series of questions in Quechua. It wasn't clear to Alex whether they were talking about him, the *Americano*, or about the incident at the checkpoint: but when he turned his steady gaze back on Alex, he seemed to be wondering whether Alex and his partner had been worth the trouble.

"So, you visit our land to look at coca," he barked suddenly. "Are you CIA? FBI? One of these agencies that thinks of us here in tiny Peru as a wild and lawless nuisance?" His Spanish was quick and fluent, and the tone was hectoring, provocative, rather than menacing, as though he wanted mainly to see how Alex responded.

"No," Alex said carefully. "I'm not that kind of person. I was born in Nicaragua and I do consultancy work in the Latin American region."

The man cocked his head as though this seemed to him unlikely or unwelcome. "The *Americanos* I can't trust because they want to uproot my crops and cut off my supplies and shoot down my aircraft. The Peruvians, *el Gobierno*, are worse. They hold out their hand for money and then betray me behind my back. Perhaps, as a Latino, you're more like them. Perhaps I have to be doubly cautious of a man like you."

Alex's heart was beating fast, but he held eye contact with the man and managed a faint smile. "*Señor*, I understand your feelings, but I'm not a government man of any kind. I'm a private citizen, an academic, a researcher. I'm interested in the phenomenon you call the burn, *la Quemadura*. We want to know about this in case it is an illegal attempt to poison your agriculture and your people."

"But here in Peru you are working with government: ENACO, the Ministry, the military..."

"As a foreigner, I can do nothing without government help."

The man stood frowning, pondering, for a moment, his breath misting in the cold air. He turned suddenly to the driver and spoke a few words. The driver set off across the concrete floor towards the inner reaches of the hangar.

"Do you know who I am?" he said, returning his sharp gaze to Alex.

Alex shrugged. "You are a man who has big responsibilities and who works on his aircraft in the middle of the night."

The man suddenly broke into a grin, revealing a gold tooth. "I am usually called Yupa. It is short for Yupanki."

"Which means?"

"It means honor. And it's important that you understand that I am, indeed, a man of honor. I can do nothing in this town without respect and honor."

"I'm glad to hear that. I'm called Alex, which is short for Alejandro. And I, too, like to believe that I am a man of honor."

"Then, if you are a man of honor, and if you accept my hospitality and guarantee of safety here in my territory, you will not betray me."

"Of course I will not betray you. In fact your identity, your business, your activities here, are not my concern. I only want to know about the burn."

"Remember Pizarro, my friend." His mouth cracked open in the same broad grin, but his eyes were cold. "He rode into these lands at a time of smallpox, pretending to be a god, and betrayed the hospitality of the emperor. You also come at a time of strange diseases."

Alex spread his hands. "Yupa, I'm not pretending to be something I'm not. And if my country has sent disease to this land, as part of some kind of attack on coca, then that's what I want to find out. I am a scientist trying to help, nothing else."

Yupa stared into his eyes for a moment and then nodded. "Go and get your friend. Sapaki is making coffee. We will talk about the burn."

***

A few minutes later they were seated at an old mahogany table in a room at the back of the hangar, drinking sweet thick coffee. Ramon had somehow recovered his laconic good humor.

Yupa, when he got going, was eloquent. He spoke about cocaine as 'our product'. From his tone of voice, it was as harmless as ENACO's coca toothpaste. He didn't use it himself, and had banned it within his family, but it brought wealth to the region.

When he described the arrival and impact of the burn, his sense of anger and injustice was palpable. What had he done to deserve this? Where had this disaster come from? It must surely be another of the plots concocted by the imperialists, the fanatics, the puritans, who, like the *conquistadores* themselves, had no regard for indigenous peoples, and whose countries were being consumed by crime and social degeneration. They had done something to coca, surely, poisoned it somehow, even though he'd found nothing wrong with recent coca harvests. This had to be a new, devious, move by the *Americanos*. But if the burn persisted, and showed up 'downstream', and was associated with 'our product', then his reputation would be ruined and his many dependents would suffer from the loss of their livelihood.

Alex asked him to describe cocaine users' symptoms. They were familiar: pain in the throat when 'our product' was snorted or smoked as crack. Even those who injected a solution of cocaine did not avoid the reaction in the throat, although the eyes, lungs, stomach might be affected as well, making the misery even greater.

"But the worst case," Yupa said, "was a boyfriend of my daughter. A friend of my son, Tico." He paused. "He died."

Alex looked at him sharply. "From the burn?"

"From our product. So his mother says. She was very clear about it. We killed her son."

"What did you say to her?"

"I told her that her son was one of those who didn't properly control his use of this thing, and that he must take responsibility." Yupa's face showed not only his contempt for weakness, but also a hint of contrition. "I told my daughter that she should have nothing to do with a man of this kind. And I believe she obeyed me. But anyway: he died. Imagine if this is going to happen often. Imagine the trouble in this community. Death we are used to. But this is a matter of trust."

Alex glanced at Ramon. The doctor was staring at the table with a faint, ambiguous smile, obviously intent on what Yupa was saying. He looked up suddenly.

"So you want us to talk to the mother?"

Yupa turned to look at him. "You are quick, my friend."

"You want us to convince her that the burn exists in other parts of Peru, and that her son's death is not your fault."

"Yes, that is what I want. And I would also like to know how this death happened, and whether we can prevent other people from dying. And what has been done to our coca."

Ramon looked at Alex. Alex hesitated, then suppressed his doubts. They needed as much information as they could get. He heard himself saying, "As well as the mother, we'd like to talk to a couple of other people who've experienced the burn, and take blood samples, and get samples of your coca."

Yupa stood up and extended his hand. "God go with you, *conquistadores*."

CHAPTER THREE

The afternoon flight from Lima to Miami was three-quarters full. After takeoff, Alex moved across to the window seat and tried to stretch out. Some of the tension accumulated in the preceding days began to ease. He looked out of the window as they climbed the Andean slopes and headed north across the *altiplano*. It was impossible to spot the villages and coca plantations which hc had visited: from here, as they gained height, one species of vegetation blended into another, at last turning brownish-red in the fitful sunlight; the place that had briefly dominated his life was as remote, suddenly, as Mars.

Alex turned his head away and closed his eyes, fatigue gathering. The aristocratic face of Yupanki, businessman and apologist for coca production, and the equally handsome faces of other members of his family, came into his mind. Those middle-of-the-night conversations seemed far away, scarcely real; but the death of the young man, from complications of the burn, had been poignant, undeniable. The mother's grief was painful to confront, and it had been hard to get the full story. She had acknowledged at last that her son had suffered from asthma, and that he saw coca, and cocaine, as a treatment for his condition, not as something that would exacerbate it. So apparently he had gone on taking the drug even when his breathing was badly affected.

If the burn ever shows up in places like the United States, Alex thought, similar outcomes will be likely; which was perhaps the most alarming information to come out of his visit.

He dozed off after half an hour. When he woke up he felt disoriented. He stretched and looked at his watch. An hour to go. An hour and he was back in America. He briefly recalled the circumstances of his life at home in New Brunswick, New Jersey, the collapse of his marriage, and found himself relieved that he was instead headed for Miami, where in spite of the occasional stiffness he felt in his relationship with his uncle, he would at least be able to concentrate. What he had to do now was clear the decks, emotionally, and find an explanation for this phenomenon in Peru. It was serious, significant, and interesting; and it might even represent a career opportunity.

* * *

When he got off the plane, he felt thick-headed and only half-awake. He showed his passport at the Immigration desk, stumbled through to the baggage carousels and picked up his suitcase, and moved on into Customs. He handed his form to a uniformed official, who studied it and then gave him a strange look.

"You're bringing in biological samples for research?"

"Yes."

"See the permit, please?"

Alex dug in his pocket for the document issued to him by the CDC. The official studied it.

"Passport?"

Alex handed it over. His sleepy mood was receding, giving way to irritation at the attitude of the official. Cool it, he told himself. This isn't because you're Hispanic. This is going to be fine.

"Follow me, okay? And bring your bags." The official held up his passport and permit as though he was directing traffic and headed off for a door at the side of the Customs area. Alex grabbed his suitcase and flight bag and followed him through the door. He was in a small holding area with stainless steel tables and several cubicles along the wall. The official with his passport spoke to another uniformed man and handed over his documents. The second official was friendlier than the first and made eye contact.

"Apologies for this, Mr. Morales, but we have reasonable suspicion that you may be attempting to bring in a contraband substance. I'm going to ask you to put your bags on the table and then pick a cubicle and strip down to your underwear."

"What?" Alex was taken aback. "Are you kidding?"

The official shrugged and turned away.

Alex angrily put his bags on the table and went over to a cubicle and pulled off his clothes. Another official, wearing rubber gloves, entered the cubicle and looked him up and down, without speaking, as though gauging his skin color or his body type. He turned to Alex's clothes and went through them item by item, paying particular attention to the soles of his shoes.

"Turn, please."

Alex turned his back on the guy, thinking that if he tried an invasive body search, he would probably hit him. But the official merely patted his genitals and buttocks in quick experienced motions, and then said, "Get dressed," as he went out of the door.

When Alex made his way back to the friendlier official, he found his belongings spread out on a table, and the official tapping at the keyboard of his laptop.

Alex watched for a moment, his heart rate climbing. "Doesn't this infringe my Fourth Amendment rights?"

"No," the man said, not looking up from the screen. "It's called the border search exception."

Alex waited another minute, grinding his teeth. “Can I repack my bags?”

“Okay. Leave out the samples.”

Alex slowly gathered up his things and put them back in his travel bag. His samples were in two sealed plastic boxes: one box containing about a dozen smaller bags of coca leaves, the other containing an insulated flask of blood samples. He had to wait another five minutes while the official explored the files on his laptop and wrote a couple of notes on a pad.

At last he pushed the laptop across the table, still open and running. “Put that away and follow me.”

Alex understood that he was being taken somewhere for another interview and he took his time shutting down his laptop and putting it in his attaché case. What the hell did they want to say to him now? Should he refuse? He sensed that the official still in possession of his passport and permit could delay matters indefinitely if he chose to do so. He gritted his teeth and followed.

Back in the baggage hall, he threaded his way around an Asian family with an improbably large collection of electronic apparatus spread around them and followed the official through a door marked ‘No Entry’. Inside was a narrow corridor with glass-paneled doors. The Customs official led him through an open doorway into a small office with a solid table, some chairs, and a young man sitting in front of an open laptop computer. The light came from a fluorescent tube on the ceiling.

The customs official handed his passport and permit and a slip of paper to the young man and gave Alex an ironic salute as he went out the door. The young man looked first at the slip of paper and then opened the passport absently and stared at it, waving vaguely at a chair. Alex put his luggage on the floor and sat down, keeping the sample bags in his left hand. He tried to hold his anger at bay and breathe steadily.

The young man was dressed in suit and tie. He was heavily built, his face broad and low-browed, but the blue eyes sharp.

"Alejandro Morales," he said, pronouncing the names badly. "Born in Managua."

Great, Alex thought. We're back to that stuff. Next it's something about me not being really American. "And you are?" he said.

The young man raised his eyes for a moment and seemed to think about that. "Dave Creasey," he said. "May I call you Alex?"

Alex shrugged.

Creasey studied his screen, taking his time.

"You're an assistant professor of molecular genetics at Rutgers?"

"If you say so."

Creasey gave him a sharp look. "I'm going easy on you, Alex. Don't make me change my mind."

Alex felt his anger leaking through the barriers that he'd carefully maintained through the years of casual discrimination. He stared back at the other man. "You know what, Dave? I don't care if you change your mind. Just get on with it. Tell me what I'm doing here."

"Hey, gutsy." Creasey got up and came around the table, still holding the passport. He loomed over Alex for a moment and then leaned back against the table. "Macho stuff. Are you usually this aggressive, Professor?"

Alex could feel a pulse beating in his temple. "No. I'm reacting to events. And I have the distinct impression that I'm being messed around."

"Let me tell you something, Alex, if you were getting messed around by me, you'd know about it, okay?" Creasey leaned forward and waved the passport at him, his expression intended to be threatening, but failing to contain real authority.

"Fine. Let's make some progress, shall we?" Alex kept his gaze on the other man, struggling to keep his temper from running away with him, afraid he had already gone too far, but to his surprise Creasey turned away suddenly and went back to his seat. He tapped at his keyboard, pretending to be completely absorbed by what he was seeing.

"So, you're Nicaraguan," he said without looking up. "When did you first come to the United States?"

"When I was eleven."

"Because?"

"My parents died. I had an uncle in Miami."

Creasey looked up. He had recovered his poise enough to attempt the tone of patronizing menace with which he had begun. "You were lucky, Alex, uh? Getting away from a civil war. Nicaragua was a dangerous place. Which side were your parents on?"

Alex hesitated. He didn't like to reveal that his father had been involved with the Contras. It had come as a shock to learn, after his death, of his father's secret allegiance. He said reluctantly, "I think my father may have supported the Contras."

"Good choice, Alex. That must have helped get you in to the US of A. Pity that you screwed up in high school."

"Excuse me?"

Creasey took his time. "It says here you were busted for possession of cocaine, age seventeen. That's a serious offence."

Alex pursed his lips. "I was a kid, for Christ's sake. And this was Miami."

"Are you still a user?"

"I was never a user. I experimented. Didn't you?"

"What were you doing in Peru?"

"I was on a consultancy assignment."

"For whom or for what?"

"Senator Robert Camilleri."

Alex watched Creasey closely and enjoyed the response: the other man flinched very slightly, turned his gaze to a corner of his desk, and pretended to think for a moment. When he looked up again, the alpha-male swagger had been dialed down to the concerned official doing his best.

"The Florida senator?"

"The same."

"Have you got some documentation?"

"I can give you a number for David Van Hoyle, his chief of staff."

"We don't do calls, Alex. It's up to you to prove you're bona fide."

"I guess the Senator figured my status and my permit would do that."

"What did the Senator ask you to investigate?"

"That's confidential."

Creasey picked up a ballpoint and began tapping it on the table. He looked irritated and unsettled, a young man out of his depth.

So, Alex thought, these guys hadn't picked up on him in Peru, or they would know he was working for a senator. But the Customs guy had seen from his laptop that he was investigating the burn, and had passed him on to Creasey for that reason.

"Bring that stuff over here," Creasey said. "Let's take a look at it."

Alex stood up and put the sample containers on the table. Creasey got to his feet and dug a couple of bags of coca leaves out of the box and held them out in front of him with a look of distaste.

"I just hope whatever you and the Senator are doing doesn't bring solace to the guys who grow this stuff."

Creasey dropped the bags on the table as though unhappy not to be throwing them in the trash. He waved at the containers. "Open up the other one."

Alex took the vacuum flask out of the cooler bag and unscrewed the top. A dozen capsules of blood were packed upright in blue-ice. Creasey stared at them for a moment and then waved them away. Alex screwed the flask shut and took the containers back to his chair and packed them away in his travel case.

"Can I go now?" he said.

Creasey had sat down and was trying once again to be cool and in command. "Alex, a small suggestion. You're a smart guy, a scientist. A geneticist. Big career in front of you. You have no operations background, right? You were never in the military."

"I'm sure you know that I wasn't."

"So, why get involved in this stuff? Your friend the Senator needs a report, so he brings you in, but frankly, it's unfair to you. You're out of your league. This is the drugs business, mean and nasty, people getting killed. A long way from critiquing student essays and growing cultures in a lab. You know what I'd do? I'd go back to Rutgers and get on with my life and leave this stuff to the crazy people who can't do without their regular fix of adrenaline."

Alex almost smiled at the irony of these words. Yes, that was what he ought to do. And maybe would do, some time or another; but it all depended, didn't it, on what kind of a life you had to get on with.

He nodded slowly and raised his eyes. "That's probably very good advice."

Creasey looked relieved. He jumped to his feet. "Grab your bags, Alex, I'll get you out of here."

CHAPTER FOUR

For the second time in ten minutes, Greg Halder sprang up from his high-backed leather chair and stared out of the window at the Washington traffic six floors down. He glanced at his watch. What were the odds against the Vice President arriving on time? Ten to one? Twenty to one? In fact, had the lazy bastard *ever* arrived when he was supposed to?

He sat down again and glanced at the thick report on his desk and then tilted his chair back and frowned at the door, older dissatisfactions surfacing. His office was grand, with Drug Interdiction Commission logos on the floor and the walls: but in the two years since the Vice President had secured his appointment as commissioner, he felt that he had not yet gained real control of the organization.

In the Navy, by comparison, it was simple: everyone jumped-to, followed orders. Even in the White House, during his time on the National Security Council, there had at least been a clear sense of purpose. But the DIC was a new agency, set up by the President at the beginning of his first term as a statement of intent, a means of skirting some of the tired old Drug War practices and prejudices. They'd achieved a few things, developed personnel around the country, many of whom Halder had met in his tours of the field offices, but a real sense of identity and mission had yet to emerge; and Halder wasn't sure he was going to find the mechanisms to create them. At times it seemed to him that the whole enterprise was nothing but a means by which the Vice President, appointed to the nominal office of Drug Czar by the President, could throw his weight around.

A phone on his desk buzzed. He sat down and picked it up.

"Your daughter's therapist," Margaret said, her voice disapproving.

He gritted his teeth. "Tell her I have an appointment with the Vice President."

"I think you should speak with her." The disapproval had deepened.

Halder gave an unhappy growl, just to make a point, but he had long ago ceased to argue with Margaret. She was one of the few people in the building whose loyalty was unquestioned.

"Put her on."

"Mr. Halder?" a woman's voice said.

"Thank you for calling again, Miss Cromwell, but my answer is still no."

"You understand that Kimberly herself is requesting that you visit her here at the clinic?"

"I do."

"You're not concerned about her mental health?"

Halder closed his eyes. An upwelling of anger and anguish flashed by like a fire truck on a freeway. He turned his mind away from it.

"Not really. This isn't the first time she's attempted suicide."

"I see. You don't think she's serious."

"Maybe, maybe not. But it's her decision. Look, Miss Cromwell, if Kimberly gets off the booze, once and for all, six months clean and sober, AA certified or whatever you call it, I'll talk with her. I'll even join in the therapy. Until then, there's nothing I can do. There's nothing anyone can do. Okay?"

Halder ended the conversation and sat staring into space. Oh boy, the joys of life in a family of alcoholics and substance abusers.

Margaret buzzed and told him that the Vice President had arrived. He got up after a moment and threaded his way around the soft furniture and opened the door of the office. The Vice President was leading a small procession along the corridor, trying as usual to look even taller than his God-given six foot two.

Halder waved him inside and nodded at the Secret Service detail and shut the door. His guest was handsome in a thin-lipped, aristocratic kind of way, with a full head of silvery hair. Jack Pendleton was from a long lineage of East Coast money whose record of public office was so stellar that being Vice President ranked as an under-achievement.

"What can I get you, Mr. Vice President?"

"I don't suppose our funding for this place runs to a decent bottle of scotch?"

Halder turned and opened the drinks cupboard, suppressing a smile. It was a typical Jack Pendleton remark. He picked up a bottle and pretended to read the label. "I guess 'Distilled in China' is not the kind of endorsement you're looking for."

"Jesus, Greg, come on. My advice would be to pour that down the sink."

"I can offer you Jack Daniels."

"Bourbon."

Actually no, Mr. Vice President, Jack Daniels is a Tennessee whiskey, but who am I to tell you that? He made do with an ambiguous nod.

Pendleton said okay in a tone of resignation and settled himself on a couch. "I take it that in your drinking days, Greg, you were not what you might call selective."

"I could tell the difference between gin and aftershave. Well, maybe not always. Ice? Water?"

"No, thank you."

Halder picked up the glass and handed it to the Vice President. "There you go, sir."

Pendleton took a sip and drew his lips back in distaste. "So, Greg, what do we need to discuss?"

"It seems that Senator Bob Camilleri sent some guy, a Rutgers professor, down to Peru to do some research."

"Did he, by God." Pendleton fixed Halder with a baleful stare. "Because of the burn?"

"We're not sure, but he brought back a bunch of samples for analysis."

"Which will tell him what?"

Halder pretended to give that careful thought. "If he's lucky he may find out something about the mechanism driving this thing, maybe stuff we don't know ourselves. But we think that's unlikely. He was only in Peru a few days."

"So the question is, assuming this guy at least confirms the phenomenon to Bob, what is Bob going to do about it?"

"Exactly so, Mr. Vice President. As you said a while ago, we don't want the health agencies like SAMHSA and CDC getting into the act just yet."

"Indeed we don't. And we must take steps to prevent that happening."

"So what do we do?"

"Bob is the chairman of the senate subcommittee monitoring drug war issues. That means his views will be on record. I'll get someone working on that. I suggest you have a word with the FBI. Just in case there's anything in his background we ought to know about."

Halder looked sharply at the other man. "Really? You think the Senator..."

"There's always something, Greg. Meanwhile you'd better keep an eye on this researcher."

CHAPTER FIVE

An American flag was flying from a tall pole in front of Senator Camilleri's waterfront home in Key Biscayne when Alex drove into the parking circle. A cop took him down a path beside the home and introduced him to David Van Hoyle, the Senator's chief of staff. Van Hoyle took him past the Senator's large, crescent-shaped pool, where an assortment of visitors were relaxing, and into the cool of a small staff building. Four other staff members were working at computer screens. Beyond was a small conference room with strip blinds shielding the windows.

"The Senator's running late, Alex." His mouth turned down at the corners. "What else is new? Can I get you some coffee?"

"Coffee would be great."

Alex settled himself at the conference table, charged-up and nervous. His uncle had known the Senator a long time, mostly as an occasional fund-raiser. Alex remembered meeting him a few times when he was growing up; he had even played baseball with the Senator's twin sons. He thought of him as a kind and paternal figure, but working for him was a new departure, and he wanted to make a good impression.

The Senator's arrival in the building was greeted with the sound of conversation and laughter from the adjoining office. Alex stood up. After a moment, the Senator came into the conference room and grabbed Alex's hand in a firm shake. His appearance was defiantly commonplace: baseball cap, once-boyish face sagging into heavy lines around the mouth, gut protruding over the out-of-fashion floral shorts. He asked after Alex's uncle, and for a few moments they chatted about family developments.

David Van Hoyle came in and sat at the end of the table, notebook open. Alex gave his presentation. Camilleri showed every sign of listening intently. When he described his treatment at the airport, the Senator looked surprised. "I don't understand what that was about." He turned to Van Hoyle. "Can we get this Dave Creasey checked out?"

"I'll get someone on it."

The Senator gave Alex a rueful look. "So he wants you to go back to Rutgers. Abandon your friend the Senator and get on with your life. What do you think about that?" Before Alex could reply, he went on, "Seriously, if you have any doubts about carrying on, just tell me. We can get a lab to analyze the samples and you're out of it."

"I'd like to finish the job, Senator. It's a fascinating and potentially serious phenomenon. As for the stuff at the airport..." He shrugged. It still irritated him to think about it, but he knew he should keep it in proportion. "Probably they were just reacting to the fact that I'm Hispanic, coming back from cartel territory with prohibited substances."

"That's my boy." The Senator reached across and gave Alex a light punch on the arm. "But I want you to tell me if things get out of hand. Okay..." Camilleri stood up and turned restlessly and grasped the maple-wood chair-back in both hands. The jowls of his face settled into heavy lines. "Let's go back over a couple of points. This disease, condition, syndrome, you describe... The pain in the throat... Are you saying that coca itself is not the likely cause?"

"Coca, either chewed or as cocaine, is clearly a necessary element. But coca doesn't seem to be sufficient in itself. Like I told you, Senator, I tried chewing it myself and got nothing. Of course there is a possibility that you need extended exposure to develop the allergic-type reaction."

Camilleri straightened up and did a slow turn, snapping the fingers of one hand. "The locals, of course, think their coca has been poisoned and they blame us. Is that right? They put it down to the ravages of defoliation, or some clever new bio-war agent."

"Yeah, I'm afraid so. And I guess there's a possibility that they're right, although the mechanism remains obscure."

"Let's hope you can prove otherwise, because if it turns out we're looking at some kind of hidden USG operation, I'm going to have some explaining to do to the Latino friends of mine who help me win elections."

"I'll do my best to find the cause, Senator."

"I appreciate that. Anyway, great job, Alex. Talk to David about your ongoing lab expenses. We'll look forward to the full report and then we'll see where we go from there." The Senator raised his head, and the folds of his face seemed to re-arrange themselves in mischievous lines. "Come on, I'll introduce you to some of the girls."

Outside, as they walked towards the swim-suited figures, an aide appeared and spoke a few words to the Senator, who turned and said, "Wait here, Alex, I'll be right back," and bustled off around the pool and into the main house.

Alex shrugged and sat down on the edge of a recliner. After a few minutes he noticed the Senator waving at him from the back porch of the house. He got up and and made his way over.

"Alex, you remember the Linda Pendleton story?"

"You're talking about the Vice President's daughter?"

"The same."

Alex thought for a moment. "She disappeared?"

"Right. There were various theories, of course, including suicide, but the insider opinion was that she hated her father and everything he stood for, and just opted out of the Washington scene, college, the whole deal."

"And you've found her?" Alex said.

Camilleri looked at him. "Linda? Oh no. But the cops keep me in touch with this stuff, given my nominal friendship with the father, and they've turned up a hooker who might know where she is. Apparently this kid had some information about where Linda was living, or had been living, and she used it to parlay her way out of some kind of racketeering charge. That didn't yield anything really useful, the trail had gone cold, but the cops thought it might be worth my while talking with her. Pretty girl, Hispanic, and if you don't mind joining in, well, who knows, it might help. How's your good cop, bad cop, routine?"

"Rusty."

Camilleri laughed. "Of course, returning to our own particular concerns, the fact that Linda is probably a cocaine addict, and Jack is the President's drug czar, shouldn't escape our attention. Who says politics isn't a dirty business?"

The Senator trotted down the steps of the porch and disappeared up the side of the house. Alex watched him go, thinking about Jack Pendleton and his reputation among his Rutgers colleagues, who rated him as one of the most hawkish drug czars in recent history. Turning up a daughter who was a cocaine addict would not be a good career move.

The Senator returned a moment later, followed by a girl of below medium height with dark, tangled hair. Alex stood up. They crossed to a table with a with a sun umbrella not far from the pool. A uniformed cop was hovering in the shade of the house. The girl wasn't what Alex was expecting. She was wearing a faded tee shirt and jeans and her face was without make-up. Her skin, despite some racial coloring, looked pale and flat.

Instead of introducing her, the Senator dropped her almost roughly in a chair, and went around the table and sat down opposite her.

Alex took a seat discreetly, but the Senator didn't glance at him. He was staring at the girl with something like distaste. "Can you believe this kid?" he said without taking his eyes off her. "What, twenty-five, twenty-six years of age, not stupid, looks like she came right out of a TV commercial, and–you see the nose? How much coke do you do in a day, Faymi?"

"Can you believe this guy?" she said, staring straight back at him. "Fifty, sixty, seventy years old, centuries in the United States Senate, looks like he came straight out of–" she tilted her head a little to show her contempt for his flowery shorts and shirt–"an old Chevy Chase movie... What the hell are you insulting me for?"

Senator Camilleri went on staring and then threw back his head and guffawed.

"You see the nose?" Faymi mimicked. "How many whisky sours do you do in a day, Senator?"

"This is Alex Morales," Camilleri said, "he's a whiz-kid scientist and professor. If you tell any lies he'll see your brain cells changing color... The ones that are still working."

She gave Alex a glance and then a slightly longer second look. Her eyes were compelling, large and very dark. Her expression didn't change as she looked at him. She was sizing him up, not offering her acquaintance. After a moment she switched her gaze to the Senator.

"You're holding out on us, Faymi," Camilleri said.

"No I'm not."

"Linda had moved on from the apartment you told us about. Probably a while ago."

Faymi shrugged.

"Nothing good is going to come out of giving the cops, and me, and the Vice President of the United States the runaround."

"I said what I know. It's up to you now."

The Senator leaned forward menacingly. "Listen up, Faymi. You probably heard of Guantanamo Bay, right? Torture and all that? Well I got something worse lined up for you. Something that only a man in my position can authorize."

"What's that, Senator?"

Camilleri held it for a beat, and then settled back. "An hour alone with my wife."

Faymi pressed her lips together and stared at the table. Alex couldn't tell whether she was expressing her disdain or trying to repress a giggle.

"Don't laugh," Camilleri said. "She'll have your parents over from Santo Domingo, the local priest herding you off to confession, she'll have you signed up for social programs and drug rehab and horticulture courses on weekends. For someone in your position, it's a fate worse than death."

"I'm not frightened, Senator. I already do weekend classes."

Camilleri sighed. "Alex, this is one tough cookie. I'm not sure she's going to crack."

"Faymi," Alex said slowly, "*Era simpática, esta Linda?* Did you like her?"

"Not really."

"Why not?"

Faymi paused, looking at Alex again with her appraising stare. "She was a rich bitch, basically. Mean as they come. Mind you, she was doing a lot of crack. That doesn't help." She dropped her gaze and began scratching at the surface of the table with a fingernail. "Not that I'm saying I knew her."

"Alex, can we take a walk for a moment?" The Senator was rising as he spoke. Alex got to his feet and followed. He noticed that David Van Hoyle, over by the chalet, was signaling to the Senator. "I'm in trouble on my schedule and I never learn. What's your feeling about this kid, one Hispanic to another? I'd say myself that she was lying, but does she know anything useful?"

"I don't know, Senator. It's possible." Alex hesitated, and then said, wondering where the idea had come from, "If you like I'll try and approach her on an informal basis. Even if she won't give up Linda right away, she could certainly give us a read on what's happening in the cocaine-using community."

"Great idea, Alex. Whatever it costs, meals, taxis, nightlife, put it on expenses. I'm in Washington for a few days, but I'm back soon. David'll find a time slot for you. We can talk some more."

The Senator pumped his hand warmly and gave him a pat on the back and headed off for the office beyond the pool. Alex stood for a moment, allowing a faint smile to linger on his face, then turned and headed back towards the girl. He was in time to see her disappear back into the house in the custody of the cop.

CHAPTER SIX

Alex's uncle still lived in the Coral Gables house he remembered from boyhood. It had high brick walls with red ceramic tiles on top and sliding wrought-iron gates. As a kid he would ride his bicycle up the drive and punch in the code and sneak in as soon as the gates had separated by a couple of feet. Then he had to wait and close the gates behind him, because his uncle had taught him that leaving the gates open was a serious and dangerous thing to do. It was the Somoza era and Miami was full of unreliable gossip about reprisals against Nicaraguan expatriates. His uncle kept a handgun locked in a hall drawer, and another one locked in his safe; and as soon as Alex was old enough, his uncle made sure that he was trained in their use. Alex found that exciting at the time, and he became a good shot, but the symbolic effect of guns in the home was to emphasize the absence of the love and care he had known in Managua.

Alex spent part of his day in his uncle's walled garden, under a sun umbrella by the pool, working with his laptop and making calls. Most days he also went in to the lab he'd been assigned at the Miller campus of the University of Miami.

Since leaving Peru, he had been mulling over his data and his experiences, trying to make sense of them. The most obvious anomaly was that he was unable to generate the burn for himself, in spite of apparently using the same materials and following the same rituals as the coca farmers who suffered from it. He had suggested to the Senator that prolonged exposure to the diseased or genetically damaged coca was required before the burn appeared, but he didn't find that a very compelling model. There would have been much more variability, people with mild cases of the burn, others more seriously affected, according to frequency and length of exposure: whereas, in reality, the burn seemed to be an either-or phenomenon; you got it or you didn't.

A disease model sounded more appropriate: bacterial, something lurking on the coca leaf, or viral. If it was bacterial, he should have ingested the bacterium in Peru, and he should get the disease. He could test for that by chewing coca every few days and checking whether he now got the burn. But looking at the patterns of spread, and thinking from first principles, he was inclined to think that a viral disease was more probable; and this would also explain why he hadn't experienced the burn. A virus could pass through a population quickly and leave nothing infectious behind; in which case he could simply have arrived in Peru too late to catch it. But a virus *could* leave organic changes behind, even genetic changes, and such secondary effects might conceivably be implicated in the burn phenomenon.

Finally there was the small possibility of bio-war attacks or defoliation chemicals inducing genetic changes in the coca crop, which was the explanation favored by the Peruvians themselves, and the one that most worried the Senator and his constituents. In theory, if that was the case, he should again have experienced the burn himself, but he decided he would have to be thorough and do the work anyway.

A few days into his routine, he got a call from David Van Hoyle, the Senator's chief of staff. After a few minutes talk about his research, Van Hoyle said:

"By the way, I did some checking and Dave Creasey, your friend at the airport, doesn't seem to exist."

"Is that right?"

"At any rate, nobody is willing to acknowledge him as their own. The Senator isn't too happy about that."

"So who warned me off?"

"In terms of agency, our best guess is the Drug Interdiction Commission. A kind of bastard offspring of the DEA. Jack Pendleton, the Vice President, seems to be fairly closely involved with it. He probably sees it as more malleable than the unruly parent. Anyway, we're going to do a little more pressing on that. The Senator has some DIC contacts. Meanwhile, we suggest you don't worry about it too much, but tell us if you notice anything suspicious."

Good advice, Alex thought as he ended the call, but not worrying about it too much might be easier said than done.

***

As Alex drove south towards the address which Faymi had given him, he found himself full of expectation and excitement, the memory of her tangled hair and the teasing, veiled light in her eyes drawing him on; while at the same time he was profoundly suspicious of these newly-conceived emotions. He'd met the girl once. She was a hooker. An Hispanic hooker, a strikingly attractive hooker, but still, a hooker. Okay, she might be useful, she might know where Linda Pendleton was, she would likely, as he'd told her on the phone, know some potentially interesting things about cocaine use in Miami, but she certainly wasn't a romantic prospect of any kind. She was a total contrast from his blonde and Waspish wife, of course, and that couldn't be bad. But a hooker. Jesus, come on.

She had also shown no interest at all in being friendly, getting acquainted, meeting him for a free dinner. He'd had to call her a few times just to get this vague meeting, of unspecified purpose, in a part of town which, he could see from the buildings he was passing, was running to seed. But still he felt the excitement creating tension throughout his body. Maybe it was because she had resisted, held herself back, not behaved in the least like a hooker. Or maybe it was because he sensed a strong and controlled personality under the surface, something to be admired. Or maybe it was because she gave him a fleeting sense of being a lost soul, something not a million miles away from the way he sometimes felt about himself.

He took a right turn and watched the street numbers. These were detached homes or little condo blocks on small lots with rusting autos and clothes-lines in the yards. He found the house he was looking for, the street number clearly written on the mailbox, which stood on a post in an overgrown neglected yard. Fir trees screened the yard on each side. The house had a long front porch faced in cedar shingles, some of which had fallen off, and a tar paper roof. A black man lounged on the porch.

Alex drove by and turned and drove by again and parked a little beyond the house. A few other cars were pulled up on the shoulder of the roadway, which had no curb or footpath. He waited until five past five, hoping for a sight of Faymi, and then got out of the car. The sky was split in two, with angry brown rain clouds to the east, lit garishly by the setting sun, and blue sky to the west. It was a sky he never saw in the north, a Miami sky: It was pouring with rain, probably, a mile or two east, and the rain might catch him here any moment.

"Does Faymi live here?" he asked the black guy on the porch.

"Faymi?"

"Eufemia."

"Never heared of no Faymi."

"I'm supposed to meet her here."

The black guy went on looking at him.

"You want to go inside? Going to cost you ten bucks."

"Ten bucks?"

"To you, my friend, eleven bucks." The black guy laughed a lot at his joke. "Pay the dude inside the door."

Alex looked around again, but the neighborhood was sleepy quiet. A couple of teenagers walked by, looking at him. He felt a burst of irritation with Faymi and himself, and opened the door.

The smell hit him first, and the furtive gloom, a feeling that he had abruptly penetrated some very private, and very far-advanced, party. He closed the door and fumbled in his pocket for some money, at the same time fighting an instinct to get the hell out as fast as he could. If this was where she wanted him to come he would see it through, and then eliminate her from his mind. He scarcely saw the man who took his money: the gloom was too deep, the alien atmosphere too overpowering. He stumbled onwards. Arched openings led to right and left. There was no color in the light that filtered weakly into the rooms around the drawn blinds. He sensed the grime beneath his feet, the damp discoloration of the walls, more by smell and touch. The reek of crack mixed with human oils and excretions seeped through the room like a noxious disease. Figures, dim, unsexed, undulated before his eyes, lying, moving, weaving past, wraith-like, inhuman, as though perceived through already intoxicated senses. He tried not to see the features, this was not Faymi, that was not Faymi, impossible...

Now a face was close upon him, thin, as colorless as the room, wisps of hair down across the eyes, a girl, he realized, young and old, but mostly young, much too young, pressing around him, against him: it took him a shocked moment to understand how definite and knowing was this pressure. He moved back. She followed, reaching with total and impersonal intimacy, so that he turned away in defense, seeing as he turned the desperate and unprivate clutchings of two figures in another corner of the gloom.

"Don't be afraid," the girl said, "I'll give you anything, just buy me a hit, I'll make you happy, any way you like it, just give me a hit, I *need* it, you see, I need it, but I'll make you happy, buy me a hit, sweetheart..."

"I'm looking for Faymi," he said helplessly.

"Don't worry, buy me a hit..."

He felt sick, fending her off, reaching in his pocket for another bill, thinking, I'm buying drugs for a school kid, instead of hauling her out of here by her hair and handing her over to... Who?

She had found the bill in his hand. "I'll be back, sweetie, but I need this hit so bad," and she had gone, through to some other room where cocaine base, he assumed, was being brewed and dried and powdered.

He knew he was on the verge of violent rage, of maybe breaking the place up, and he was frightened. They wouldn't like that, the owners of this business. Not now, he told himself, not like this. Don't think about that girl. Just get out of here.

Don't be late, or I won't wait for you, Faymi had said. Okay, here I am. He looked round defiantly, his eyes seeing more and more that disgusted him, gritted his teeth and turned to the other room and stared again into the fetid gloom. If she was here, it was better not to see her: he would feel ill for the rest of his life.

His fury bubbled up suddenly, and he turned, shaking, and made his way out of the house, not looking or thinking until he was in his car.

You bitch, he thought, you little bitch.

It began to rain suddenly, pounding hard on the roof. He lowered a window and smelled the clean tropical vapors. His phone rang. He dug it out of his pocket and looked at the number. He put the phone to his ear and said, "Faymi?"

"Yeah. It's me." Her voice was flat, giving nothing away.

"What the hell? Where are you?"

"Across the street."

He looked up sharply. The homes on the other side of the road were as Miami-ambiguous as the weather: neither wrecks nor happy suburban. A small cabin was wedged into a space between bigger homes.

"In the place with a palmetto behind?"

"Maybe."

"Maybe?" Alex felt his anger breaking through. "Faymi, for God's sake, what's going on? You gave me the address of a crack house."

"You said you were interested in cocaine."

"That doesn't mean I want to go into a crack house and have some pathetic kid hit me for money, to the point where I'm mad enough to..."

"To what? Break the place apart?"

"Do something stupid, anyway. Probably get myself beaten up."

Faymi said nothing.

"Faymi, for crying out loud, if you don't want to meet up, why not just say so? Why send me into a fucking crack house? For the record, I was looking forward to seeing you, but okay, you don't want that, so say so, I can take a no and get on with my life, but this... This is ridiculous."

Alex could feel himself trembling with anger. He cancelled the call, put the phone in his pocket, and started his car. As he drove away, he thought, Nice going. You've lost your temper with the girl the Senator wants you to cultivate, our only connection with Linda Pendleton, plus as first dates go, you scored a zero. No wonder you couldn't hang on to a marriage.

For a second he thought about turning back, but after a brief hesitation he shook his head firmly and drove on.

CHAPTER SEVEN

Faymi called him the next morning, as he worked in his uncle's courtyard.

"Are you still mad at me?"

"Faymi?"

"Yeah. It's me."

Her voice, as he remembered it from the previous day, was cool and flat, but there was the hint of an apologetic tone. In fact, the crack house visit had festered in his mind, and he hadn't entirely forgiven her, but he realized that calling him must have required a special effort, and he tried to banish any resentment from his voice when he replied.

"I was hoping to meet you. I guess I was kind of… you know…"

"I could do lunch. If you want."

"Really? Seriously?" She said nothing, so he added, "Where?"

"Dadeland food court. One o'clock."

"And you'll show up?"

"Yeah. I'll be there."

"Okay. I mean, sure."

She broke the connection and he put his phone away, thinking, Maybe I can salvage this, maybe I can still get something for the Senator. At the same time, as a faint echo of the previous day's excitement began gathering at the back of his mind, he told himself to be a little less trusting, this time around.

***

Dadeland Mall, where the Palmetto going south met U.S.1, covered a lot of real estate. Inside Alex followed the signs to the food court. It was busy and most of the booths and tables were occupied. It was a couple of minutes after one. He began wandering amongst the tables. He saw a girl who looked a little like Faymi, seated by herself at a table for two, but she didn't have the vibrancy he remembered, and she was immersed in a book. He circled again. He looked back once, from across the hall. The girl had raised her face for a moment. Suddenly he sensed a familiar symmetry in the features.

Faymi. No doubt at all: but he hesitated. She looked very remote. She was dressed simply in a white blouse, and her hair was brushed, but the beauty was muted. He remained suspended, uncertain, for another few seconds, wondering how great a force she represented. Is this what I really want? She's a hooker, and her behavior is unpredictable. He started a slow indecisive trek across the hall, as though being reeled in on a line, ending up beside her table. She raised her eyes.

"I was just going to quit on you," she said.

Quit then, he almost said. He sat down without speaking.

She looked down, put a hand defensively on her book: no rings, no bracelets, but a pretty hand, small, with a clear firm structure and lightly-tanned skin; well-kept nails, but no polish. He looked back at her face: it was closed, with no indication of feeling, but a flicker of her eyes, up and down again, showed him something surprising: she was nervous. In fact the whole cast of her body, slightly tensed, the hand braced on the book, indicated a primitive kind of fear.

Here was a girl, he thought, who met and bedded strange men almost every night of the week, and she was nervous of him. Perhaps, in a way, it was a compliment: she had lowered her guard enough to be nervous.

"Are you okay?" he said.

"Sure."

"What are you reading?"

"Nothing special." She pulled the book a little towards her.

"You're sure you're okay? You don't mind being here?"

"As long as you're not still mad at me."

"Why did you do that?"

She dropped her eyes. "I told you I didn't mean it to work like that. You looked so mad when you came out of there. And it started to rain. I was planning to meet you at some point, but..."

"Why did you give me that address in the first place?"

She shrugged.

"Tell me," he said.

"I wanted to see if you'd go in there."

"Why?"

"I didn't know how important it was..."

"For me? To find you?"

"I'm lying. I just thought you might like it in there. A lot of guys do."

Alex settled back in his chair. He thought he understood what she was saying, and it proved again how hard it was for her to do what she was doing: meet an ordinary guy in an ordinary way.

"What do you want to eat?" he said.

"I already ate."

He was taken aback for a moment. "Don't give me that. I've been watching you for... twenty minutes."

Her eyes flickered. "At home."

"Then eat again. If I don't see you eating, I can't ask you any questions."

"I'll have a cup of coffee and some frozen yoghurt. Peach."

He went around the stalls collecting a double cheeseburger for himself and the food for Faymi. He looked across at her once and saw she was reading her book again. He brought the food back to the table. He sat down and took a bite out of his cheeseburger. She poked at her yoghurt.

"Okay," she said. "Let's hear your questions."

"You've got to start eating first."

She dabbed at the yoghurt and put the spoon in her mouth with an elaborate gesture. "Okay. Talk."

"I told you I was in Peru last week... Maybe you know they use the coca leaf raw down there, they chew it in a sort of plug, mixed with lime... and what's happening is that they're getting a nasty reaction to it, like a burning pain in the throat, or the upper respiratory tract... They call it the burn. What I want to know is whether there's any sign of this kind of thing arriving here in Miami. Among cocaine users. It's probably too soon, but with all of the connections with Latin America, we figure Miami could be in the front line."

Faymi scratched at the surface of her book with her index finger. "I don't do coke myself, you know."

"Okay."

"But sure, I heard some stories. Mostly from the girl I share with, Paloma. She's into coke. She talks about bad product, stuff that really hurts when you snort it. She even had a friend who died."

"Died? Really? Was this recently?"

"Oh yeah, this girl's funeral was maybe a week ago. The bad product stuff not much longer, and maybe getting worse."

He turned his gaze away and thought hard. Could it be true? The burn had arrived in the United States? If so, there were all kinds of major implications. More suffering, more lives at risk. More pressure on him to figure out a mechanism. Maybe other scientists or agencies, the CDC, NIH, not to mention the DEA, getting into the act. His brain jumped from one thought to another.

"You could talk to her if you want," Faymi added.

He swung his gaze back on her. "You wouldn't mind? I'd certainly appreciate it."

She held his gaze for a moment. "You're married, right?"

He raised his eyebrows, then slumped back with a small sigh. "How did you know?"

"I get lots of practice."

"You mean... your guys?"

"I like to guess. Usually I'm right." She paused. "Me, I'm divorced."

"You were married?" he said stupidly. He realized he'd never thought about her life, as though being a hooker was all he needed to know.

She nodded. She picked up her coffee cup and sipped at it. Alex had a feeling that her mercurial personality was changing, that she was letting the tough-girl defensiveness subside. There was a hint of mischief in her eyes and she spoke quickly, as though going for a ride on memories of happier times.

"We had a really cool ceremony in church. Honeymoon in Niagara Falls. I became really house-proud. Polishing stuff that didn't deserve it. You know what I liked best about being married? Changing my name. Some feminist, me. I went around telling myself, gee, I'm Mrs. Eufemia Alonso Rodríguez de Soto. It seemed really really neat. I wrote notes and signed myself Mrs. Eufemia Alonso Rodriguez de Soto. When I took stuff in for dry-cleaning, I'd give my name, Mrs. Eufemia Alonso Rodríguez de Soto. I really felt grown-up."

"How old were you?"

She thought for a moment. "Eighteen."

"You were married at eighteen?"

"Sure. It didn't work, of course. I was divorced at twenty. Or twenty-one. Everything kind of faded away. It's funny, I can't even remember what he was like. I probably wouldn't know him if I ran him over in the street."

"Did you love him?"

She looked away, her expression vague. "Maybe. He was really nice looking." She took a sip of coffee. "What about you? Do you love your wife?"

He hesitated.

"Mrs. Alex Morales," she said. "I bet she's cool... maybe blonde... lots of education, really brainy... with one of those oval faces like the heroines in comic book romances..."

"She's blonde, yeah... maybe brainy isn't quite the word..." He shook his head emphatically. "But anyway, she's history, now. She left me for another guy."

"When?"

"A few months ago."

"And... you loved her, right?"

He dropped his gaze. "Yeah... Sort of. Yeah. Of course." He drew breath and blinked a couple of times. Then he looked across at Faymi. The change in her was now complete. Her raised face, eyes fixed on him, was open, innocent, no longer withdrawn. She looked as though she was deeply absorbed in what he was going to say, and as though she cared about the nature of his problem. He felt caught out, suddenly uncomfortable. The roles had been reversed: he was now the one with the problem, defending himself against damaging intrusions.

It was the moment, he realized soon afterwards, when he fell in love with her.

***

The Kendall apartment to which Alex was admitted a couple of days later was a spacious four-bed filled with soft furnishings, upholstered footstools, and deep cushioned wicker, plus the usual clutter a pair of successful career girls would accumulate. There was nothing, to his eye, suggestive of their trade.

Faymi let him in and took him into the living room. He found himself watching her intently, trying to gauge her mood. She had taken more trouble with her appearance than on their previous meeting: her blouse had an elegant blue motif, and her black hair was brushed smooth; but the openness had retreated behind a self-conscious hauteur.

"I made some punch," she said. "Or there's frozen yogurt. Or I could make coffee."

"Punch would be fine. Thank you."

"Paloma will be here in a moment," Faymi added, and then disappeared through an arch. He turned and stared out of the picture window. He had half forgotten that he was here to talk to Paloma about the burn, so focused was he on Faymi and the kind of reception she would give him. He shook his head in irritation and made an effort to switch gears. This was important. He needed all the information he could get.

Two girls soon entered the room. The one in front of Faymi was a flurry of movement, arms and hips swaying, her Indian-bright sarong swirling around her legs.

"Hi, real sorry, real sorry, Alex?" She came up close to him and reached out to shake his hand, her gaze intimate and direct. "Hi, I'm Paloma."

He briefly held the offered hand, which was warm and slightly moist. Paloma was taller than Faymi, attractive, but without the other girl's startling beauty. She pirouetted away, turned to examine him again, glanced at Faymi.

"So, Faym," she said, "you seriously telling me this guy isn't a client? Pro bono, if necessary? Jeez, come on, you waste your time on sleaze balls with pot bellies when you could be dancing the samba with this guy?" She waved her hand at him, a dozen metal bracelets sliding down her bronzed arm.

Faymi looked blank and said nothing.

"Anyway, Alex, did I mention that my name is Paloma? And that I'm a great fuck and tons of fun?" She was on the move again. "Welcome to our home, and don't listen to anything I say. Faym will tell you, I've got a big mouth. And just at the moment I really don't *feel* like I'm a lot of fun, so forgive me if I talk a lot of crap. You know how it is with coke, it should pick you up, but sometimes it goes mean on you and you just feel shitty. Sit down, Alex, Jeez, what are we doing, standing around, sit down and relax."

Faymi turned and went through the arch.

Alex sat down in a wicker armchair with bright yellow cushions. "Faymi says you know people who've been getting some kind of a bad reaction when they use cocaine."

Paloma kneeled on a leather-covered ottoman and then got up again. "Mostly it's what I'm hearing secondhand, someone gets hold of some bad product and has this horrible burning sensation at the back of the throat that gets them very mad and frustrated. Like, screaming at their dealer and demanding their money back. I can't tell you it's happening real often, maybe everyone's repeating the same old story, but we're all kind of nervous about it. Except a few super-controlled personalities like Faymi who don't even smoke cigarettes."

"I guess Faymi told you I've been investigating something similar in Peru?"

"Yeah, she said something."

"The peasants there chew coca leaves, and most of them are getting a pain in the throat which they call *la Quemadura*, the burn. Cocaine users get the same thing. If there's no connection with what you're talking about here in Miami, it's a hell of a coincidence."

"Yeah, I'll say. So is there something wrong with the coca crop?"

"That's a theory, but there's a problem. I didn't get the burn myself, and I tried chewing quite a lot of the Peruvian coca."

"So what is it?"

"Good question."

Faymi arrived with tall glasses on a tray. Paloma took hers and chose another ottoman to sit down on. She stared moodily at her fruit punch. "Your boyfriend's getting me spooked about this damn thing. I think he's telling me that it's going to get worse and lots of us are going to start getting wasted."

Faymi glanced at him, as though inviting his comment.

"It's possible," he said.

"So what do we do?"

Alex took the glass which Faymi offered and stared at Paloma. "I think you said you weren't feeling too good just at the moment?"

"Oh that. It's nothing. I'm okay. A touch of flu or something. Hey, don't get me going. I can dream up anything."

"This is a shot in the dark," he said slowly, "but there is a possibility that the burn is caused by a disease of some kind, probably a virus, which is nothing when you get it, a lot of people won't even notice it at the time, but which then leaves behind this sensitivity to cocaine."

"What, permanently?" Paloma's voice rose into a squawk.

"I don't know. But viruses can cause permanent changes, or they can hang around in a dormant state, like the herpes virus."

"Now you're really cheering me up. Jesus Christ, Alex, I hope you're going to tell me there's a cure for this thing."

"A vaccine would be possible in theory. And this is all pure guesswork at the moment. But when you said you're not feeling very well, I just thought it was possible that you're in the first phase of this thing."

Paloma stared at him. "Oh God, don't tell me. Look, I often don't feel good. Ask Faymi. I'm a real hypochondriac. I mean, it's just in my head, I imagine stuff."

He held her gaze for a moment. "So you don't have a fever, for example?"

"Oh shit, no. I don't think so. No!"

"Any symptoms at all to do with the nasal passages, the back of the throat?"

"Listen, ask me for something and I've got it." She moved her head back and forth, opened her mouth, sniffed a couple of times. "You see? Now I think it's a little bit scratchy, no pain or anything, but..." She opened her mouth again and swallowed. "No, it really isn't anything."

"Would you mind if I take a look?"

"Oh Jeez... I guess. Whatever turns you on."

He took out his phone and keyed the flashlight. Paloma let her head roll back and opened her legs suggestively. He moved close and directed the beam.

"Can you stick out your tongue?"

"I can stick anything out, sweetheart." She added some orgasmic sound effects as she did as he requested.

He picked out a faint roseate flush decorating the back of her throat. Surprised, he moved the beam backwards and forwards.

"More orgasms," he said.

Paloma obliged.

He stepped back and put his phone away.

"So, nothing, uh?" she said, pulling her knees delicately together with her hands.

He glanced at Faymi, who was watching them both with a look of total detachment.

"Paloma," he said, "I'm sorry, there's something there. Just a slight reddening at the back of the throat. Nothing to worry about, but I do think it could be significant."

Paloma rolled her eyes and sighed loudly. "Oh God, come on, you're kidding, you're not saying my head is going to explode every time I snort a line or two? I'm not good with these things. My doctor says that pain is bad for me. And what about Carmen? Did Faym tell you about Carmen?"

"The girl who died?"

"Right."

"Tell me more about how it happened."

"Her friend, the girl I know, says she was the sort of girl who panicked a lot. She was also heavily into coke. So my friend has the idea that when the burn came along, and she was getting these pains in the head instead of the hit she was expecting, she maybe started injecting instead. Would she still get the pain if she injected?"

"Very likely, yes."

"So then she panicked and just went totally crazy. She was alone, that was the trouble. Nobody really knows."

"The official cause of death was what? Cardiac arrest brought on by a cocaine overdose?"

"Yeah. That sounds right."

Alex thought about the mother of the dead boy he'd met in Peru. Addicts could behave in unpredictable ways, and occasionally, reacting even to mild trauma, that could be fatal.

"Paloma, listen, I need your help. If I could take a swab from you and maybe a dozen other girls experiencing the same kind of symptoms, I might be able to track this virus down."

"A dozen girls, uh?" Paloma said, struggling for a flirtatious tone, but sounding flat: "Gee, Alex, you're quite the guy."

"Will you do it? My guess is we need to move quickly, because this infectious stage might only last a few days."

Paloma drank some punch, her expression resigned. "Okay. For Carmen's sake, I'll see what I can do. Figure out your end and give me a call."

CHAPTER EIGHT

The Senator's home looked strangely deserted: no cars parked on the sweeping half circle of driveway, no aides to look after people, no buzz of activity from the direction of the pool. It was just after noon. Alex rang the bell. The Senator himself opened the wide carved door and pumped his hand and pulled him inside. Alex was aware of light from high cathedral windows. He followed the Senator through to a long kitchen-breakfast-room at the back with windows and French doors overlooking the pool. A woman of about the Senator's age, almost as casually dressed, with bright eyes and an amused expression, was stripping a lettuce at the sink. She peeled off a rubber glove and came forward to shake hands.

"Who says that politicians can't hang on to their marriages?" the Senator said. "This lady, believe it or not, is my wife. Twenty-six years in the Senate and I present to you with pride the first, the original, the only, Mrs. Camilleri. As an achievement, I rate that right up there with amending the constitution."

"His achievement, you notice," said Mrs. Camilleri, smiling without rancor, "not mine."

The Senator now had a paternal hand on Alex's shoulder. "What's my secret, Alex? You've got to pick 'em right to begin with, which means a little common or garden horse sense. After that, I found there's just two things you've got to pay attention to. Throw away that feminist garbage about doing the dishes and sitting down to rap sessions every evening. Just two things, Alex: change your socks regularly, and don't make fun of your mother-in-law."

The Senator began to laugh, and crossed to his wife and gave her a hug.

"I guess I ought to tell you, Alex," his wife said, turning to him, "that he makes fun of his mother-in-law all the time."

She poured coffee for them and he and the Senator took their coffee mugs through to the Senator's study and settled in deeply-upholstered leather armchairs, each at an angle to the Senator's massive desk. The photos on the walls seemed to contain every president and major political figure of the last quarter century. A pair of bronze Labradors guarded the picture window looking onto the front yard.

"There's something I need to ask you right away," Camilleri began. "Have you been followed? Anyone been asking questions at the lab?"

"There've been a couple of times when I've kind of wondered. Cars hanging in behind me. At the labs, one of the technicians is friendly, keeps an eye on what I need. But she doesn't really ask questions. Why, what's happened?"

The Senator studied him for a moment. "I think I've got to tell you about this, Alex, even though it may be unwelcome and upsetting for you. It may not even be true."

Alex felt the stirrings of disquiet. "Go ahead."

"This information came out of CIA files, apparently genuine, delivered anonymously to David at my Washington office. It's about your father. Again, let's keep an open mind on this. The allegation is that the light aircraft in which your father and mother died was not making a routine flight back to Managua, but was on its way to the United States with 120 kilos of cocaine on board."

Alex was too stunned to speak.

"And that it didn't come down by accident but was shot down by Sandinista government forces. It's not clear why your mother was on the flight, but it suggests to me that neither of them knew what was going to happen. They were lured across the border to Costa Rica by the Contra command and then given no option but to make a drug run."

Alex was back for an instant in his parents' home in Managua, running from room to room, window to window, waiting for news.

He pulled back from the memory and looked up. The Senator was watching him. "Even if this is true, Alex, you've got to remember that Reagan was in the White House and cowboys like Oliver North were devising increasingly crazy ways of getting round the Congressional ban on funding the Contras. One of those ways was to funnel back the proceeds of drug smuggling. How's that for a cynical betrayal of the drug war? I think it shows you where this kind of drug policy leads you in the end. Everybody gets corrupted. Anyway, you can't blame your father. If he flew that plane-load of cocaine, he did it to raise money for what he believed in."

Alex dropped his gaze and nodded, still not trusting himself to speak.

"The issue we've got to look at, Alex, is why this information was sent to me. I think we've got to see it as another effort to discredit you. Or maybe worse. I don't want to alarm you, but David thinks that with that drugs conviction you blundered into, which I don't care a damn about, by the way, but it's there in the record... David thinks that with both those things they might be able to attack your citizenship status."

"My American citizenship?" Alex said.

"Just a possibility."

"So they're sending us a message to back off. Stop the research."

"I'm worried that might be the case."

"*They* being the DIC, Pendleton, the drug war people."

"Yes. Probably."

"And the reason is simply that the burn will be useful in prosecuting the drug war."

"I'm afraid so."

Alex felt his muscles tighten. "Senator, I value my American citizenship, but if these guys want to take it away from me, I'll revert to Nicaraguan and go somewhere else in the world to pursue my career. It's not a big deal." As he spoke, he realized that he was making some big assumptions about his resilience and adaptability, but he didn't want the Senator to think that he was intimidated.

"So you want to carry on?"

"We're at a turning point. In fact I've set up the basics for a study that could really give us some answers."

"Tell me."

Alex leaned forward and began to talk.

***

Bent over at his lab desk, Alex stared at a series of images on the screen of his laptop. They were grey, slightly blurred, often difficult to interpret, but rich in meaning. He liked to bring them up just to confirm that they were real, and to look for details that he might previously have missed.

They were electron microscopy micrographs, digitized into computer files, one for each of his specimens. Every file contained a series of overlapping views, and there were eleven files altogether. He'd obtained the specimens in ones and twos, as and when he could link up with the girls whom Paloma had persuaded to participate. The procedure had never been straightforward: although the girls were motivated by stories of the burn, they tended to be skittish and to worry about their cocaine use getting back to the cops. Obtaining an informed consent signature was touch-and-go, and a couple of times he gave up, making do with a name and a phone number. He used a flocked swab for more efficient removal of biotic material, but a flocked swab at the back of the throat was ticklish and irritating, and the girl might gag and swear and generally complain. He used his best bedside manner and pacified them as far as he could; but when he finally put his swab into the tube of viral transport medium and shook it vigorously, it felt sometimes like he'd drawn blood from the proverbial stone.

Back at the lab he took half of the VTM and froze it, and used the remainder to prepare an electron microscope slide.

Gradually, he became excited. A round shape–in fact, he knew, icosahedral–kept showing up: about a hundred and ten nanometers across, with spiky extrusions. Not only was it clearly a virus, it was, he suspected, a new virus. He spent hours examining library pictures of viruses, and although many of them were icosahedral, none of them was an exact match.

Paloma quit when he'd done eleven, telling him that he was the lousiest customer she'd ever procured for: eleven girls and nothing! Not a single dollar changing hands! In any case, it seemed that the infection in her particular community was dying out and moving on. Most of the women he took specimens from showed signs of the roseate flush at the back of the throat, but the last couple were the weakest of the set. Two weeks had gone by since he had taken the first specimen from Paloma, and he figured that at least that long would be needed to develop antibodies and secondary symptoms like the burn.

His phone's ringtone sounded. He took it out and glanced at the screen and put it to his ear.

"Faymi?"

"Yeah. You busy?" Her voice had largely gone back to the colorless, formal, tone he remembered from their first conversations.

"No, I'm okay."

"It's Paloma."

"What about her?"

"She's... you know... not too good. This coke thing."

"The burn? You mean she's getting the burn?"

"Yeah. I guess so."

He took the phone away from his ear and sat rigid, a dozen thoughts chasing through his mind. It was only one case, one instance, nothing like a statistically significant data point, but he felt no doubt: this was it, the thing had happened. More than elation, the emotion that gripped him was fear, deep in his gut.

"Faymi, sorry, I know we thought this could happen, but it's kind of a shock when it does. How bad is she?"

"She's complaining a lot, but... I don't know. It's kind of difficult to talk right now. She doesn't want me telling you this stuff. But I'm working on her. Maybe you can come by tomorrow and check her over."

"Yeah, sure. And you? Will you be there?

"Maybe. I don't know."

The coolness in her voice nearly made him blurt out something needy and stupid. He clamped down on his feelings and said, "Okay. I'll call you later."

He continued to sit rigid for a few moments, focusing on the news of Paloma, new thoughts developing, all of them based on that sudden certainty: Paloma's low-grade virus had led to the burn. He had to reexamine his habits, his preconceptions, and take account of a lot of things he had tried, until now, to suppress.

He glanced at his watch and jumped to his feet, looking around the cubicle to see what he needed to do. He put his laptop in his valise, checked the locks on his cabinets. On a sudden impulse, he went out into the lab, collected an insulated thermos container, filled it with dry ice, and returned to his cubicle. He put on gloves, opened his freezer, selected two specimen tubes, pushed them into the dry ice, closed the thermos, locked up the freezer. He put the thermos in his valise and stood thinking. After a few seconds, he put the gloves and the gown in the bin, and set off for the exit.

Five minutes later he was in a southbound Metrorail train, looking out at the plazas of downtown Miami. He got out his phone and brought up Dennis Carver's number. He'd spoken with Dennis a couple of times since going to Peru, but he hadn't said much about his work. Time, surely, to hear what Dennis had to say about his mysterious virus. But he hesitated before pressing dial. I'm getting paranoid, he thought. Then again, maybe I need to get paranoid. He put the phone back in his pocket.

At University station, he found a phone outlet and bought a cheap Nokia and fifty dollars of prepaid time. He got in his car and drove to his uncle's home and made his way to the umbrella by the pool. He got out his new phone, keyed in Dennis's number, and pressed dial.

Dennis's hello sounded mildly suspicious, which didn't surprise Alex: Dennis was protective of his privacy, and this was an unknown phone number.

He chose a formal and urgent tone of voice. "Are you in a secure location, Dr. Carver?"

"Alex?"

"Yeah. I'm using a throwaway phone, like they do in the spy movies. Seriously, are you somewhere you can talk?"

"About what? Plots to bring down the government? NSA can spot that kind of thing on *anyone's* phone."

"Okay. What about viruses? Can we talk about viruses?"

"You bought a throwaway phone to talk about viruses?"

"Yeah. One special virus, in fact. Which just might be responsible for the thing I was looking at in Peru."

"Are you serious?"

"Yes."

"And you think some interested party is hacking in to your regular phone?"

"Okay, I'm paranoid, but yes, it's possible."

There was a slight pause at the other end. "For the record, I'm at home waiting for the kids to get in from baseball practice. And nobody is hacking in to my phone. We don't do that kind of thing in Princeton."

"Of course not. Listen, if I sent you a micrograph of a specimen virus... icosahedral with spikes... could you tell me if it's something new and unknown?"

"No. I could tell you if it was unknown, recently, on the eastern seaboard of the United States, maybe, but unknown globally... No. I don't have a Chinese-type visual memory. Send me the base pair sequence."

"I thought you'd say that. I might get it done in two or three weeks."

"In two or three weeks, I'll be in Florida. We're bringing the kids down to Disney World, as long as Flo can get the time off. We should meet up."

"That'd be great."

"Keep me in touch, bro."

CHAPTER NINE

Alex got to the girls' apartment a few minutes after four. Paloma answered the buzzer and he made his way up to the tenth floor. He was relieved to see, when she opened the door, that she didn't look as haggard, resentful, or sick as Faymi's stories had led him to believe. Desperation was discernible deep in her eyes, but she was wearing the gaudy beads and bracelets he remembered, and she'd done an efficient job with her makeup.

She took hold of his arm and drew him into the living room. "Faymi had to go out, Alex, one of her regulars called, but whatever she told you about me isn't true. I'm fine, fine, enjoying life in my own crazy way, which means that whatever happens with cocaine, I don't give a fuck. I will rise above it. In other words, get high in some other way. Anyway, stay a while, Alex, have a drink, for Christ's sake, mellow out a little. Don't look so serious."

"Faymi said you were doing okay," he said, "and I'm glad about that. Apart from anything else, I wanted to thank you for your help, and give you an update. It seems three or four of the other girls have got the burn."

"And that's good?"

"It means I'm on the right track."

"Sweetie, you'll be on the right track when you find the cure." Her voice rose into a screechy lament. "When are you going to find the cure?" Her normal voice returned. "But I'm fine, I'm fine, aren't I sweetheart?"

Her eyes were directed over to his right. He turned, and only then noticed the other person in the room, a man sitting in a corner by the window, half hidden by a couch.

"I'm going to get you a beer," Paloma said, heading for the kitchen. "Say hallo to Jerry Henckel. He's interested to meet you. He's a physician."

Paloma swished around him before he could comment. Henckel, taking his time, was raising himself from his chair and making his way around the couch. He was boyishly good-looking, but not quite as young as Alex had first thought. He was dressed in a fine cotton shirt with a discreet monogram, and fashionable cream slacks; clothes that said money without being vulgar. His smile was warm, the handshake cool and firm.

"You're a friend of Faymi, Paloma tells me. Nice girl, Alex, very nice girl. I admire your taste. Paloma, now... You know what I like about Paloma? She lays it all on the line. Watch her face and you know what she ate for breakfast. Am I right? Faymi, now, she's the opposite. She covers over. But they're both good kids." Jerry Henckel's voice was pleasant and relaxed, and the boyish smile fluttered occasionally. "Have some potato chips, Alex." Henckel reached down and picked up two bowls. "It's a real nice dip, fresh, that deli on Sunset, you know? It's healthy, take my word..."

Alex found himself reaching for a potato chip. He was intrigued by Henckel's obvious charm, but he felt he'd been caught on the back foot. How much did this guy know about his work? Had Paloma already blown his cover in the medical community?

"You're a physician, did Paloma say?"

"Most of the time." Henckel replaced the bowls on the table. "I give the girls a little advice now and then, but I also like to think of Paloma as a friend. As you know, she's been feeling kind of down lately, which is why I've been coming by."

Paloma returned with a beer for Alex and something clear with ice for Jerry Henckel. He put his arm round her and gave her a hug, and she clung on to him, showing off her intimacy with him.

"So, Alex, how you going to figure this coke thing?" He put his hand to his throat and made a face. "I'm not much of a user, a little at the weekends sometimes, but man, it's like the revenge of the vampires."

Alex was beginning to recover his balance. It was clear that whatever kind of physician this guy was, he wasn't exactly aligned with law enforcement.

"You got it yourself? The burn?"

Henckel gave a self-deprecating shrug. "Just the once. That was enough. What do you think it is? Pal tells me you've been doing some investigating."

Alex sipped his beer, thinking fast. If Paloma had told this guy about his research, there wasn't much point denying it.

"The work I'm doing is kind of unofficial. So I've got to ask you, Jerry... Can you please keep this to yourself, for the sake of the girls, and the sake of what we're trying to achieve?"

"Absolutely no problem. I'm just glad that someone is trying to do something. I'm starting to see a lot of this thing, not just with my patients, even with my friends. Which is why I'm right behind you in your efforts to identify and contain. Did you learn anything positive from the girls?"

"A virus still looks like the probable cause. But there's a lot more work to be done."

"Listen, Alex, if there's anything I can contribute, give me a call." He produced a card and handed it over. "I really mean that. Call me."

"Sure." Alex nodded and put the card in his pocket, thinking it doubtful that Henckel was a guy he'd want to talk to again. A moment later he made his excuses and Paloma showed him to the door. Jerry was still smiling and eating chips when he waved goodbye.

***

"Alex? Have you got a moment?"

Alex looked up from his screen to see Professor Chang, his nominal supervisor, peering into his lab cubicle. Alex had only run into the Professor on a couple of occasions, and their conversations had been brief; the Professor was usually in a hurry. This time the busy look was overlaid with something more serious.

Alex got up and followed him out into the corridor.

"If you're free," Chang said, "I'd like to take you to meet the Executive Dean of Research. Kind of a formality, I guess."

"Sure." Alex took off his gown and gloves and followed Chang, who set off at a brisk pace, out of the building and across to the Jackson Medical Towers. As they rode up in the elevator, Chang made a perfunctory inquiry about Alex's work, but otherwise said nothing.

Alex was getting an uneasy feeling in the pit of his stomach by the time they got into the Dean's spacious, book-lined office. He wasn't encouraged by the serious demeanor of the middle-aged woman who half rose from her chair, shook his hand, and waved at a chair. Chang introduced her as Sheila Baumgartner, a name Alex vaguely remembered from academic papers on the sociology of medicine.

Chang took a pace backwards. "Do you need me, Sheila?"

"Stay a moment, Don, would you mind? I don't think we'll be long. Dr. Morales, I confess I'm surprised and embarrassed to be conducting this interview, but certain circumstances make it necessary, I'm afraid." She hesitated. "To come directly to the point, it has been made known to me that you are conducting a clinical study on drug users here in

Miami without fulfilling the statutory and legal requirements necessary for such an activity. Can you comment on that?"

Alex had half-expected something like this, but it still came as a shock. He took a long slow breath. "I guess my first reaction, Ma'am, is to wonder where this information has come from."

"Yes, I understand your curiosity about that, but I'd rather not say at this time. Do you acknowledge the basic facts?"

He dropped his gaze and thought for a moment. "Yes," he said, his eyes on the front of her desk, "it would be discourteous to you and the school to deny something that is fairly apparent, at least if my activities have been monitored by somebody, which I assume is the case. What I would say is that..." He raised his eyes at last. "...there are good reasons for the way I've done this work, which go to matters of protecting the volunteers from undue attention, and also to the unusual importance and sensitivity of what I'm doing. I could go into the details of all that, subject to approval from the sponsor and funder of my work, Senator Camilleri. In fact the Senator might be willing to speak with you himself."

"As a matter of fact, since the Senator is an important contributor to the welfare of this institution, I spoke with him already."

Alex stared at her, less and less happy with the direction this was taking. "And?"

She fidgeted with her papers. "He acknowledged that he knew roughly where your investigation was headed, and he agreed with you about the potential significance..." She looked up. "But he said he didn't realize you were breaking the law. He said he would never have condoned such a thing."

He was aware of his heart rate rising. His hands had tightened on the arms of the chair. Okay, what did you expect? He's a politician. He's not going to take the fall for a guy like me who's pushing the boundaries. But he felt betrayed all the same. If Camilleri had exerted himself, could he not have bought him a little time at least?

"If that's what he told you," he said, trying to keep the anger out of his voice, "then I won't attempt to dispute it. I presume you're closing me down."

"The Senator was anxious that nothing negative should appear on your record as a researcher, so we'll try and reach an accommodation with you, Dr. Morales. Don, you told me there's no contractual basis for his work in your department?"

Professor Chang, who had remained standing, nodded unhappily. "He was given lab space as a courtesy to the Senator." He turned towards Alex. "Alex, I'm sorry, but I think the deal should be that I supervise the destruction of your samples and core records, to protect us from any future liability, after which, of course, the facilities are withdrawn from your use. But as Sheila says, in response to the Senator's request, we won't make any report to your supervisors back at Rutgers."

Alex looked from one to the other. He was frustrated and angry about what was happening, but he knew that neither of them was really to blame. They were protecting their institution.

"I'll cooperate in whatever way you think best," he said. "Tell me one thing: did the complaint about my work originate with the Drug Interdiction Commission?"

From the quick glance they exchanged, he guessed that his stab in the dark had hit the mark.

"And they were insistent, were they not," he went on, "that my work should be destroyed?"

"We really can't get into that, Dr. Morales," Baumgartner said, leaning back and putting her hands on the desk. "The point is, we're offering you a very fair compromise."

"I appreciate that. You might like to consider, however," he said, turning towards Chang, "that the DIC is somehow getting information out of your lab. I'm not sure that kind of thing encourages free and open research."

***

Chang didn't attempt to censor what was on his laptop, a concession, Alex felt, to the murky circumstances of his dismissal. Alex also laid claim to all the material originating in Peru, and he again agreed, his attitude suggesting he just wanted to get this over with. Alex managed, in sorting through the glassware, to sidetrack one tube of viral DNA which he had succeeded in purifying, placing it in the Peruvian group. He felt slightly uneasy at deceiving the other man, but then Chang was obviously uneasy himself about the whole business, willing to observe the overall intent, but not the detail. When they were done, he waved at a lab assistant to get rid of the box of discarded biomaterials, escorted Alex from the building, finally shaking hands with an apologetic nod of the head.

On the Metrorail train going south, anger suddenly washed over him and he bunched his fists and swore to himself. They, Dave Creasey and his miserable agency, had been watching him the whole time; had found out where he was working; had sneaked in and examined his work, or recruited someone, or talked with someone; had maybe tracked him when he visited the girls; had even been smart enough to hack in to Velos, the clinical management system on which he was supposed to record his activities. And Senator Bob Camilleri, family friend and patron, had more or less thrown him to the wolves.

It was the middle of the day when he got home. He went out for a run in spite of the heat, pounding the streets for half an hour and sweating out some of his anger. He was clearly at a decision point. He could talk to the Senator, but he didn't think that Camilleri was going to suggest a new way forward. A new way forward would have to be even more clandestine than the last way forward. He wasn't even sure he wanted to tell the Senator that he'd preserved a couple of samples of the live virus, and had sneaked out the DNA. It might be safer just to keep quiet.

On the other hand, without the Senator, without funding, without a lab, what could he hope to accomplish? The drug war cops, thinking they'd shut him down, might leave him alone, but more likely they'd still keep an eye on him. He'd have to do some clever maneuvering, remain constantly on his guard. Maybe he'd be better off back at Rutgers. At least he could still use the med school labs, and there'd be a few friendly faces around and about. Except that the drug war agents were everywhere, and there would still be the problem of finding cocaine users and recruiting people for the follow-up research that was going to be required.

He swung around a fountain in a small park and pounded on. The sun was in and out behind heavy clouds, giving relief and then sudden glare. One thing, he thought, about running instead of driving through the streets: neither vehicles nor humans could follow him without making it obvious. He reached into his shirt pocket and took out his phone. That was another way they could know where he was. He was about to turn it off, but hesitated and put it back in his pocket instead. Safer, surely, to preserve a facade of innocence.

He became aware that, consciously or not, he was within a couple of miles of the girls' apartment in Kendall. It wasn't, of course, just the lab he was losing. If he was forced to relocate, he was losing Faymi as well. Or the possibility of Faymi, since his hopes and feelings had so far found no way around the barriers. He decided to run on and see if she was at home.

CHAPTER TEN

The hot wind gusted around him as he jogged up the entrance way into the building. Following the Florida Power and Light guidelines, the girls kept their apartment at 85 degrees during the summer: a nice cooling drop in temperature, but still warm. Faymi wore shorts and a halter top.

No Paloma. Just Faymi, turning in that off-hand way, showing that smooth curve of thigh and hip, asking him if he wanted a drink.

"Sure," he said. "Thanks. Maybe a cold beer?"

Faymi padded off to the kitchen, returning in a moment with two amber-filled glasses. He took his glass and sat on the couch. Faymi remained standing, giving him a glance and then turning away, sitting finally at the other end of the couch.

It was the first time since their lunch at the Dadeland food court that they had been alone together in any meaningful way. Looking at her now, he wasn't surprised to sense a constraint, a tension, in her posture. He eased his way around it by telling her what had happened at the Miller.

"So you've got no lab? Nowhere to work?"

"No."

"What are you going to do?"

"Good question. I might have to go back to Rutgers."

She turned her head and looked into his eyes.

"I'll miss you," he said. "Maybe you don't know that. Maybe you don't know how much..." He broke off. "Anyway," he said after a pause, "I don't know that I can get the job done at Rutgers. The DIC people can get to me just as easily up there."

"What about the Senator? Doesn't he outrank this Miller woman?"

"Not exactly. Not on her turf. But I could have hoped for something more, given the circumstances. Basically, he seems to have hung me out to dry."

"Have you spoken with him?"

"No."

"Give him a try, Alejandro. At least make him feel bad."

He looked across at her. Her posture had softened. She was looking at him with a faint smile. Bad idea, he thought, putting down his beer glass. Wait. But his body didn't wait. And it was so easy, so easy to move the few feet, to reach out and touch. She took his left hand. His right hand moved on to her neck, her bare shoulder. His lips found her cheek. Then the reaction, the subtle change of state, as her muscles hardened and her body signaled its disquiet...

He had been half-expecting that. He drew back, wanting to engage her eyes. She didn't look at him, hanging her head briefly in embarrassment or defeat, but tightening her hold on his hand. Stalemate, for a moment: then she jerked to her feet, turning and getting her other hand on his wrist, pulling him up, her eyes still lowered, but clear decisiveness on her face.

He allowed himself to be drawn to his feet and led around the couch and through the door to Faymi's bedroom, a room too feminine for the Faymi he knew, more in keeping with the romances she read: silver-grey broadloom, double bed and vanity and mirrors in white and gold.

She pulled him across to the bed and began undressing him, not with caresses but with fussy impatience. He stayed neutral, like someone playing a patient in a first aid drill. There was more artifice to the way she removed her own clothes, showing him the contours of her body as her halter top and shorts dropped away. It made him faintly embarrassed. He reached out for her: she came and lay beside him with a touch of the impatience, reaching her arms around him and pulling at him as though everything should now follow an allotted course.

Alex slowed her down, touched her, kissed her; but she wanted him on top, wanted action, wanted no pause for thought. This cooled him rather than excited him: he slowed her again, caressed her hair, kissed her lips. Gradually she seemed to subside, give in to him. Or give up on him? The life was going out of her, her body becoming heavy, inert. His fingers touched and explored and stroked, but it became apparent that he was on his own. She was not responding to him. The momentum she had tried to inject was lost. He was failing her and he didn't know why.

He passed his hand down her back and around and found her hand. "Faymi..."

"It's okay," she said, the flat voice.

"It's my fault, I guess."

"Oh yeah." Sarcastic.

He shifted a little, allowed her head to come up, watched her face. "If I knew what to do..."

"Get yourself another girl."

"I like this one."

She raised her eyes. "Paloma's right, you must be nuts."

"Faymi: I see you, the real you, as a very special person."

She looked down. "I can't do it, Alejandro."

"What, you can't do it. What do you mean?"

"I can't do it. Make love. Sex. It's... it's... No, it's no use talking about it. I can't do it, that's all."

"But..."

"But what?"

He raised his hand and touched her hair.

"But I do it all the time, right?"

He said nothing.

"Work is work, Alejandro. It's different, isn't it? It isn't me, it's just him, some john I don't give a damn for. There are things you do. It's like milking a cow. A squeeze here, a squeeze there, a condom... But when I'm me... like this... I clam up. I know I'm not going to be any good. The truth is I don't want to be any good. I back away. There you have it. I'm in denial... living my little fantasies..."

Alex felt out of his depth.

"You don't feel any... arousal?"

"It disappears. Flies away like a bird. The point is... I'm not a woman. Do you understand that? I'm not a woman. I get dressed up in women's clothes, and men look at me and whistle, but I don't feel like I'm a woman. I'm a fake. Good for nothing but..."

She pushed herself fiercely off the bed and began to get dressed.

Alex fumbled helplessly for his own clothes. "Maybe you're going to have to give that up if you're going to get over the problem..."

"Oh yeah? What would I do? I may not be a woman but I'm a good hooker and I make good money."

"We could find something..." It didn't sound convincing, even to himself. Least of all to himself.

Faymi said nothing, her hurt and embarrassment fading as she got her defensive mask back in place. Don't feel sorry for me, she seemed to say as she marched out of the room. He sighed and did up the buttons of his shirt. When he got back to the living room there seemed to be nothing to do but say goodbye and go.

***

At home, he poured himself another beer and sat by the pool. He felt as though a powerful energy source had been withdrawn from his life, a bereavement of a kind. He wouldn't accept, he decided, Faymi's pessimism, her sense of defeat. She had a strong personality and a capacity to feel for others. She was a fighter. With time and help, she could surely make progress. The problem was, she didn't trust him yet. And why should she? Did he trust himself? Did he love her enough to go through the tough times with her, maybe while she continued to work as a hooker? Did he understand what that would involve?

He took Faymi's advice and tried to reach Camilleri later in the afternoon. The Senator was in Washington and tied up in committee work, David Van Hoyle told him; but the Senator had been expecting his call and had several messages for him.

"Bob is aware, and I'm quoting him here, that he ran for cover the moment the enemy opened fire, and he's sorry that he so manifestly exhibited all the worst features of a politician with a thin majority... All the same, Alex, he believes he did the right thing in letting them shut you down. This is simply getting too risky for you. It was supposed to be a skirmish at the edge of the field, so to speak, just to get them thinking, and it's now like they've wheeled on the big artillery and gone all nasty on us. He wants you out of there and safely back in your own world. It's already pretty clear that the burn isn't to do with bio-war agents, so he's got a lot of what he needs. Send us the accounts so that we can take care of all of your expenses. Bob says he'll look for other ways of getting up the noses of these guys. We can also think about bringing in other agencies. If he needs any technical detail we'll come back to you, but his final message is to lock this stuff away, get on with your life, and please forgive him for his failure to see just how it would turn out."

Alex pondered these remarks for the rest of the day, not quite satisfied, but mollified to the extent that his anger moved away from the Senator and focused back on the drug war people, whoever they were, who had watched him and threatened him and sabotaged his work. It stuck in his craw that they were determined to suppress knowledge of a disease that might spread around the globe and cause suffering to millions.

He woke up at 2.30 in the morning and began obsessively reprising all the events that had led him to this point. His anger burned hotter and hotter, until at length he found himself banging his fist into his pillow. He didn't get back to sleep. In the morning he felt washed out, but calm.

At breakfast, he said to his uncle, "I don't want to worry you, *Tío*, but what I told you yesterday about giving up work on the virus... I was wrong. I've got to carry on. It's too big to just let it go. I think I can find people who will help me. But it's going to mean I have to take security seriously, and that could have an impact on you. The last thing I want is to disturb your life and your home, so I think I should move out."

Henry leaned across the table towards him. "*Alejandro*, I had a feeling you might go that way, and although I fear for you, I also admire your decision. I think it's a good cause, and I think Hispanics in general would agree with you. *So vaya con Diós*. And no, I won't have you moving out. That would arouse suspicion. What, kick my nephew out when he's in a bit of trouble? Please. Stay here and use whatever facilities I have."

Alex looked at the well-defined, ascetic features of his uncle's face, and realized that emotions were stirring there which he had missed or refused to see before.

"I suppose, *Tío Enrique*," he said, "when I first turned up, it was hard, it changed your life..."

His uncle seemed to stiffen.

"I mean as a boy, when, after... the death of my parents..."

"I wanted you to come. I thought it was the best thing. Of course,

I wasn't used to children."

"What I mean is, Uncle, I probably didn't make it easy for you."

His uncle looked at him. "You had lost your parents. What could you do? You resented it very much."

"It showed?"

"Of course it showed."

"I'm sorry."

"Don't be sorry. We managed, didn't we?"

"You managed. I'm still learning."

"We're both still learning. Which is the way it should be."

Alex nodded slowly. "But please tell me, *Tío Enrique*, if anything happens that worries you or threatens your peace and security. I don't want to cause trouble."

Later, Alex thought again about the loss of his parents, particularly his mother. Was that why his failure with Faymi had been so upsetting? Even if he didn't leave Miami, he saw it as another loss, the very loss he had hoped to avoid. But this didn't need to be true, he told himself. This wasn't a death. He could remain in touch with her. The future remained open. It was a commitment he'd half made, a responsibility, and he had no intention of setting it aside so soon.

CHAPTER ELEVEN

As Alex ran through Coconut Grove towards the Brickell skyscrapers, he felt as though he was passing through a portal into a new world. The giant columns of blue glass, or pink-marbled concrete, glowing like fantasy castles in the distance, hadn't been there when he was a boy. He pounded onwards, watching them grow, until finally, on the wide pavement canyons between them, their massive bulk seemed to bend the light and shift the force of gravity.

He headed to Brickell Bay Drive, and then to a forty-five story colossus standing close to the waterfront. Riding up thirty-five of those stories in an air-conditioned elevator, he took a towel out of his back pack and wiped the sweat off his arms and legs. Leaving the elevator and hiking down a corridor, he found Jerry Henckel standing at an open door. The boyish grin, the pleased look, was more in keeping with a teenager left in charge by his parents than with the owner of a two million dollar condo.

Henckel shook hands and drew him inside. Alex found himself in a white hallway with sculptured bronzes and modernist copper light fittings.

"Come on through, Alex. If you run across any kids who look like they're on a vampire training course, don't let it bother you. They're not mine, they belong to my patients. I clear 'em out now and then, but somehow they get back in."

Alex followed Henckel into a very big room with cream broadloom wall to wall and glass doors to the terrace. The expensive stuff on the walls was pop art and collectable posters: and the stuff standing on the floor consisted of realistic dragons and ape-men, and big screen games consoles, several of them alive and flickering. He didn't see any trainee vampires, although it was obviously a space that kids would enjoy. In the distance was a kitchen modeled on the control room of a spacecraft. Henckel was half way over there.

"Can I get you a beer?"

"Great. But I don't want to keep you from your patients."

"It's no problem. When they want me, they call me." Henckel took two bottles of Sam Adams from the Bosch refrigerator and opened them. "Let's sit out on the deck. We get a nice breeze up here and it's really not that hot."

They went outside. There was a big sun awning and furniture in teak and canvas. Alex sat down and squinted at the heat haze. The terrace faced north-east, and he could see Key Biscayne and the Atlantic ocean to his right, and more skyscrapers to his left.

Henckel took a swig of beer. "So, Alex, you tell me they chucked you out of your lab at the Miller."

"That's right." He looked across at Henckel, some of his earlier suspicions returning. Henckel owned and operated a couple of clinics, as well as ministering to selected clients, but even so his wealth seemed slightly excessive. "Fortunately I hid a couple of live virus samples at home. But yeah, I'm without a lab, and I'm probably under surveillance by the DIC. I'm sure they didn't follow me here, by the way, I took some fairly unusual loops and short cuts. And if they're monitoring my cell, well, they'll only hear me telling a couple of people how I've given up my Miami project and will be back in Rutgers soon. I'll always use a clean phone to call you."

"Good thinking. Listen, I've got a suggestion for you. But first, would you mind showing me that stuff you were talking about? Especially the virus pictures? I'm really intrigued."

"Sure. No problem."

Alex reached into his backpack and pulled out his laptop. He set it up on the hardwood table, the afternoon sunlight behind them blocked by the top ten floors of Henckel's condo. Henckel drew his chair in close. Alex spent twenty minutes going through the best micrographs, telling Henckel which girls were involved with each set.

"So there's one, maybe two ambiguous ones," Henckel said, "but otherwise this spiky football shows up on samples from all the girls who subsequently got the burn. Right? Jeez, Alex, there's got to be a frigging good chance you're onto something."

"I think so too." He closed the laptop and stowed it away.

Henckel swung his chair round and leaned back on the cushions and picked up his beer. "Let me go back to your lab problem. My idea ain't perfect, but nothing is. What about you set up a lab at home? I can help with that. I can order stuff, equipment, chemicals, more or less anything. And I can get it anonymously delivered on soft drink trucks or whatever. What do you think?"

Alex thought for a moment. Would this be fair to Uncle Henry? And where could he set up to operate safely? The cellar? Too flood prone. The pool room? "I could probably manage on that basis. But I'd also need commercial lab services, particularly DNA sequencing."

"We're hooked up to most of the big guys, so I should be able to cover you on that. I'm going to suggest we use the girls' apartment as a drop-off point. You can leave something for me, and I can leave something for you. They might arrest one or other of us for living off immoral earnings, but I don't think they're going to connect us."

Alex nodded slowly. It sounded workable.

"So have we got a plan?" Henckel's expression was bright, carefree, as though they were organizing a holiday outing to the Hialeah race track.

Alex frowned. "I haven't told you about the tricky bit. What I showed you is really just an indicator, a possibility of a mechanism for the burn. But I'm a long way short of proof. To get a paper published, which is really what is needed to get some credibility, I've got to do something more. Here's my suggestion, and please tell me what you think about it. We get blood panels from maybe a dozen more cooperating cocaine users. I say 'we', but in practice I guess you're the one who would have to manage this. Half of those, roughly, would be suffering from the burn, half not. You give them to me blind. If it was possible for you to be blind as well, that would be better, but I don't want to complicate this too much. Meanwhile I develop an antibody test which I can validate with my live samples. Then I look for these antibodies in your bloods. If I find antibodies only in the patients who are suffering from the burn, then we've got a result. Not perfect, but I think it would be enough for a short paper somewhere."

"I follow what you're saying," Henckel said, nodding, "and it sounds okay, but what about the fact that you've had to work against the regulatory system, you've broken the law, in fact. Wouldn't that make it hard to publish?"

Alex took a pull on his beer. Henckel was right: without institutional support, he was compromised.

"There must be places on the internet," he said at last, "where this kind of thing, even if anonymously reported, would... go viral. No pun intended."

"Yeah. And I can see the benefits of that. If people are warned about something, they can take steps to avoid it. But it's not quite the big enchilada, is it? Tell me about the prospects for a vaccine."

"Pretty good, as long as somebody somewhere will spend the money, but there are big issues. If the virus is constantly mutating, like flu viruses, then, as you know, you have to constantly update the vaccine. If the virus is stable, then you can hope to eliminate it, but if the first phase symptoms are very mild, as with this virus, it's hard to get ahead of it, because nobody takes precautions, and almost everyone gets it in the first wave. My guess is that about 80% of the Peruvians who chew coca have now had the disease and are suffering from the burn. So a vaccine isn't much use to them."

"What you're saying is that to stop the burn moving through countries like the United States, you've got to move fast."

"Exactly. Assuming it's a fairly stable virus and you've got a shot at catching it. Which is why the tactics being used against me by the drug warriors are so goddamned infuriating and evil. We need to get going on a vaccine program now, as soon as I've backed up my findings."

Henckel jumped to his feet. "I'm getting another beer, Alex. Want one?"

"Sure. Thanks." Alex stared out at Key Biscayne. Senator Camilleri's home was somewhere there amidst the luxury properties, although he couldn't identify it. His anger was fizzing up again. Didn't the Senator understand what these drug agency people were doing? Throwing down these road blocks? Didn't he see that now was the time to stand up and fight them?

Henckel returned with the beers and some nuts in a bowl. "Alex, if you're prepared to take the risk, I'm ready to gamble on your efforts being productive in some way or another. I'll even pay for the stuff I provide you with. The quid pro quo is that I get to access and use anything you turn up: live virus, data, DNA. If I can find some pharma entity willing and able to invest in making a vaccine, then I'm allowed to sell them all that stuff, say on a fifty-fifty basis, half the money to you, half to me. You get to keep the intellectual rights, if you want them. How does that sound?" Jerry tossed a peanut in his mouth and began to chew.

Alex reached out for some nuts. "I've got no problem with financial arrangements like that. I'm not in this for the money." He paused, returning his gaze to the ocean. It was obvious that the pharma entity Henckel was talking about wasn't Roche or Pfizer. It was more likely an organization with a stake in the drugs trade, directly under threat from the burn. He turned back to Henckel. "What I need to know is that whatever we turn up is made public. Your guys can have a license to make a vaccine, but it's got to be in everyone's interest that people know it's a virus, and that there are ways to combat the transmission of the virus. If that information is out there, it seems to me that public health authorities will be forced to pay attention and get into the act."

Henckel popped a couple of nuts in his mouth and nodded. "I don't see a negative there. What we want to do is control the virus, by any means. I'll draw up some kind of memorandum of agreement, just so we know we're on the same page."

"Okay. I've got to talk with my uncle about all this, but I think he'll go along."

And will I go along? Alex thought, reaching for his beer and looking at Henckel across the top of the glass. And do I really have any choice?

CHAPTER TWELVE

It was after his makeshift lab had been up and running for a few days that his uncle's security alarm went off in the middle of the night. By the time Alex had struggled out of bed and gone downstairs, Henry had already arrived at the control panel and reset the system. They spent a few minutes studying video from Henry's security cameras, but there was no sign of an intruder, animal or human.

"Probably a cat," Henry said. "Or a pair of cats. Usually the system gets it right, but just occasionally they can set off the motion sensor."

Alex slept fitfully after that, and in the morning when he went into the pool room, he checked everything carefully for signs of a break-in, but nothing had been disturbed, as far as he could tell.

He was working on the sixth blood sample supplied to him by Jerry Henckel. He'd got a positive response to his antibody test, indicating antibodies for the Paloma-Blow virus, as he was informally beginning to call it, were present in the blood, but he ran the test again to be sure. He got the same result. He put it down as a plus in his notebook. Alex would rather have reserved these findings until they had done the full twelve, but Henckel was keen to know the results one by one, and so he had relayed each result to Henckel after doing the test. Of the first five bloods, two had tested negative for his viral antibodies, and three had tested positive. Henckel told him this was a perfect score: all five correct;

the two testing negative had not had the burn, the three positives were suffering from it.

Alex had also tested the blood samples he had brought back from Peru, and all tested positive for the virus except one. He and Henckel were building a data set that proved that his virus was a factor, and probably the causative factor, in the etiology of the burn, and while this result gave him a good deal of satisfaction, it also made him feel vulnerable. The implications were huge: and even with a smart operator like Henckel in his corner, he wasn't sure he could deal with all of them effectively.

In the afternoon, taking a break by the pool, he got a call on his cell phone.

"Did you ask for Faymi, Señor Morales?"

"Yes I did," he said, smiling.

"Okay, *cariño*, I'll be with you in a few minutes."

"I'll look forward to it."

Faymi, he presumed, had something for him from Henckel. It had been a surprise and a relief, after the humiliation she had suffered at his hands, that instead of retreating behind her defensive barriers, she had done the reverse, and opened up her real, mischievous, personality, treating him like a client or an ex-lover or a wealthy patron as the mood dictated, and basing these inventions, it seemed, on the stories she read and the Mexican soap operas she watched. It was as though, having revealed the depth of her problems to him, she had been freed of the burden of self-protection and deceit, and could flirt with him or make fun of him instead.

He told his uncle exactly who Faymi was, and to his surprise his uncle seemed more charmed by her beauty than disapproving of her profession.

He went into the kitchen and mixed up a fruity drink for her. He let her in through the side gate a few minutes later and took her round to the pool. She sat down and put her hands on the table and stared at them, not seeing the drink. It was suddenly apparent to him that the mischief had gone, and that she was deeply upset.

"It's Linda. Linda Pendleton. I think she's dying. She's completely lost it and she won't listen to anyone."

He was momentarily confused. "Linda Pendleton? The Vice President's daughter? You're saying you're in touch with her? You've been looking after her?"

"I did what I could. But it wasn't enough. What I'm saying, *cariño*, is that there's no point trying to help her any longer. She's got to go into a hospital."

"And this is because of the burn?"

"The burn and a bad coke habit."

"Are you asking me to help?"

She gave a little shrug. "I don't know what to do. Maybe if she was in a private hospital they wouldn't rat on her. I can't afford that, and obviously she can't. Not the way she is at the moment."

He thought hard. "I suppose you don't want to hand her over to Senator Camilleri?"

Faymi made a face. "Are you kidding?"

"What about if I speak with Jerry? Jerry would know where to take her, and could maybe help us raise some money."

"Okay."

He got out his clean phone and spoke to Henckel for a few minutes. Faymi seemed to relax a little. She put a hand on the tumbler in front of her, as though noticing it for the first time, and raised her eyebrows at him. He nodded. She picked it up and took a couple of sips.

He took the phone from his ear and said, "Jerry says there's a place in Belair which is discreet. An upscale detox clinic. He'll help with the money. But they'll need to know who she is. Not to tell anyone, just to cover themselves legally. They've got all the HIPPA stuff to worry about."

"What choice have we got?"

He spoke with Henckel again. "He wants to know if he should send an ambulance. It'd be safer than doing it in my car but we'll do it that way if you want."

"No, we'd better go for the ambulance."

She gave him the address, which he relayed to Henckel. When he closed the call, she asked to borrow his phone. He heard her talking to somebody about the ambulance arriving and the handover.

After that she sat slumped over, her face sad. "I don't know how we kept it going so long. Linda really didn't appreciate what we were doing. But you know? I hope she makes it. It's a bad thing, Alejandro, to have a parent you hate."

***

It was twilight and raining, and close to supper time, when he returned to the girls' apartment the following day. Faymi had sent him a coded message to pick up a package from Jerry. Paloma was out and he sat in the kitchen with Faymi while she cut up a chicken.

"I went to visit Linda today. Maybe you guessed." She looked up briefly.

"I thought you might have some news. How was she?"

"Okay. It's a swanky place. Lots of flowering potted plants. She was pretty knocked out and hooked up to a drip, so she didn't say much, but she seemed... Peaceful. Probably that's an illusion. She was never peaceful."

"What's going to happen to her? What's she going to do when she gets better?"

"You mean, is she going to tell her story? Tell the world about the burn?" She dumped some leftover bits of chicken in the trash bin.

"Faymi, you know where I stand on that. It could destroy the Vice

President's career, which would be nice, and give publicity to the burn, which would be even better, but it's her life. She's got to do what she wants."

"You don't think Jerry will set her up somehow?"

"You know him better than I do. I doubt if he could force her to say things she doesn't want to say."

"Maybe not." She washed her hands at the sink. "I guess I just worry that she'll end up on the front pages with no more control over her life. Not that she had any control anyway. Come on, I'll get you the memory stick from Jerry."

***

The following morning, in his bedroom, he downloaded the contents of the thumb drive onto his laptop and began to skip through the contents. Henckel had used one of his commercial labs to sequence the DNA of the Paloma-Blow virus, and it was exciting to Alex to see the results come up on his screen. There were close to a thousand pages of the letters C, G, A and T. His virus contained, it seemed, more than two million nucleotides, which made it modest in size. He used software tools to break the endless stream of nucleotides into codons, and then more software to hunt for known genes, of which there were quite a large number.

He pulled out his Nokia and called his friend Dennis. "Are we still on for Tampa at the weekend?"

"The kids, not to mention my wife, will murder me if I postpone this trip again, so yeah. What about you?"

"I've got a few more bloods still to come, and then I've got to do some cleaning up, but I don't see anything to stop me. Listen, I'm looking at the DNA right now. If I send you a copy, would you have time to look it over before you leave? We can chat about it when I'm with you."

"Sure. I'm intrigued."

They talked a little more about Dennis's trip to Florida, and then he went to the mall and sent the DNA file to Dennis from an internet café.

He got a call from Jerry in the middle of the afternoon. "Alex, I'm still trying to get to the bottom of this, but there's bad news: Linda is gone."

"What?"

"Her dad marched into the clinic about an hour ago, said he was taking her home, and nobody had the guts to say no."

"Shit. Poor kid." He thought about Faymi's sad predictions. "How did he find out?"

"I think we can assume that someone blabbed, but who and why, we don't know. In fact we'll probably never know, because there's a lot of people working at the clinic, and most of them would have heard about their special guest. Even with a tipoff, it still shouldn't have happened, of course, given the girl's constitutional rights: but I guess it's a lesson in political theory; everyone has constitutional rights, but vice presidents have more constitutional rights than other folks. It probably helped that he threatened to bankrupt the place if word of his actions got out."

After ending his call with Henckel, Alex sent a message to Faymi telling her that they ought to meet. He wanted to see her again, and he thought he should tell her the bad news about Linda in person.

CHAPTER THIRTEEN

Alex chose the Tamiami Trail, Highway 41 through the Everglades, to cross to the west coast. He had driven it a couple of times as a student, usually with friends, and they would stop a time or two and have a beer and go looking for alligators. The Tamiami Canal tracked the two-lane highway on the right, sometimes as wide as a small lake, sometimes flanked by grassland, sometimes by cypress forestation. Alex liked the open, endless sense of space, clouds chasing across a big sky. There was no traffic, just a few passing cars.

He was relieved to have finished the last bloods from Jerry. Henckel had cleared the lab equipment out of his uncle's home by sending a van with a plumbing company's logo on the sides. His perfect record of predicting who was suffering from the burn had been maintained in the results from these final samples. He'd joined Henckel for a meal at a Brickell restaurant in which he had stake. And now he was escaping at last from some of the tensions that had built up over the last days and weeks. It wasn't clear exactly what he would do when he returned from his meeting with Dennis in Tampa, but Dennis was a good friend and very smart guy. If Dennis could back up the idea of a newly-evolved virus, and elucidate the mode of action and the secondary effects, they'd have a lot more ammunition to work with. Summer was passing, Labor Day not far away. Whatever Henckel managed on the vaccine front, they had to get some publicity for what they'd done; even if that meant using addicts themselves to spread the word.

There were a few palms beside the highway, the land rising slightly. He passed the gas station at Royal Palm Hammock. At Naples he would transfer to Highway 75 and head north for St. Petersburg. A Highway Patrol vehicle passed him going east. Alex gave it no special attention, but glancing in his mirror, he saw that it had stopped and was turning round. He felt a sudden flash of alarm. There seemed no possible reason for this maneuver, no other car on the road. He mentally checked his car for possible violations, glanced at the status of his lights, his speed. He was within the limit. In the mirror, the FHP vehicle was further behind him but had finished turning and seemed to be following him. Unwelcome possibilities flooded into his mind, all of the nervous paranoia of the last several weeks coming back to life.

He was carrying the Nokia in his breast pocket, ready to phone Dennis. The numbers he had been concealing, Dennis and Jerry and a couple of others, were contained in its memory. He could see now that a light was flashing on the roof of the cruiser. He pressed the button to lower the passenger-side window, took the phone from his pocket and flung it as hard as he could through the window.

Would they have seen that? He watched the mirror. The cruiser was still a long way behind him. So probably not. But they were driving fast, closing the distance. His next thought was flight. He would outrun them. But immigrant habits restrained him. He wasn't going to win a contest like that. And maybe, he thought, trying to counter his rising sense of panic, they had taken an emergency call and were headed back to Naples, this whole thing a coincidence.

He took his foot off the gas and let his car slow down. The cruiser soon drew level and the cop in the nearside seat waved him over. He pulled onto the gravel shoulder and stopped. He stared straight ahead, gripping the wheel. The cruiser pulled in a few yards in front of him.

He could see now that there was a dog in the back, a big German shepherd, ears cocked, eyes eager. The uniformed men got out of the cruiser, unhurried, confident. The driver walked over towards Alex. The other man raised the rear door of the cruiser and let the dog out, holding him on a tight leash.

Alex lowered the window and handed over his driver's license. The cop who took it from him was a big man with a sergeant's stripes on his pale mauve shirt. He studied the license for a moment and handed it back. He put both hands on the window opening of the door and leaned forward from the waist and took a careful look inside the car.

He stood up again. "I'm Sergeant Delamara," he said in slow even tones, "and this is Trooper Kerzik."

Alex nodded. "And the dog?"

Delamara gave a thin smile. "K9 Fury," he said. "Dr. Morales, we'd like you to get out of the car and turn around and put your hands on the roof of the vehicle."

Alex had wondered for an instant, when the Sergeant introduced himself, whether this was going to turn into something routine, but that possibility looked increasingly remote. He complied warily. Delamara patted him down.

"Please step away from the car."

Alex turned and took a couple of paces towards the rear of the car. The roadway was close beside them and there was limited room for maneuver. He watched as Trooper Kerzik led the dog around the open driver's door and let him sniff the interior. He was struggling to catch up with the unfolding situation. The dog meant that this was an FHP drug interdiction team. Who had organized that? And what the hell were they expecting to find?

The dog was excited, pulling on its leash, panting, trying to get into the car. Alex felt his own heart rate increasing in equal measure. Surely to God this couldn't be what it seemed. Surely they wouldn't resort to this. But since when did he believe these guys played fair?

Kerzik pulled the dog back. Delamara turned to Alex. “Dr. Morales, we have good indications that there are contraband substances aboard this vehicle. We would like your permission to search it.”

Alex stared at the dog for a moment, gaining time. He returned his gaze to Delamara. “No,” he said.

Delamara’s expression didn’t change. “We’ll do the search anyway. We have probable cause.”

“What, the dog?”

“And other information.”

“What information?”

“Sir, we’re going to search the vehicle. Any attempt to interfere will be seen as obstructing a police officer.” Delamara’s hand moved suggestively towards his gun holster.

Alex turned away. In spite of the late afternoon heat, he could feel his face turning hot as blood rushed to his head in a sudden fit of anger. He didn’t trust himself to speak. Nor did he want to watch the search process. The result was preordained. These guys knew exactly what they were doing. He drifted a couple of feet further from the car and hung his head, struggling to contain his anger, anger directed as much at himself as at these probably innocent stooges.

He heard the dog whining and snuffling, and saw Delamara coming back from the cruiser with a tool kit. Alex turned his back on the operation and stared at the tall palms beside the highway.

“Take a look, please, Dr. Morales.”

Alex turned round and saw Trooper Kerzik grinning and patting the dog, which seemed in as good a humor as its master. Delamara stood tall and stiff, his expression unreadable. Alex saw that the trunk was open, the spare wheel compartment exposed. Two bags containing white powder sat side by side in the center of the tire. He was expecting something like this, but he still felt a shocked burn in his gut.

He looked up and held the Sergeant's gaze. There was something unsettling in the other man's expression: not so much pride as a kind of righteous glow; this guy really believed in his mission.

"How did you know where to look?" Alex said.

Delamara turned his head to indicate the dog, now being taken back to the cruiser.

Alex was thinking, So the DIC, who'd probably been following his car around for weeks, had obtained a key, or used some kind of master key available to them, to open the trunk and slip in these bags. There were plenty of occasions when they could have done that. Maybe the evening he was at the girls' apartment. Or maybe at home, if they'd improved their knowledge of his uncle's alarm system and got in some night without setting it off. He gave a small, disbelieving nod.

Delamara took out a penknife and made a small hole in one of the bags and tasted the powder. "Guess what?" he said with the thin smile.

"Cocaine?" Alex said.

"About what, four kilos?"

"How convenient," Alex said.

Delamara's expression hardened. Alex now saw that he was controlling anger of his own. "Are you saying this wasn't by the book?"

"No, I would say the search was well conducted."

"So what are you saying? That you're not in the business of moving cocaine back to a student campus where a lot of kids will buy it from you and think you're a cool dude?"

"Yes, that's what I'm saying."

"And you're not going to tell us how much is in here, total?" Delamara waved at the interior of the car.

"I've no idea," Alex said.

Delamara stared at him. For a brief moment, Alex thought the anger in him would erupt. Kerzik came back from the cruiser and began taking pictures of the open trunk. Delamara sighed and stepped back.

"Play it how the hell you want. Dr. Morales, you're under arrest."

***

Alex didn't fully understand that he was going to jail. In spite of having his car and its contents impounded, and the uncomfortable ride to the Collier County Courthouse in Naples, his hands handcuffed behind him, he still believed that he would be booked and maybe interrogated and then sent on his way, to be arraigned later back in Miami. He still believed that his status, as essentially non-criminal, would count for something.

The Sheriff's deputy to whom he was handed over by the FHP cops treated him with routine indifference, taking him back into the bowels of the courthouse, and issuing monotone instructions about placing all his personal items on the table and stripping down to his underpants. Alex's anger and resentment, still boiling away inside, prevented him from responding in dutiful silence. He stared at the deputy.

"What is this?" he said.

The deputy gave him a sleepy-eyed look. "You never been arrested before?"

"No." Alex remembered only vaguely the circumstances of his arrest as a teenager, but it had seemed like something very different.

"You'll come up before the judge in the morning. Or maybe Monday. Meanwhile we put you in a cell."

"I don't get to talk to anybody about this?"

"Who would you like: Rush Limbaugh?"

Alex dropped his gaze, overwhelmed by a bleak sense of impotence. "Don't I get to call a lawyer or something?"

"All in good time. What color uniform do you want?"

Alex frowned before recognizing the humor of a bored official getting through the day. "What about prison red?"

"Sensible choice." The deputy pointed at Alex with the ball-point pen he was holding. "You can start with the watch, loose change, keys. You'll get it all back. Some day."

Alex began putting his personal belongings on the table. The deputy wrote on his clipboard.

"Okay. Strip."

Alex removed his clothes, putting shirt, slacks, shoes on the table. The deputy checked each item, wrote something down, put the clothes in a bag. He looked Alex up and down for a moment, and then tossed him the uniform: shirt, overalls, and canvas shoes. Alex hesitated and then slowly put them on, unable to purge himself of resentment over the indignity. This guy is just doing his job, he told himself: but he wanted to throw the clothes to the floor.

Instead, he submitted silently to the remaining procedures: fingerprinting, photographs, a machine that pricked his finger and took blood.

The deputy finally pushed a telephone towards Alex. "Two calls. One to your lawyer, and one to your family. Keep them short."

He hesitated. There weren't many options. He didn't know any criminal lawyers. They'd probably give him a yellow pages, but that was hit and miss. He remembered his uncle's landline number, but old habits made him uneasy about asking his uncle for help.

He shook himself and reached for the phone. His uncle had to know. And his uncle, in fact, would want to help; as long as he understood what was happening. The deputy was watching him: still bored, but mildly curious, perhaps, about what he was going to do. He dialed the number. There was a good chance, at any rate, that the deputy didn't speak Spanish.

Alex was relieved to hear his uncle's voice at the end of the line. He took a deep breath. "*Buenas tardes, Tío. Estás ocupado?*"

"Alejandro?"

"Uncle," Alex said, continuing in Spanish, "I'm afraid this will be upsetting. Are you alone?"

"Yes, of course. What's happened?"

"I'm at the Collier County Courthouse in Naples. I was stopped by the Highway Patrol near the end of the Tamiami Trail. They found bags of cocaine in my car. It looks like I'm going to spend the night in jail."

There was a shocked silence from his uncle. Henry had reacted badly to his teenage arrest for possession, but that was a long time ago; Alex didn't think he'd be misled by that childhood indiscretion. He glanced at the deputy. His thin face and pale brown hair did not suggest Hispanic origins, and unless he was a very good actor, he had already lost interest in the foreign language conversation. Alex continued with increased confidence:

"It was a setup, of course. All they had to do was get into the trunk of my car and put the stuff in the spare wheel compartment. Probably they planted a tracking device as well, so they knew when I was leaving town."

There was another brief silence from his uncle. Alex doubted him for a split second, but when he spoke, there was nothing but concern in his voice. "And this is because of your work on the... perhaps I shouldn't speak of it?"

"No, better not. I'm calling on the Courthouse phone. Call it my project. And yes, I think that's what this is all about."

"Isn't it time to tell the Senator?"

"Uncle, I'm not sure that's the best first move. What I need is a lawyer."

"A lawyer, yes... Are they treating you well?"

"Apart from the fact that they think I'm some kind of dirt-bag coke dealer, yes, I guess so. More or less by the book. Of course I'm mad as hell, but that is something I've got to control."

"What happens next?"

"It seems I'll be arraigned in the morning. Or Monday. I don't know much about these things, but I assume that's when I should get bailed out. I need to get a lawyer over here if possible."

"It's a long time since I had need of a criminal lawyer, Alejandro. I will make enquiries."

Alex glanced again at the deputy. He had turned away and was writing on the clipboard. Alex's mental energy had been released by his uncle's immediate acceptance of his situation, and by the trust in his voice.

"Uncle, you know the guy who was helping me with... with the project? I have a feeling he'd know the right kind of lawyer. I'll tell you how you can reach him. If I describe someone as the person who wouldn't swim in our pool, because he or she couldn't swim, do you know who I mean?"

"Yes, I know who you mean."

"You'll find the number on the pad in my room. Call it and ask for this professional guy's number. Maybe you can borrow someone's phone to do that. And then, if you don't mind, Uncle, give the professional guy a call and tell him the situation. I think he'll want to help."

Uncle Henry spent a moment making sure he had the details of Alex's arrest correct.

"If any of this comes back on you, Uncle, I will be very upset."

"Nobody expects this kind of thing, Alejandro. Not even us, Hispanics. As for me, I can look after myself. The important thing now is to get you through this."

Reluctantly, Alex said goodbye and put the handset back on its base.

"That it?" the deputy said.

Alex nodded. "One call is enough."

Already the energy he had felt when talking to his uncle was fading away, a bitter sense of injustice returning.

"Sign here," the deputy said, holding out the pen to Alex and pointing at the clipboard.

Alex glanced through the list of his personal effects and signed.

"Okay, let's go. I bet you can't wait to meet Murphy."

"Murphy?"

"Your cell mate. He's a little bit nuts. But he didn't attack anybody yet."

PART TWO:
MIAMI HONEYMOON

CHAPTER FOURTEEN

In the valleys between the gently rolling hills, some fields were thick with tall ripe corn, and some were stripped bare, reduced to stubble. Apple orchards hugged the southern slopes. Greg Halder listened for the commands of his on-board GPS navigation system and negotiated a right turn into a hard-topped lane marked by a "No Entry" sign. At the barrier he shouted a code word when a tinny voice asked for one, and the steel bar swung aside. He drove on.

People in Washington had told Halder, who was from Ohio, that northern Virginia wasn't part of the real Virginia. By which he took it they meant the South. But then Jack Pendleton was an East Coast aristocrat, so he probably didn't want to be in the real Virginia. And wherever this place was, it didn't seem to have an inferiority complex. As Halder emerged from the trees, he found himself confronted by an old stone farmhouse, much extended and renovated, with a pool, tennis courts, stables and paddock clustered round. Some very expensive-looking horseflesh was standing quietly in the paddock.

A man in a suit trotted briskly down the stairs from the porch, introduced himself, and guided him into the house, apologizing for the Vice President's absence on pressing business, and assuring the Commissioner that he would not be kept waiting long. Halder had been counting on an hour or two in a back parlor somewhere while the Vice President shot some vermin or won a tennis match or sold a few thousand bushels of grain on the CME, so he was neither surprised nor put out.

The aide led him down some worn and polished wooden steps, to a long low room at the back of the house, half-paneled in oak, with a stone fireplace and chimneybreast. Pictures of horses, framed in brass, adorned the walls above the paneling, and the soft furnishings, spread about in casual profusion, looked as though they had been put together from worn saddle leather. There was no air-conditioning, and the sash-windows to the stone-flagged yard were half open. The aide brought him tea and biscuits on a tray, and Halder sat down on a big stuffed armchair and opened his attaché case and took out some briefing papers.

He sat up suddenly, aware that someone had entered the room. A girl stood before him, poised, it seemed, for flight. She was thin, her features, especially her eyes, magnified by the pared-down emaciation of her face, on which a nose stud was the only embellishment. She wore jeans and a faded pink chemise and her dark hair was untidy.

Seeing that he was aware of her presence, and had made no move to discourage it, she took several quick paces and sank to her knees within several feet of his shoes, her hands clasped together in front of her.

"Oh God, this is so terrible. My dad will kill me. Don't say I was here, okay?"

Halder felt he was seeing a ghost. A frightened ghost: among the emotions transparently on display on the girl's face, fear seemed uppermost. "Linda?"

She nodded."

Halder stared at her. Talking with Linda was something he had wanted to do, for several reasons, but the girl's closeness disturbed him.

"You're Greg Halder, aren't you?" the girl went on. "You're head of the DIC. The anti-drug people. You probably want to arrest me. I'm harmless, though. Really. And I can't do that stuff any more. Not with coke anyway." She put her hands to her throat and her expression turned to agony. "Aaaagh!"

"Yeah. The burn. We know about that. I guess it was tough."

"Was it you?" Linda's face mutated into angry lines. "Did you create that thing?"

"No. What makes you say that?"

"It helps you, doesn't it? Helps the DIC. Helps my dad. People stop using coke."

"We don't work that way, Linda. I'm sure your dad has told you."

"Oh yeah, sure. My dad telling the truth? When did that last happen?"

"In fact," he said, "the burn arose naturally. In Peru, we think."

"Is it some kind of contaminant?"

He hesitated. The girl in front of him was not at all as he had imagined. He had pictured Linda as a sophisticated college kid with a rebellious streak. This girl looked lost, unstable and frightened. "Exactly what does it do to you?" he said, trying to project sympathy. "How does it feel?"

"How does it feel? Horrible! Like you're swallowing acid. Then it goes all round your head. Like it wants to explode your brains. I used to think I was having a fit."

He found himself thinking: *this is what you get when you do stupid things, selfish things; this is what addicts need; this is what my parents should have had.*

"And then what happens?" he said. "It dies down?"

"If it didn't die down, I wouldn't be here."

"But it taught you something. Didn't it? You're off cocaine, you're recovering your health."

Linda's eyes flashed with anger. "I can't *get* cocaine, I can't get *any* drug, I'm not allowed to do anything for myself, my dad just keeps me here to punish me, for being a lousy daughter, for screwing up, for destroying the family name, for letting him down personally. Sometimes I think he'd rather I was dead."

Halder was shocked into silence.

Linda's hands fluttered up around her head, her mercurial expression changing again, the fear returning. "Oh God, I'm so stupid, I didn't mean to say all that stuff." She pulled herself forward on the wood block floor. She was now within touching distance. "I just wanted to talk to someone. I thought you might understand. You know my dad. And I met you before once. Maybe you don't remember, I was a teenager, I guess. I just thought, if you know my dad, if he, like, tells you what to do, then you'll know what he's like and maybe you'll understand."

He instinctively pulled in his feet. "Linda, I don't see... I mean, what about your mother?"

"Mom's no use, she's like me, she's scared of my dad, she's worse than me, she pretends it isn't happening, at least I managed to run away. Mr. Halder, I've got to get away from here, please help me, I could hide in the trunk of your car, or the back seat maybe, if you give me the key I could leave it by the front wheel."

The girl was edging closer. Halder felt his situation veering between desperate and ridiculous. He looked up at the windows, worried that this encounter would be overseen.

"Linda, you must know I can't do that. Whatever the rights and wrongs of the situation. You need therapeutic care."

"You can arrange that. I don't care where you take me. You can do anything you want. I'll go to bed with you if you like. I know you use hookers, but I'm free, and I'm good, and I won't talk. Seriously, you can trust me."

He felt an electric current running up his spine. What? Where and how had she got hold of that? He tried to keep his face blank, uncomprehending; instead, he found himself getting to his feet, moving past the girl towards the windows.

"Linda... please... just go." He turned to face her. She had stood up and was watching him. "Your father will be here at any moment."

"I can tell him about the hookers, you know... if you won't help me." Her face had morphed again, was now looking pinched and hard.

"If he thinks as little of you as you claim... he won't believe you." His defensive jab found its mark: Linda's face crumpled. "And you too," he said. "You shouldn't believe everything you hear."

Linda ran suddenly to the door and disappeared. Her young ears had perhaps detected sounds inaudible to him: a few seconds later, the Vice President entered the room.

Halder looked at him with intense and critical scrutiny, for once not enjoying the frisson of a narrow escape.

"Have you seen the latest from our friends across the border, Greg?" Pendleton was saying, waving some documents. "A birthday party! Kids! Aged twelve and upwards! Shot down like rabid dogs. Fifteen of them! And another twenty or so injured. And for what? All the survivors can say is that the men doing the shooting appeared to be looking for someone. *Looking* for someone, I ask you. Can you believe the mentality, Greg, the sub-human indifference to life? You think there's a rival drug-dealer at a kid's party and you go in and start shooting."

Halder could see that the Vice President was expressing genuine moral outrage. The irony almost made him smile. "Ciudad Juarez?"

"Where else?" Pendleton sat down on a swivel chair and waved at Halder to make himself comfortable. "It's like Syria or Iraq in that town. We hit what, close to three thousand murders in Ciudad Juarez last year, and it's *getting worse*. It's getting worse, Greg!"

"I know."

"It's getting worse because American addicts keep on funding this illegal business to the tune of twenty billion dollars or thereabouts. So what did you want to tell me about Alex Morales?"

Halder, who had resumed his original seat, blinked and drew breath. "As you will have learned by now, Mr. Vice President, he's in jail on a drugs trafficking charge."

Pendleton's righteous-crusade expression didn't change. "That sounds useful to me, Greg. Given that cutting him loose from the Miami lab didn't seem to work."

For a moment he held eye contact with the Vice President. The message was clear: *if you arranged the arrest, okay, but I don't want to know*. He dropped his gaze.

"Yes sir. His laptop was in his car."

"And?"

Halder took his time. He was still trying to erase the image of an angry, threatening, but pathetic girl, whose sufferings with parents had perhaps been greater than his own. And the call girl habit, which had grown into another form of addiction… How the hell had she got to know about that? Only by knowing some call-girls right here in Washington. My God, she must have been a hell of a teenager.

"We're still going through the files," he said, forcing himself to concentrate. "We only got the laptop yesterday. But I think you should know that Morales was working on the idea that a virus is the principal cause of the burn."

"A virus?"

"Yes sir. A virus which is not in itself harmful, but which leaves behind the unpleasant sensitivity to cocaine. Which is certainly plausible, according to my Chief Scientist, Jon Vasco."

Pendleton's brow furrowed in thought. "A virus was always the likely culprit, Greg, and of course it's good news. A virus can easily spread globally. So what are you going to do now?"

Halder noted in passing that Pendleton didn't seem surprised, or even much interested, in his news. What else was he learning about this deceptive man?

"Of course we need to keep this virus idea under wraps. We don't want other people investigating, and we don't want Morales's work passed around."

"Hasn't he passed it around already?"

Halder heard an accusatory tone in Pendleton's voice. "We're checking into that, but we think not. If we can keep him sealed off in prison, discredited, we might stop it going any further. That means, of course, denying him bail." He stressed the final words and gave his boss a look. "The arraignment takes place on Monday morning."

"Who's the judge?"

"Arabella Costanza."

"You want me to speak with her." It was more a statement than a question.

Halder gave a small sigh. He hadn't believed it would be this easy. "We would appreciate it, Mr. Vice President."

"I don't know her, and of course she'll assert the independence of the judiciary, but she probably believes something a little bit different. Brief me on the legal details, Greg."

Halder did so and then paused. "There's one final issue, Mr. Vice President: our friend the Senator. He obviously knew what Morales was doing. Can we presume that your recent conversation with him will continue to keep him in check?"

Pendleton smiled thinly. "You should have seen his face, Greg, when I showed him those photos of him with his arm round the intern. Ashen. Of course they're not particularly compromising photos in themselves, but he clearly got the message. So no, I don't think Bob will give us any problems over Morales. He's the most uxorious man in the entire Senate."

Halder decided to take the bait. "Uxorious, Mr. Vice President?"

"Unusually or obsessively devoted to his wife. No, Bob isn't going to put his marriage at risk. He's already shown that by not intervening over the Miller business."

"Got it."

"By the way, I hope you told Gordon how much we appreciate his cooperation. Trust the FBI to squirrel away something useful. We certainly owe him one."

"I'll make sure he knows that, Mr. Vice President."

CHAPTER FIFTEEN

By the time Alex had spent a half-hour with his new lawyer, Rebecca Adelstein, a woman Jerry had recommended; been badgered by a couple of unsympathetic agents from the DIC; and been denied bail by a cold-eyed judge whose mind seemed to be elsewhere, he had slipped into a mood of bitter anger. He paced around the cell, blaming every institution he could think of. He had finally become, he realized, one of those ethnic victims routinely abused by the war on drugs: a fate he had sympathized with in others, but had never expected to suffer from himself.

A couple of days later, with nothing to do but listen to the half-insane ramblings of his cellmate Murphy, his mood had changed again. He became anxious and claustrophobic. He'd agreed with his lawyer that they should apply for the trial venue to be relocated to Miami, but when word came that the transfer would be made the next day, he began to remember the bad things he had heard about the Miami Pre-Trial Detention Center and to wish he hadn't been in so much of a hurry.

There was no reprieve. They gave him back his belongings and escorted him out through the back of the court house building. The Collier County vehicle, an unmarked black sedan, was air-conditioned, but the big man sitting beside him in the rear seat had a body odor problem that seemed to get worse with the passage of time. Maybe he's scared I'm going to strangle him with my handcuffs, Alex thought sourly.

For a while he watched the scenery, trying to appreciate and remember detail, in case it was a long time before he saw the Everglades, or any other part of the natural world, again.

His companion was fiddling with his smartphone, checking his messages, composing and sending something, finally putting it away. He seemed suddenly watchful and uneasy. Traffic on the Tamiami Trail was thin. Up ahead, where a track led off to the left, a white van was parked and a couple of men in overalls were working with a big coil of electric cable: one was half way up an electric pole, and the other was beside the van. They were obstructing the east-bound lane, and there was a temporary road sign sitting on the roadway about twenty yards this side of the van. The driver slowed down.

"You know anything about this?" the driver said.

The big man next to him was leaning forward intently. Alex could see the gun holstered at his waist. "No. Looks like nothing, though."

The workman holding the roll of cable was signaling them to stop and waving on another vehicle approaching from the other direction. The driver seemed undecided about what to do, but slowed further. The other vehicle was a heavy sports utility four-by-four traveling at a steady pace. Alex's driver had no choice but to pull up in front of the portable road sign.

"You'd better call this in," he said to the big man. "These assholes can't–"

The four-by-four had stopped beside them with a squeal of brakes. A rear window went down and a gun came out. At the same moment, the back of the white van flew open and two men in stocking masks jumped out, commando style, and ran towards the Collier County vehicle, bringing automatic weapons up to their shoulders.

The driver seemed to lose it: he screamed an oath and put his foot down. The car shuddered and leaped forward, clanging against the road sign.

"What the hell you doing?" the man beside Alex screamed.

The four-by-four responded immediately and reversed to cut off the escape route of the Collier County vehicle. There was a thud and the car rocked but continued to move forward. Alex saw the two men in stocking masks tracking back and lowering their weapons. There was a quick burst of gunfire. Alex felt the car buck and settle and grind to a halt.

"You want to get us killed?" the man beside him yelled into the ensuing silence.

The driver slumped down behind the wheel in a state of shock. "Jesus," he muttered.

Alex found himself crouching forward, straining at the handcuffs. This was how they were going to kill him. They'd push him out of the car and these guys would shoot him and they'd say he'd been trying to escape. A figure loomed at the window.

"Let him out!" someone yelled.

"Dan!" the big man shouted. "Release the damn locks!"

The driver turned his head and stared blankly.

The big man suddenly threw himself forward across the front seat and scrabbled at the control panel. "What the hell you trying to do to us?" he said.

Alex heard the locks click. His muscles knotted and froze in panic.

The door to his right suddenly swung back and he felt himself being pulled out of the car. Unable to balance himself because of the handcuffs, he fell over onto the edge of the roadway. *Now*, he thought, bracing himself for the bullet. Rough hands pulled him to his feet and half-carried, half-shoved him along the road towards the van. He caught a glimpse of one of the workmen heaving the coil of cable into the back of the van, and then he himself was lifted and propelled forward onto the metal floor. He was aware of the stocking-masked men jumping in behind him and slamming the rear doors shut. The van began to move. Alex rolled over and brought his hands up to his face and inspected them in the dim light. His wrists were bruised, but his fingers were working. He struggled to raise his upper body off the floor of the van. The men had taken off their masks and were both staring out of the small windows in the doors of the van.

One of them turned around suddenly and came back and kneeled beside Alex with a grin. "*Hey, amigo*," he said in Spanish. "How do you like the prison escape service, huh?"

***

Alex was in a daze for most of the journey that followed. The van turned off the smooth roadway after a few minutes and bumped down a dirt road. When Alex was pulled out of the van into the blinding light, he could make out water and cypress groves and some kind of tourist facility. A helicopter was sitting on the dirt with the rotor gently turning. There was a delay while the men set fire to the van, and then he was helped up into the helicopter and they were off, flying low over the Everglades, away from the sun, the sprawl of Miami and the glistening blue of the Atlantic coming slowly into view.

They landed in farmland somewhere close to Homestead, Alex guessed, and he was blindfolded and put in the back seat of a car. The drive lasted about forty-five minutes. When the blindfold was removed, he found himself in an ordinary room with green walls, a bed, and a chest of drawers. A pair of sliding glass doors let in daylight. Two of his rescuers hovered close beside him. He could read nothing in their young, Hispanic, faces, neither evil nor benevolence. He felt dizzy and sat down on the bed.

"What happened back there?" he said in Spanish. "Did anybody get hurt?"

"No, no, *Señor*," one of the men said. He was a good-looking man, with a short dark beard and white teeth. Alex recognized him as the man who had grinned at him in the van. "Everything was perfect."

Another man came into the room. He had a tool box with him, and he knelt in front of Alex and fingered the handcuffs for a moment and then dipped into his toolbox and began working away on the keyholes. In a few minutes, both cuffs had sprung loose, and Alex thankfully raised and stretched his arms.

"You'd like a beer, *amigo*?" the bearded one said.

"Yes. I would."

The three men drifted out, and after a couple of moments the bearded one returned with a cold can of Heineken.

"Thanks," Alex said. He raised his eyes. "What's your name?"

"Carlos."

"Can you tell me what this is all about?"

"Wait until you talk with the boss."

"Who is your boss?"

"A very important man. A Colombian. Same as me. You will talk with him by phone. Until then, get some rest." Carlos gave him a friendly wave and left the room.

Alex popped the tab on the beer can and took a swig. Scenes from the day's adventure replayed themselves in his mind. He felt disoriented, unable to assess what had happened. Carlos seemed friendly, but was he better off here, among people who very likely had drug trafficking connections, than he would have been in the Miami jail?

When he finished the beer, he got up and went through an open door that led to a washroom containing a shower and a toilet. He used the toilet and then put his head under the shower for a moment and dried himself off with the towel on the rack. Glancing in the mirror he saw a convict wearing red prison clothes. On the chest of drawers in the bedroom he found a couple of tee-shirts and a pair of shorts. He stripped off, feeling bleak satisfaction at throwing the prison clothes aside, and put on the shorts and a tee-shirt. Then he turned his attention to the glass doors through which bright afternoon light was entering the room.

They were locked, but through the glass he could see a covered patio and a walled yard gone to seed. An old coin-operated Bendix washing machine stood against the wall to the right. A villa in some run-down part of Miami, Alex guessed.

He turned away from the light at last and lay down on the bed. He was out of the hands, at least, of the corrupt bastards who had put him in jail. As the tension in him slowly subsided, fatigue took hold. He surprised himself by dozing off.

He woke up when someone entered the room. The light from the glass doors had softened. He sat up. Carlos was standing beside the bed.

"*El Jefe* is ready to talk with you." Carlos put a chunky telephone on the bed beside him and plugged the cable into a socket in the wall. "Pick it up."

Alex picked up the handset. Like Carlos, the man on the other end of the line spoke Spanish.

"Señor Morales, welcome to my world. Carlos has told you who I am."

"But not your name."

"I am Pedro Rojas. You've heard of me, perhaps."

Alex wasn't sure that he had, but he guessed that he was speaking with one of the new generation of Colombian *cartelistas*.

"Yes."

"So what shall we do with you? I believe you must come to

Colombia. I can give you facilities, technicians, what you need."

Alex was shocked into silence.

"You have some other idea? But we can come back to that. First, there are many things to discuss. My friend Jerry has told me about the work you've done together. Señor Morales, I can't tell you how shocked I was to learn that the burn is caused by a virus."

"I see," Alex said, still struggling to get the measure of the man at the other end of the phone. "You know about the burn?"

"Of course. Our situation is similar to Peru. Until now we've been fooling ourselves that this problem will pass, that it will remain a local phenomenon, that we have only to clean up, plant new trees, improve our checks and controls... a problem for us, yes, but something we can deal with, as we've dealt with things in the past... but it seems we're deluded, the victims of our old ways of coping with things... no science, no analysis... If this is a virus, and it spreads around the world, it will be a huge disaster for us. It will be the death of cocaine. Do you agree with that?"

"I hadn't thought that far ahead," Alex said, hoping he didn't sound as slow as he felt. "It's not clear at the moment that it has that infective power. But yes, there is that possibility."

"Our customers will find other drugs, there are always other drugs, but for us here in Colombia, it will be the end. Not just my business, but all kinds of businesses. We will lose billions of dollars and many thousands of jobs. So you see you have become a very important person for me, and I am prepared to treat you with respect. Jerry tells me that you are on our side, in that you wish to destroy this virus and frustrate the efforts of those who would allow it to proliferate."

Alex cursed his naivety in partnering up with Jerry Henckel. "Jerry is right about that, Señor Rojas. This is a disease that must be beaten. All the same, the best option is surely to mobilize public health departments around the world."

Rojas dismissed this in a short, contemptuous phrase. "Can you imagine the Americans spending public money on cocaine users? Or even the Europeans? No, of course not. They'll welcome it with open arms because it does their job for them. And in addition they'll do what they're doing to you, suppress anyone who tries to understand it and stop its spread."

Alex could only acknowledge, from his own experience, that this was true.

"Anyway, I want you on my team, and as you can see I have invested a lot to make that possible. I have a good lab and here in Colombia I can make sure of your security. Also I have ways to get you out of the United States. I think a vaccine should be the first target of your research, wouldn't you agree?"

Alex closed his eyes and let his head drop. For reasons that he couldn't immediately articulate, he knew that he very badly did not want to go to Colombia and work for this man. He would prefer to go back to jail. But he understood that he was not being given the choice. He tried to speak, cleared his throat, glanced at Carlos.

"But first," Rojas said, "I want to confirm that you have all the data and samples you need to continue your work. Jerry thinks he has everything, including live virus and DNA and some of your test materials. Is that true?"

"I think Jerry got the material stuff when we closed down my home lab," Alex said, trying to think of a delaying tactic. "But the Highway Patrol got my laptop when they impounded my car, so I've lost some data. I can maybe think of a way of recovering that, if you can give me some time, but I guess I need to talk with Jerry." Would Rojas go for that? What he needed was a lot of time, while he figured out some means of escape.

"Work on it with Jerry. Meanwhile my guys will look after you, so get some rest. We'll talk again soon."

***

During the evening, the door to his room was left open, and the *compadres* didn't seem to mind if he ventured into the sitting area, which was divided from a spacious kitchen and dining area by a Spanish-style arch. The décor was beaten-up urban guerrilla chic, a couple of couches in once-flamboyant colors, rugs mired with grime, automatic rifles stacked carelessly in a corner, and a huge glistening flat-screen television set up for easy viewing. The windows, which Alex assumed were at the front of the house and faced the street, were closed and the view cut off by jalousie shutters.

He only saw three or four of them together at any one time, but he worked out that there were five of them. None of them were Americans. They were slightly in awe of the material excesses of American life, but they thought that Americans dressed like bums and the girls were fat. They spoke as though cocaine was just another product, and earning money from the unhealthy habits of rich and perfidious *Americanos* a valid response to regional injustice.

After dinner, spiced pork and rice, he asked if he might join them for a while, watching TV, and they waved permission. He sat cross-legged on the floor. It was their own exploit that morning, he understood after a moment, that was holding their attention, and they switched from one Spanish-language channel to another to try and pick up coverage.

Several mild whoops and cheers went up from the men slumped in the couches, as a shot of a burned-out white van in the middle of the Everglades came up on the screen. The commentary described the daring rescue of a Rutgers professor awaiting trial on drugs charges, and speculated, not very credibly, Alex thought, about the underlying motives. Nothing was said about the virus.

In the night he dreamed of being manacled hand and foot in a van that was slowly starting to burn. He got up soon after dawn and had a cold shower and sat on his bed, analyzing his surroundings and his situation. He found himself remembering the time in Managua, after the death of his parents, when he was waiting to be taken to America. His aunts were with him, and he was terrified of leaving them and being taken to a strange place, home of the anti-Christ Ronald Reagan. Something of that fear was with him now, as he thought about the proposed relocation to Colombia: but his rational mind was also telling him that working for a desperate Colombian drug trafficker was not a job with a bright future; or any future at all; so he had to avoid it if he could.

Bianca, a young girl who acted as cook for the *compadres*, made pancakes for breakfast, and Alex wolfed them down, with two cups of coffee, feeling slightly more human afterwards. Jerry called around 8.30, and Carlos took him back to his room and plugged in the phone.

Jerry's voice sounded completely undisturbed by recent events. "Hey, Alex, you crazy son of a bitch, what the hell are you trying to do? Get your life turned into a movie?"

Alex asked him about Pedro Rojas.

"I've known him since Columbia Medical School, would you believe. He didn't graduate, but he's a smart guy, and when he went back to Colombia he decided he was going to make some money. For what it's worth, he has his principles, and you can trust him. Well, most of the time."

"This'll sound pretty stupid, but what exactly does he do? He grows coca and produces cocaine but then what?"

"I'm guessing somewhat, but I think about sixty percent of his product he sells to the Mexicans, specifically the Zeta cartel, who smuggle it up the east coast route and into the US via border towns like Laredo. About twenty percent goes by the old routes into Florida, and he's directly in control of that. He does the distribution himself. That's where Carlos and his team come in. They're mostly Colombians and Cubans, and they blend in with the local Hispanic population. They take care of problems in Florida, like protecting the distribution routes and breaking you out of jail. The rest of his product probably goes to Europe, through one means or another."

"And he has his principles."

"I think he'll try and give you a fair deal."

They talked about whether there was any unique data on Alex's laptop that they needed to recover; but Jerry, it seemed, had acquired everything that he needed to go to work. So no delay possible there, Alex thought, disappointed.

When they had finished their conversation, Alex asked Carlos if he might go out into the yard to get some air and do some exercises. Carlos said he would arrange it. At last the youngest-looking of the *compadres* appeared, a slim youth dressed in black, shyer and less confident than the others. He unlocked the sliding doors and opened them and Alex passed gratefully out into the yard.

It wasn't like running free as a bird through Coral Gables, but he kept it up for half an hour, going through an exercise routine he sometimes used when away from a gym or a track, supplemented with some jogging around the yard, hoping to recover some of the fitness he had lost in jail. He also took the chance to study the wall and estimate the difficulties of climbing it. The youngster remained with him in the yard, sitting on the Bendix, which was out of the sun, fingering a rosary and looking a little lost.

When Alex was done, breathing hard and sweating copiously, he leaned against the wall beside the Bendix and asked the boy his name.

"Felipe."

"Where are you from?"

Felipe hesitated, then shrugged and said, "*Habana de Cuba.*"

Alex nodded slowly, bringing his breathing under control. "We in Nicaragua, the Sandinistas, that is, used to have a strong link with

Habana. Our leaders got help and advice from Fidel."

"You're Nicaraguan?"

"Yes. Until I was eleven. Brought up Catholic, like you." Alex indicated the rosary.

"Ah!" Felipe said, putting it away in his pocket. "You know what mothers are. 'Whatever you do, Felipe, don't forget that God is watching!' Do you believe that, *Señor*?"

"It's not whether you believe it, is it, Felipe? It's the fact that your mother believes it. So in a way, it's your mother who's watching."

Felipe stared at him for a moment. "I've left my mother behind, *Señor*. She can't be watching." He pushed himself forward and stood up. "And now, *vámonos*!" He led the way back inside and relocked the glass doors.

CHAPTER SIXTEEN

The evening was warm and humid, especially here by the water, but the light was fading behind the Jefferson Memorial. The tourist boat rental was done for the day. Halder saw the Secret Service agent first, then the tall figure of Jack Pendleton III loomed into view through the twilight. Halder fell in beside him.

"So Naples screwed up," Pendleton said after a moment, his tone of voice hard.

"The Morales business? Yes, sir, I'm afraid that was a major snafu. Although we think we may have found the safe house where he's being held." Halder couldn't prevent a certain smugness creeping into his tone of voice.

"Really?" The Vice President stopped and turned towards Halder: and in front of them and behind them, other shadowy figures also came to a halt. "And how did you manage that?"

"The usual way. Appealing for help and then blind luck. This salesman out of Miami was driving the Tamiami Trail just before the heist and he recognized this guy maneuvering a big coil of wire. Thought it kind of strange."

"Are you saying he gave you a name?"

"No. But he knew he'd seen the guy with the wire a couple of times, and he remembered where. A store in Little Havana. Good police work did the rest."

"So it's possible you're going to get Morales back."

"I would put it at fifty-fifty at the moment."

"When are you going in?"

"Maybe tonight."

"You're getting help from the DEA?"

"Yes sir."

Pendleton began walking again, and for a few paces he was silent. "You guys in the DIC aren't a sentimental bunch, are you, Greg?"

"That depends, Mr. Vice President. We send Get Well cards just like other folks."

"You know what I mean."

"I'm not sure I do."

Pendleton stopped again and turned on Halder, his expression impatient. "Just don't let Morales get himself into a situation where he can tell his story. This needs to be over. Is that clear enough for you?"

Halder could see that their conversation was finished, and he bowed his head. Pendleton turned abruptly and strode back down the path. The Secret Service followed, and Halder was alone. He stood still and stared at the lights around the Jefferson Memorial bobbing in reflection on the water of the Tidal Basin.

So now he was being invited to do more than put an innocent man in jail; he was being invited to murder him. Which might not be surprising, coming from a man who beats up on his own children; but which did go a little way beyond bending the constitutional rights of a fellow American, don't you think, Mr. Vice President?

Since the morning, his thoughts had frequently drifted back to a conversation with his daughter, in which she had told him that she had enrolled in her local AA. It had been inconclusive, his refusal to meet her remaining, for the time being, intact. But her attitude, tone of voice, was new. She had taken hold of her life and was setting out in a tough new direction. And his relief and pride and hope had eroded something in his own sense of mission, his own assumptions about fixing the world. Why was he bullying people and arresting people and making life miserable for people when they weren't going to change until they were ready to change?

The only cure is to recognize that you're an addict, and fight it every day of your life.

He started walking slowly back towards the Mall.

CHAPTER SEVENTEEN

Alex took out the steak knife which he had secreted in his underpants when returning his dinner dishes to the kitchen, and studied the locks on the sliding glass doors. It was a little past midnight, according to an old digital clock which Carlos had given him, and the house around him was quiet. A light left on in the yard, and a faint glimmering of moonlight, gave enough illumination for him to see what he was doing.

Locks like this were vulnerable, as a lot of people in Florida knew to their cost, and he'd jimmied a couple himself, as a kid; but the question was whether he could do it now, quietly, with only a steak knife to help him.

He chose the top lock as the more accessible of the two, and inserted the knife and began twisting it in the fashion he remembered. He was startled when the lock popped with a loud click. He pulled out the knife and stepped back, listening. The house was quiet. He sat down on the bed. If it was that easy, he'd postpone the second lock until he was ready to make his escape bid, and that was probably best attempted at about two in the morning. He slid the knife under the bed and lay back.

He woke up confused. Had he been sleeping long? Had he heard a noise? He sat up, listening.

A moment later he heard a tiny click from the door handle. “Morales?” someone whispered.

He turned, but he saw nothing. “Yes?”

“We have a little problem. Get dressed. Quickly.”

“Okay.”

He pulled on sneakers and a tee shirt and crawled to the door of the room, which was open. The corridor was dark, but he could now hear the sounds of quiet activity, the *compadres* speaking in low voices. He was startled when someone put a hand on his shoulder. Turning, he could just make out Carlos’s beard.

“Sit down at the doorway of the lounge where we can see you,” Carlos whispered. “And keep out of trouble.”

Alex crawled along the corridor and sat tight against the wall at the entrance to the lounge and watched as shadowy figures darted through the gloom, checking weapons, peering out from vantage points on all sides of the house. Carlos said something he didn’t catch, and there was suddenly a new sense of urgency. One of them had got on a chair and was pushing up a trap-door in the ceiling of the corridor beside him.

Carlos knelt beside him. As well as a gun strapped around his waist, Carlos was wearing a small backpack.

“Your laptop?” Alex said, indicating the backpack.

Carlos nodded. “Everything important from Jerry.”

“We’re evacuating?”

“Probably. Just follow orders and make sure you move fast.”

One of the *compadres* at the front of the house said in a low penetrating voice, “Fuck. They’re here.”

“A swat team?” Carlos said, jumping up.

“Yes.”

“Then shoot!”

A crashing roar of sound filled the house, and flashes of light washed over the shooter, standing marksman-erect by the window.

Alex cowered low against the wall, horrified by the suddenness of the action, convinced that it was all over: the police would win, and all of them would die or be captured.

Carlos was now pulling at a ladder that had appeared from the trap-door. He got it down and kicked the chair away and pulled the man beside him towards it.

"*Adelante!* Go! Go!"

The man scrambled up the ladder. There was another brief outburst of gunfire, punching at Alex's ears. He struggled to rise.

"Okay! Let's go!" Carlos hissed. Figures appeared through the gloom. "Berto! Chi-chi! Move it!" Carlos pushed them at the ladder. "Alex. Follow me."

To Alex, everything seemed to move slowly, time frozen, as the echo of gunfire ebbed away and silence returned. A muted burst of gunfire sounded from some point outside the house and Alex heard the thwack of bullets hitting the walls close by. He leaped towards the ladder and half pulled, half climbed his way up behind Carlos. Up here in the loft there was a dim light and a walkway of boards across the rafters. Carlos was already vanishing through a low doorway in the end wall. A thud seemed to shake the building to its foundations, followed by a splintering sound and a crash and another burst of gunfire. Alex bent low and ran for the doorway.

"*Amigo...*" It was a poignant and despairing gasp of sound.

Alex stopped and turned. He saw a figure struggling at the trap-door hole, like a drowning man trying to rise up out of the water, encumbered by a gun hanging from his shoulder. Alex recognized the boy, Felipe. A dark red stain had spread across his T-shirt just below the shoulder. Cursing his fate, Alex ran back and grabbed his shirt and locked his arm under the uninjured shoulder and pulled with a strength he didn't know he possessed. Felipe slithered up through the hole and they both fell back on the walkway.

"The ladder!" Felipe muttered.

Alex thought he could hear sounds of feet inside the house. He understood immediately what Felipe was saying and cursed again and grabbed at the top rung and pulled. Nothing happened. Suddenly he was aware of someone beside him, jerking the ladder free and pulling with him. The ladder came up and flew over Felipe's prone shape and rattled onto the rafters. Carlos dropped the door into place and wedged it with an iron bar and pulled Felipe to his feet.

Alex's nerves screamed again as gunfire broke out and puffs of insulation appeared between the rafters. With Carlos hauling Felipe by one arm and Alex pushing him from behind, they moved with clumsy speed through the doorway, which led to another pitched roof space. A fireman's pole disappeared through a hole in a second boarded walkway.

"Go, Alex, I'll hand him down."

Alex wrapped himself around the pole and found himself in an empty storeroom. He reached up and grabbed at Felipe's legs and felt the weight of him falling into his arms. Felipe seemed barely conscious. Alex glanced around. A doorway revealed basement stairs. Another *compadre* appeared and grabbed Felipe under the arms and pulled him recklessly down the stairs. Alex followed. Carlos clattered down the stairs and the two men dragged Felipe to his feet and got their arms around him and hustled him into the tunnel which opened up at the end of the basement. Alex followed them down the dimly-lit space, and helped to push Felipe up the stairs at the end. They were in a garage. The two men lifted Felipe into the back of a big four-by-four. The others were already inside. Carlos ran forward to the driver's door, peeling off his backpack, hissing at Alex and the remaining *compadre* to get aboard. Alex was last in at the back.

What about the door of the garage? Alex wondered, as Carlos started the car and accelerated into it. Alex braced himself, the car bucked and settled, the door bounced aside and they were out into the night, cornering hard into a suburban street. Alex thought he saw the shapes of two armed men in the shadows, and he heard the zing of a bullet going by. Carlos was driving without lights, weaving from side to side. They made another screaming turn, and a small cheer went up.

Alex heard his voice join with the others, felt the group spirit riding high, and was hit with a crushing realization: this is a way of life, the adrenaline highs, the short-term goals, the mutual support; this could be him, down the road, a criminalized outsider, stripped of his citizenship, demonizing the United States, reduced to living on the fringes; back to Nicaragua, but worse.

No. That wasn't him. He had a choice. But he had to take it now.

Carlos had slowed a little but was still making frequent turns. Alex was on the right-hand side of the vehicle. He hadn't a clue where he was, but it was a mixed neighborhood of villas and homes, with grass at the roadside and trees adding to the darkness. He put his hand on the door-handle. He sat rigid, gathering his courage. He sensed Carlos going into a left-hand turn, and as soon as he felt the outward swing, he raised the handle, pushed the door open, and launched himself into the road.

He hit the asphalt with both hands and the side of his face, and the force of his motion rolled him twice over and into the grass corner. He was on his feet a second later, feeling bruised but okay, and ran with all his strength, back around the corner, away from the SUV, listening for the screech of brakes that might tell him they were coming back for him. He heard only the disappearing sound of the motor, eerily calm and untroubled, and then another sound: a police siren. Carlos had more to think about than recovering his lost cargo. Alex kept running.

He got his bearings at the next intersection: he was in Westchester, a Cuban residential neighborhood south and west of Little Havana. He stopped for an instant, listening. He felt a tingling on his face and put his hand to his cheek. The side of his face was numb, but his fingers, in the pale streetlight, were dark with blood. He wiped his hand on his trousers. He could hear a car in the distance, and the siren, fading now: but the streets around him were empty of traffic.

He turned south and ran with long steady strides. He kept his eyes moving in all directions and turned his head frequently to check behind. At crossroads, where the view to the east opened up, he could see the lights of the Palmetto Expressway and hear the distant hum of never-ending traffic. The houses he was passing had moved upscale, with looped driveways and palm trees and decorative shrubs. He ran on the sidewalk, more densely shadowed than the roadway.

A pickup truck suddenly crossed two blocks ahead of him, the guttural noise of the motor only reaching him after it had broken cover. He froze briefly against a willow tree, his heart racing, and then ran on. Up ahead a major intersection was looming, with taller buildings, traffic lights and desultory, early morning traffic. Bird Road.

He slowed to a walk, a bank on his left, a Mexican restaurant in carnival-mode coloring on his right, the ambient lighting suddenly more intrusive. A noise from overhead made him turn into an alleyway behind the bank and press himself against a wall: the sullen beating of a rotor. He looked up, but low cloud had gathered and he could see nothing.

Crouching low and keeping to the wall, Alex skittered along the alleyway until he could see where it led: a parking lot and beyond that a gas station. There were a couple of cars parked at the end of the parking lot. He left the cover of the alleyway and scanned the sky: the noise of the helicopter was louder but all he could see of it was the flash of a searchlight in the clouds about half a mile away. He ran as hard as he could for the cars, the pulsing beat behind him gathering strength. He ran around the first car and dropped flat and worked his way underneath.

For ten minutes he endured the attentions of the growling beast above him, flashing its searchlights here and there, apparently at random, a couple of times lighting up the ground around the car.

He waited half an hour after the noise subsided towards the east, and then slithered out from under the car, oil clinging to his shirt. He hunkered at the roadside for a few minutes, waiting for car headlights to disappear from both directions, and ran across the eight lanes. He turned right and then left and pounded on to the south.

***

He was weary to the bone and dehydrated. The soupy air trapped by the low clouds was tantalizingly damp. He thought of his uncle's house, not far away to the east. There was no hope of refuge there, the house almost certainly under surveillance, but he imagined scaling the wall and drinking from the tap by the pool, going up to his room to sleep. Would he ever do that again?

And then it began to rain, warm and clean out of the dark air. He ran with his mouth open, savoring each drop. And pounded on, street after street, wondering at the fact that he had not seen a soul anywhere.

He turned at last into the street that had lodged itself so clearly in his mind. He slowed almost to a walk as he made his way along the overgrown sidewalk. Yes, there it was, looking dark and sinister, barely visible through the rain, the crack house where he had sat waiting in his car for Faymi; and opposite, or nearly opposite, a plain wooden dwelling sitting in its small lot like a parked container, the house from which he assumed she had been watching him. Or was it the one beyond? As Alex approached them, he felt his fatigue and despair gathering into a sense of hopelessness.

He chose the nearest. At least there was a tin-paneled garage which gave a little cover from the next house along. Feeling like a thief, he bent low and went between the garage and house to the small back yard. The fronds of a big untrimmed palmetto were just visible against the dark sky. He went cautiously along the back of the house. The windows were shuttered. He tried turning the handle of the back door, but it didn't move. He was suddenly overcome with fatigue. He took a couple more paces, found himself screened by the palmetto and the garage and sank downwards on trembling legs. He leant backwards against the planks of the house, planning to think it through again, and listening instead to the sound of rain on the roof. He fell asleep.

In his dream he had a fish's tail, and the gang were making fun of it, kicking at it, telling him he'd have to get rid of it. He was trying to carry Felipe up a ladder, his tail refusing to grip the rungs, and Felipe was bleeding all over him, the gun he was wearing pressing into his temple.

"Hey! Bum!" someone was saying, a woman's voice. "Where the hell do you think you are? On your way! Beat it!"

The gun was no longer pressing against his head, but someone or something was kicking at his foot. He woke up suddenly, pushed himself up on one elbow and drew in his feet. For a moment he couldn't get his bearings.

"You want me to call the cops?" the woman said.

The rain had stopped and the sun was shining. Alex could see the woman in profile against the bright daylight. Slim, more like a girl. A determined girl, with a hand on her hip and a gun in her hand. A well-proportioned girl, too, curves somehow familiar.

Sweet relief went through him like a drug. "Faymi," he said, and passed out cold.

CHAPTER EIGHTEEN

The little square bungalow stood on its own piece of land, one of a row, cheap rental housing for immigrants who dreamed of their own home. Faymi had found it by going around on foot until she saw a *se renta* sign: the furnishings were basic, a big refrigerator and an electric stove, bought in the owners' first wave of enthusiasm; a table and four chairs; a bed, a battered sofa, and not much else; but it was a cash deal, no identification needed; and there they were, Emílio and María Sánchez, newly-weds from Nicaragua, looking for work.

Faymi went shopping and came back laden down with groceries and cheap new clothes for them both. She insisted on an immediate change of wardrobe, already calling him Emílio, and speaking only in Spanish. She chattered on about their new life, adding details as she thought of them, and telling Alex to remember them. She cast him as clever but work-shy, unreliable, inclined to flirt with other women, and herself as the hard-working housewife. She backed this up by cooking dinner as though she'd been turning out tasty meals all her life.

Alex went to bed as soon as he'd done the dishes and quickly fell into a deep sleep. He awoke in the middle of the night, sweating and confused. It took him a moment to get his bearings. A body in some kind of shroud lay beside him, barely visible in the dim light from the window. He resisted the urge to reach out a hand and touch the shroud; but after a few minutes he began to relax, and at last he went back to sleep.

At breakfast, Alex asked Faymi why she had gone to live in her run-down little home opposite the crack house. She explained that the cops had become a nuisance, staking out the apartment, checking on their movements; so she decided to sneak away.

"They didn't follow you?"

"No. But if they search the records they could track me down easily enough. It's okay, I'm sure we got away in time."

"How come you own that place anyway?"

Faymi shrugged and looked innocent. "You know me. I whine and I wheedle until I get what I want."

"And you wanted that place?"

She threw up her hands in a gesture of resignation. "Okay. If you insist on knowing all my secrets. A client left it to me in his will. An old guy."

"Why?"

"Either because I'm a calculating hooker, and I talked him into it. Or because he was in need of a little kindness."

"Which you provided."

"Me? Kind? I'll tell you this, *cariño*, I had no idea he was going to do it. It came as a complete surprise. So work it out for yourself."

"What I'm beginning to work out is that you're the best thing that's happened to me since this whole business began."

Alex spent the morning watching the limited range of TV channels they could get on the portable left behind by the owners. There was nothing about a police raid on a house in Westchester. Nothing about a missing professor.

Faymi got out and talked to several of their neighbors. It was a supportive, Hispanic community, she said, and it was no good hiding away and never speaking and making people suspicious.

"What do you talk about?"

"Our husbands, mostly. I told them that you were a clever man, but lazy, and that we fight a lot."

"Do they wonder why I stay indoors all the time?"

"I said it's because you have to stay in and make calls to prospective employers."

He nodded weakly.

"All the same, Emílio, you should probably begin to show your face now and then. Especially now your beard is beginning to make you look different."

He took her advice, and in the late afternoon, when it was cooler out than in, he went out into the back yard, a small strip of unfenced land planted with a few small ornamental shrubs and ferns, and worked away at some necessary weeding and trimming with a couple of rusty tools he found in a small shed. At first he felt exposed and uneasy, but the activity gradually settled his nerves, and his confused thoughts began to focus on specific concerns. He had no idea what he was going to do next, but there were people he knew he should contact.

In the morning, he asked Faymi if she would buy a laptop and a pair of cell phones with pre-paid calls, promising that he would pay her back. She claimed that money wasn't a problem, and went out and bought what he'd requested. They took a bus south and found a McDonald's with a Wi-Fi hot spot. They ate burgers and drank milkshakes. Faymi chattered away at him in Spanish, chiding him for his failure to find work.

After they'd eaten, Alex phoned a Nicaraguan friend of his uncle and asked him to convey the message that he was okay and lying low. On the laptop, he created an email address with Yahoo and composed a message for Dennis. He attempted a dispassionate summary of events following his arrest, apologized to Dennis for involving him, and advised him to secrete the file of the viral DNA somewhere and wait for better times.

"I've been meaning to tell you something," Faymi said.

He looked up at her. She was fiddling with some sugar cubes, her expression serious, diffident. She was Faymi again, no longer María, his chattering spouse.

"Linda escaped from her dad," she said. "We had a chance to talk."

"This was before you left home?"

"Yeah. She was somewhere in Virginia."

"How is she?"

"She sounded pretty much together. I mean, not back on drugs, anyway. She wanted to tell me some things."

"What things?"

"Stuff about her dad, mainly. She's got the idea she can ruin his career. She was being kept pretty much a prisoner at her dad's farmhouse in Virginia, and she hid out and listened to his meetings whenever she could. There was like a den at the back of the house where people came to talk to him, and the windows were left open because there was no air-con, so she could sit under the window in this back yard and hear quite a lot of what was said. She heard this guy from the DIC asking her dad to make sure you didn't get bail."

Alex went cold inside and stared at Faymi. "You're saying... she's saying... Jack Pendleton, the Vice President, made sure I didn't get bail? Fixed it with the judge?"

"Yeah. They talked about the judge."

"And this guy from the DIC? Who was that?"

"The head of it. I forget his name, but she said she knew quite a lot about him."

"The head of the DIC, the Commissioner, is Greg Halder."

"Yeah. That's the name."

"Greg Halder," he said carefully, aware of the muscles in his body tightening up, "told the Vice President to fix it so I was denied bail."

"Take it easy, Emílio."

"The son of a bitch. The son of a bitch!" He managed to stop himself banging his fist on the table.

"Keep your voice down, *cariño*."

"Don't you see what this means? It means it's the bastards at the top who are doing this to me. Consciously, knowingly, framing me."

"What did you expect?"

"I don't know. I don't know." He picked up his coffee cup and tried to control the action of taking a sip. "What about Linda? Will she be okay?"

"I don't know. But I have a feeling she wants to stay in touch. I'm suddenly the friend who saved her life."

***

For their next excursion in search of Wi-Fi, they went further, outside the zone of Hispanic dominance, and switched to English to put on their display of marital disharmony. Alex found a long email from Dennis in his inbox:

> Hey, Alex, I can't tell you how glad I am to hear something from you at last. We caught the news of your original arrest when we were down in Florida, and Flo and I were just totally flabbergasted.
>
> This virus info you sent me. Very very interesting. In fact, mind-blowing. Because I'm pretty sure that we're looking at something that's man-made. Why do I think that? Number one, it's just a little too clever and original. Is it the sort of thing that is *really* adaptive, that is *really* likely to evolve, even in coca-using Peru?

I doubt it. Number two, okay, almost all the genes it uses are known and out there, but there are a few that are unique, and the proteins they code for don't have recognizable (to me) functions. Number three is the real oddity: a couple of sections of non-coding DNA, very short, a few hundred nucleotides altogether, so they could be just historical debris; but I don't remember running across that kind of thing before. Here's a sample:

GTTTGGAACCTGCGTGGCGCACTACATTGATTA
TGCTG TCCTTGTAATACGTCGGTATTAGTTAGCA
ATCAGTTGGCGCTGCATGGACATTTAACTAATGAC
ATTACCGT

Just for fun, I tried using the code which Craig Venter devised for turning three-nucleotide codons into numbers, letters and punctuation, so that he could put messages in his synthetic genomes. Here's the result:

JZLIOFKRYTQNTUVEGWXDBAMHJFSKZPCLET
YGO

Obviously this perfect sequence of letters couldn't have happened by chance. So make what you can of that.

CHAPTER NINETEEN

Alex skipped through to the end of the email, but there wasn't much more of a technical nature. He read the whole thing again slowly. He felt unbalanced, giddy, all his plans, his attempts at decision-making, vitiated. He stared at the screen, unmoving, for a long time. Had Dennis really got the right angle on this thing?

"What?" Faymi said.

"Sorry, honey. Here, take a look." He turned the laptop around. "It looks like it might be a job offer."

Faymi quickly scanned the screen and then pushed it back. "I don't understand some of that," she said quietly, "but I get the drift. Is it true?"

"Dennis is a smart guy. If he says it's man-made, it probably is. He knows what's at stake."

"So what are you going to do?"

"Do you realize," he said, glancing at the youngsters at the next table and keeping his voice in check, "that if this thing is man-made, then those bastards at the DIC, and maybe right up the chain of command to the President himself, are not just keeping it under the radar because they want nature to take its course, they're keeping it under the radar because they're the ones that made it."

"Can you be sure of that?"

"Doesn't it make sense? They've been ahead of me from the beginning."

Faymi was silent.

"Listen, sweetheart, would you mind if I stayed here for a while and did some research on the web? I want to see what I can find out about Halder and his team."

Faymi looked around carefully. "What about if we find another Wi-Fi spot, maybe in a bar? You'd be less noticeable. And I could go and do some shopping."

He nodded and they got up. Ten minutes later he was hunched in the corner of a dimly-lit, nearly empty bar, working the search engines on his laptop, a beer in front of him. After an hour he had narrowed his search to one man: Jon Vasco, Chief Scientist at the DIC. The papers Vasco had written, the references to him by his peers, were few and far between, but it was clear that he was a brilliant, maverick postgrad researcher at MIT who had been directly involved in the creation of synthetic genomes, even synthetic copies of known viruses. It was not clear why he had given up research three years ago and gone into forensic science, a surprising career change by any account. Alex couldn't find any hint of academic impropriety. Had he been recruited by the DIC to head up a top secret project?

At last he turned back to email. He sent a reply to Dennis, telling him what he had learned about Jon Vasco, and asking him if he had any colleagues at MIT who might know more about Vasco's career change. He decided he should also send a message to Jerry Henckel: he could see no reason why Jerry shouldn't know about Dennis's theories; in fact it was important that he did. He and Rojas's connections could help spread the word.

Faymi returned with her shopping soon after he'd sent the email to Henckel. He ordered a house draught for her and another one for himself and told her what he'd found out about Jon Vasco.

"So *now* what are you going to do?" she said.

"I need to wait and see what Dennis has to say."

"And assuming it's true, about this DIC guy, *then* what are you going to do?"

He lowered his gaze. "I don't know. I sometimes wonder whether there's anything I'm capable of doing, given the weight of the opposition out there."

"Emílio," Faymi said, slipping into her María character, "you'll never get your life back unless you get out there and face these people down. It's no good thinking you can escape to the Bahamas or somewhere, that isn't going to get your job back, or settle the issue of the virus, or give you any proper satisfaction. Sometimes I think you're living in a dream world. You've got to think about your responsibilities, and make a plan, and..."

She continued to scold him for a few minutes, veering off the point here or there, and continuing to refer to him as Emílio, but making him think that much of her emotion was real, and intended for him. She broke off at last and said, "Don't pay any attention to me, Alejandro, I'm just scared most of the time. And don't ask me why. Shall we go?"

***

He woke up in the morning to find one of his arms flung across her, his mouth clogged with her hair. He moved back gently, thinking she was asleep, raising a hand to smooth away her hair; then he saw her eyes open, watching him.

"I'm sorry I got mad," she said suddenly.

Alex came more fully awake. "It's okay."

"I'm the one who lives in a dream world. And I know how it screws you up."

"Do you want to tell me about it?"

There was a long pause. "Would you believe me?"

"Why wouldn't I?"

"Everything I've told you about myself so far is lies."

"Faymi… I understand that. You live in a fantasy world because the real world was unbearable."

She gave him a sudden push in the chest. "Turn over, I can't talk if you look at me." A moment later, when he had turned on his side, she added, "I can't do anything if you look at me."

"Why not?"

"I don't know." She paused. "I guess it began when I was a kid. I was always sneaking off on my own. My mother thought I must be raising all kinds of hell somewhere, but I wasn't. I just liked being on my own. What I really hated was people coming to the house and saying stuff like, 'Oh what a pretty child.' Maybe I'd already seen that my mother used her looks to get what she wanted and I didn't want to be like that.".

"Where are we talking about?" Alex said. "If this isn't the Dominican Republic, or Mexico, where is it?"

"Texas. I was born in Texas."

"You don't have a Texan accent."

"I did when I was small. But my mother and father were Mexican, and my mother took me back to Mexico when I was ten. I hated it. We weren't in a big violent city like Nuevo Laredo or Monterrey, but we were in the middle of the drugs trade and everything was corrupt, poor, unfamiliar. Plus I'd lost my dad."

Faymi paused for a moment, and Alex had to prompt her. "Go on. I'm fascinated."

"He's not exactly a weak man, my dad, but he didn't stand much chance against my mother, who took him over and used him and his relations to get started in Texas. He worked as a clerk in a trucking business, and for a while we did okay, I guess, but my mother wasn't satisfied. I don't know where she got her ambition from, but it gradually got worse, my dad told me, and she pushed him into getting a better job, and when they still weren't getting rich, she pushed him into the business that was beginning to dominate the border regions: cocaine. Of course I was too young to know what was going on, but apparently my father was useful in keeping double sets of books and hiding the money that was coming in from drug consignments. I could tell he was worried and unhappy, but he didn't talk about it, and I just sort of kept away from both of them.

"Anyway, they caught up with my dad in the end and he went to jail, and my mom figured she might be next, since she'd got herself involved in some of the deals, so she went back to Mexico. And got herself even more mixed up in the drugs business, because that's where the money was, and now she didn't have an income from my dad. My mother was still a good-looking woman at that time, and that was the card she played. She could always get herself noticed, introduced, and she got to know the big players. She chose one of them, Jorge Aguillera, whom she thought she could turn into a kingpin honcho. There was a wife, but she got rid of her, and then she set to work on Jorge. Do you understand the plaza system in Mexico?"

"No."

"The plaza is kind of like an unofficial license to manage the drug trade in your area. The local police chief decides who gets the plaza, and of course you have to feed back a lot of money to him and his friends. Believe me, it's totally corrupt. So my mother decides she's going to get the plaza for Jorge. I was about sixteen by then, and I guess I was pretty whether I liked it or not, and I had some admirers and one of them was Eduardo, the son of the police chief."

"Oh, shit."

"Yeah. Big time, oh shit. He wasn't bad looking, as a matter of fact, and of course he had status, and I might have been interested, except that I totally didn't want to get married. And so my mother..."

Faymi was silent for a long time. Alex became aware that she was crying, although he could hear only a tiny occasional snuffle. At last she started again, her voice tight, all but minor tremors eliminated:

"I don't know whether I can talk about this, Alejandro. I never told anyone. Not even Paloma."

"Just take it slowly, Faymi. Take as long as you want." He waited and then added, "Your mother forced you to marry this Eduardo?"

"Yes." A sharp, dry syllable.

"Did it work? Did this guy get the plaza?"

"No. Not that I know of."

"And the marriage didn't work either, I suppose."

"He taught me to be a whore, Alejandro. That's what he taught me. That's what he gave me."

"Faymi..."

"I wasn't any good in bed, of course I wasn't, I was shy, I knew nothing, and I didn't want to be married. I was only seventeen. So he raped me, and he raped me, and he raped me..."

Now her tears burst out in bitter sobbing. "So I had to learn. I had to learn how to manage his lust. I had to defeat him by fooling him and teasing him and taming him until he wanted what I had to give, wanted me on my terms, wanted the strippings and flauntings so much that he stopped the violence..."

"Faymi? Can I hold you? Just hold you?"

"It's okay. I'll hold you."

He felt her nuzzle up against his back, one arm over his waist, one arm around his neck, her limbs tense and trembling. The image that came into his mind was of an infant chimpanzee clinging to its mother's back. He found one of her hands and held it, and she responded with a tight grip. He waited as she gradually settled down, some of the tension ebbing away.

At last she spoke in a quiet resigned voice, close to his ear. He could feel the warmth of her breath. "The worst thing was that my mother knew what was happening, she could see I was bruised and beaten up, but she did nothing. She just looked the other way... I can never forgive her for that."

"How did you escape?"

"I knew I was entitled to an American passport. But it took me a long time to get everything together, make my secret excursions to the American Embassy in Guadalajara. I wheedled and pouted and pretended I needed clothes and that Guadalajara was the only place to shop. And then when I finally crossed the border and found myself back in the place I'd grown up in, everything tidy, in order, people looking prosperous... I cried and cried. I made my way to Miami and I thought it was so beautiful... And then of course I felt flat and sad and miserable and worthless. And guilty. That was the worst thing, the guilt."

"Why did you feel guilty? You had nothing to feel guilty about."

"I left such a mess behind. I told myself that's their problem, but your mother is your mother, whatever you think of her."

Faymi cried again and then finally went quiet. Alex listened to her breathing, which became slower and steadier. The hand holding his own gradually lost its grip and he let it slide away. He eased himself away from her limp embrace and turned to look at her. Her head had fallen forward and sideways onto the pillow and her face was half covered in dark hair. Her eyes were closed. Her expression was peaceful. He bent down and kissed her lightly on the forehead. She didn't stir. He crept out of the room and began making coffee in the kitchen.

CHAPTER TWENTY

The next day, they changed buses twice and found another suburban community and a Dunkin Donuts with a hotspot. There was a message from Jerry Henckel in his inbox:

> I passed your stuff on to Pedro. I think it mollified him, although it took me a while to really explain about vaccines and viral coats, and I think they still feel you could have been an asset. But what really softened him up is the story from Carlos about saving Felipe's life. Pedro might even half-forgive you for running away. Carlos and the others are safe, by the way. You probably guessed that from the absence of news coverage.
>
> Take care, *amigo*, and let me hear from you sometime. If you're in a hurry, and want to call, this is a secure number...

He memorized the number and showed the message to Faymi.

"You didn't say anything about saving someone's life," she said a moment later.

"I probably didn't want to think about it. Anyway, it was nothing.

Felipe was wounded, I was the guy nearest to him. I didn't really have a choice."

"There's always a choice, Emílio."

They bought a *Miami Herald* on the way home, and after lunch he went through it quickly. He didn't find any references to himself, but he found an article headed, 'Good and Bad News for Cocaine Users'. He studied it with a sense of helpless frustration.

> The street price of cocaine may have gone down, but the woes of users in the Miami area seem far from over. According to a spokesperson from the Miami-Dade County Health Department, an unpleasant reaction to cocaine, nicknamed 'the burn' by users, has been endemic in parts of south Florida for several months. Tests by CDC on cocaine seized in the Miami area have so far not revealed the nature of the contaminant thought to cause the painful side effect. A CDC official, speaking off the record, suggested a possible connection with a similar problem in Peru, where the coca plant has a medicinal function. But the fact that the symptoms have not shown up in other jurisdictions suggests that the toxic additive will be hard to trace, and may no longer be present in the latest shipments.
>
> Regular users continue to suffer, however. Dr. John Melzer of the Jackson Memorial Hospital, Opa Locka, a specialist in community health, says that they continue to get admissions of addicts who cannot control their use of the drug in spite of suffering from the burn, and who can develop life-threatening complications. A recent trend has been the growing use of cortico-steroids, of the

> kind used to treat respiratory diseases such as asthma, as a counter-measure, but Dr. Melzer warns that such a combination is largely ineffective and can sometimes exacerbate the condition, and in one case was indicated as a cause of death...

Alex threw the paper aside in anger. So wouldn't they want to know that this thing is caused by a virus? Should he try and get a message to this reporter? And also to this Dr. Melzer? Or suppose Dennis were to send the DNA and other material to CDC, wouldn't they have to take it seriously, since they were apparently aware of the problem?

No, CDC would want to repeat the work he'd done, and in Miami at least the virus was now hard to find.

He and Faymi walked to a Tex Mex place for supper. Alex found a message from Dennis waiting in his inbox.

> I spoke to a friend at MIT, and he asked around. Jon Vasco was definitely a high grade synthetic biology guy. But just a tad unstable. And gay. That means nothing these days, but there's a story going round that he was OTT in love with a guy of somewhat dubious provenance, a drug user, maybe into dealing a little as well. I think we might take the big leap and assume that the drug in question was cocaine, don't you? Anyway, this guy died, nobody seems clear whether as some consequence of the drug-taking or not, but Vasco was badly shaken up. He finished the year at MIT but that seems to have been when he moved into forensic science.
>
> That's about all I found out. Hope it helps. Let me know if there's something else I can do.

Alex read this through a couple of times. Vasco definitely looked to be in the frame. Had Halder recruited him on the basis of his MIT work? Or was it the other way round? He remembered the message that Dennis had found in the virus DNA and he turned back to the earlier email. The string of letters decoded by Dennis was:

JZLIOFKRYTQNTUVEGWXDBAMHJFSKZPCLETYGO

It was immediately obvious to him that the sequence started with the first letter of Jon Vasco's name and ended with the last. He began to study the remaining letters. After a few moments, he blew the air out of his lungs and settled back in his seat. Faymi asked him what he had learned. He turned the screen and showed her.

"Does it help?"

"It gives me leverage. It gives me something to work with. If I can get Halder into some kind of compromised situation, where he has to listen…"

"I can do that."

"What do you mean?"

She slowly finished the French fry she was chewing. "There's something I didn't tell you about Greg Halder. Something Linda told me." She looked up. "He uses girls like me."

"What do you mean?"

"Hookers, call-girls."

"Good God," he said. "So that's the kind of guy he is. No wonder he doesn't care if drug addicts suffer." He stopped, watching her expression. "How does Linda come to know this?"

"She didn't tell me in detail. So I'm putting it together. But Linda is a hell-raiser. She's wild. She was into drugs early. I'm guessing that she escaped the constraints of being the Vice President's daughter, which she hated anyway, and got to know other drug users in Washington.

Who would have included a few call-girls. Also she was motivated to find out bad things about her dad and his circle, so she picked up the scuttlebutt. She would have liked it better, of course, if it was her dad who was using hookers, but a guy like Halder was close enough to be interesting."

Alex breathed out. "So what are you saying?"

"I'm saying I'm a call-girl, so I can get to him."

"You know the people who organize these things?"

Faymi poked in the bag of French fries. "I do business with a couple of madams in Washington. They send me referrals. And Linda will probably have figured out the connections, so she could well know the agency and the person who supplies him with girls. So yes, I think I can get to him."

"No. You've done enough. Why should you take the risk?"

"Because you need to get off your butt and do something."

He pulled back with a grunt. "All the same..."

"I'm offering, Emílio. Take it or leave it."

CHAPTER TWENTY-ONE

When the doorbell rang, Alex whispered, "Good luck," and retreated into the bedroom. The apartment in which he and Faymi had been waiting for the last half-hour was lavishly furnished in French-style draperies, with lots of gilt on mirror-frames and statuary, giving it a louche, faded empire feel. The bed was a four-poster with lace curtains.

They had been living in Washington for over two weeks, in a cheap apartment a few blocks east of Union Station. It was above the street level offices of a friendly black entrepreneur, in a Victorian row house, with its own entrance up an iron staircase at the side. They had one big room with kitchen and bathroom, a big bed, and a bay window.

The surrounding streets, burdened by summer heat, decayed housing, and obese no-hopers, had increasingly got on their nerves. Alex half-expected to be jumped on by a squad of armed agents. But the worst thing for him was idling away the days while Faymi got dressed up and went out, mostly in the evenings, but sometimes by day, and sometimes late at night, to ply her trade.

She told Alex that there was no alternative: she had to convince Veronica, the madam identified by Linda as the main supplier of girls to Greg Halder, that she was a top-class hooker, and that she was working her way towards a luxury holiday, for herself and her man, in Washington and elsewhere. It was clearly no good, she said, to ask for a liaison with Halder; that would immediately create suspicion. She had to make such a strong impression that Halder, whom Linda said liked variety, would choose her on the basis of her pictures and Veronica's recommendation. And that meant being patient.

Alex found to his discomfort that watching Faymi go off to her assignations, instead of dulling her appeal, seemed to intensify it. He was fascinated by the black shine of her tangled hair, the beads of perspiration on her upper lip and her naked arms. A few days into his ordeal, he was making some iced lemonade for them both when she brushed by him to get at some cookies. He reached out suddenly and put a hand on one of those naked arms. She stopped. He let her arm go, mildly shocked. He apologized. For several days she seemed unsettled, giving him a wary look from time to time. He apologized again, and assured her that he was fine; and after a while things continued as before.

All the same, he was reaching the limits of his endurance when finally the word came through from Veronica: a client called Greg Halder; could Faymi fit him in the following evening? Yes, she said, she could.

***

Alex checked the camera in his hand for the tenth time and stood listening at the door. He heard a man's voice, Faymi's welcoming tones, and at last the key phrase: "And let me introduce you to Mr. Alex Morales."

He opened the door and stepped through into the reception area, glossy with shiny fabrics and brass fittings. A man in a dove-grey suit was standing in the middle of the room, frozen with shock, staring in his direction. Faymi, in a thin, peach-colored, robe, moved close up against him and put her arm around his shoulder. Alex remembered the script and raised his camera and shot a couple of frames. Then he put the camera in his pocket and advanced slowly into the room, taking care to avoid any sudden or threatening movements. Faymi moved gently away from Halder, but Halder, while still showing signs of surprise, gave no indication he was going to fight back or pull out a gun; in fact his expression was beginning to show traces of something that Alex could only identify as resigned amusement.

It was not what he was expecting from a man whom he had identified as enemy number one, a man whose corruption and indifference to human rights would surely be written across his face. Instead he saw a man with a military bearing and a watchful acceptance of the unexpected. Alex told himself not to trust these first impressions. "Mr. Halder, I hope the situation is clear to you. I am in a position to destroy your career. But I have no interest in doing so. All I want to do is to talk."

Halder looked at him, and then back at Faymi, and the amusement in his expression turned suddenly into a smothered laugh. "Talk is fine, Mr. Morales, talk suits me just fine. And you must forgive me if I don't seem to be taking the situation seriously. But I was with the Vice President only half an hour ago, and he told me if I wanted to keep my job I'd better find you. So you'd have to agree there's something ironic about the timing of this."

"You're admitting the Vice President's involvement in these trumped-up charges against me?"

Instead of answering, Halder turned and waved at the room around him as though trying to figure something out.

"How the hell did you manage to set this thing up? Wait a minute, wait a minute..." Halder turned. "You're Eufemia, right? Linda's friend. Yeah, now I got it. I thought Linda might tell her dad about me, but I didn't see it going further than that. So good work, guys. It's a fair cop. And I plead guilty to putting you in jail. But believe it or not, now that the burn looks like being a busted flush, I've been looking for a way to get you off the hook. I told the Veep just now that it was time to give you your life back."

Alex took a pace forward, anger finally kicking into life. "You expect me to believe that, when you've got an illegal government program to protect? And when this virus you made can be amped up and rereleased?"

"What are you talking about?"

"I'm talking about the burn, of course. You have to know that the burn is caused by a man-made virus, because you're the agency that made it."

Halder was staring at him in amazement. "Are you crazy? I know that the burn is caused by a virus, but as far as I'm aware, it's a virus that arose naturally in Peru."

"Bullshit! You have to know that–" He broke off and pulled back. "Faymi, maybe you could pour Mr. Halder that drink you were going to offer him. Mr. Halder, I want you to sit down and listen carefully to what I have to say."

***

Alex got his laptop and they sat side by side on a silk-upholstered couch with blue tassels. Halder explained that he didn't drink, and Faymi made coffee. Alex showed him the emails from Dennis, and the material they'd dug up on Jon Vasco. At length he brought up the sequence of code which Dennis had translated into letters:

JZLIOFKRYTQNTUVEGWXDBAMHJFSKZPCLETYGO

"You may already be able to see that this has to be a man-made list, from a man-made piece of DNA, because in nature the codons would not all translate into letters. Nature doesn't use all possible codons, there being only twenty amino acids, so natural DNA would translate into a subset of numerals, letters and punctuation marks, signifying nothing. Do you follow that?"

"Kind of. But supposing they were using a different code?"

"Then you'd still get garbage. No. Any code-breaker will tell you that when you see meaning, you know you've got the right code. And this letters-only list is meaningful, because the underlying cipher contains numerals and punctuation marks, as well as letters. So you can't get letters-only by chance. You see?"

Halder paused. "You're saying this bit of DNA *has* to be man-made, to a very high level of probability?"

"Yes. And that it was devised by using Craig Venter's code."

"So all I have to do Alex, is trust that you didn't devise this bit of DNA yourself, and stick it into your file."

"You have a copy of this file on the laptop which you impounded from me. You can check. You'll find this sequence is present. If you think that I knew that I was going to be arrested and doctored the file to confuse you in some way... well, I'd have to conclude I'm not talking to a rational man."

Halder was silent. "Jon was very keen to destroy that file, fix it so that another virus would show up, make you look stupid. I said no, but maybe he destroyed it anyway. If you're right about him, he probably wasn't figuring on anyone isolating the virus this soon, so it was a shock when you did it. Okay, I may not be as rational as you, but I accept the provenance. Is there more?"

"Yes, there's more." Alex took a ballpoint pen from his shirt pocket. "I want you to take a look at this sequence of letters. You may already have noticed that it starts with a J and ends with an O." Alex pointed with his pen at the screen.

"I hadn't, but I do now. And, hey presto, Jon Vasco starts with a J and ends with an O."

"Exactly. Now let's go through the sequence. The fifth letter is an O. The twelfth letter is an N. The fifteenth letter is a V. The twenty-second letter is an A. The twenty-seventh letter is an S. The thirty-first letter is a C."

"JON VASCO. Shit, this is going too fast for me. Couldn't this just be chance? They're not at regular intervals."

"The point is, as you'll find if you study the sequence, the letters making up the name occur only once. This makes the odds against them appearing like this by chance astronomical. It's got to be a message. But a message that's only decipherable if you know what you're looking for. In other words, there must be hundreds, or thousands, of other names that you could get out of the sequence. But none of them, we may presume, are synthetic biologists employed by the DIC."

Halder took a deep breath and remained still. At last he got up and began slowly walking up and down, head bent in thought. After a few minutes he stopped and lifted his gaze.

"Alex, I'm inclined to believe at the very least that you're sincere. You believe what you're saying. But frankly, it's mind-blowing. I just can't take it on board. A man-made virus would not be something I would approve of. I go along with the natural version because it's out there, a given, kind of an ecological corrective. But something created to give cocaine users a hard time... it would be criminally irresponsible. And now you're telling me that my own guy, Jon Vasco, is somehow involved. Is even advertising, in a devious sort of way, that he's involved. I don't know."

"What don't you know?"

Halder took a few more paces. "It's true, Jon is a pretty weird mixture. He'll grab hold of a white board and write out equations, processes, anything. There's a huge ego in there. But all the same, it seems like a strange thing to do. Unless he's taken leave of reality, which is possible, I suppose... You don't think he could have done this whole thing, created the virus, got it out there, on his own?"

Alex shook his head. "In my opinion, no. That's why I thought it had to be you guys at the DIC."

"Do you believe me now that it wasn't?"

Alex stared back at him. He couldn't dispel a lingering distrust of the man, but the weary figure in front of him seemed to be struggling with genuine incredulity and shock

"Is there any possibility," he said, "that the Vice President knows that the virus is man-made and somehow forgot to tell you?"

Halder frowned as though trying to cope with another difficult idea. "You're suggesting it's a project buried deep in the military or somewhere, with only the President and the Vice President in the loop. But in that case, what is Jon Vasco doing in there? Even if he was the genius behind the concept, they wouldn't have him working at the DIC. They certainly wouldn't let him put his name in the thing."

"So who could be employing him? Who would make a thing like this?"

"I don't know."

"Can you find out?"

Halder had been pacing again. He sat down on a striped armchair and leaned forward, elbows on his legs. "This is where we try and figure out where we go from here, right? Alex, I may believe you to be sincere, but you've given me a hell of a lot to try and absorb. This is my career, my future, my loyalties... I'm not too stuck on my career, to be honest, if I had to resign, it wouldn't kill me. So your threats to expose me are maybe not the issue. What is the issue is whether you're seeing this whole thing right, and if so, what I want to do about it. I need a couple of days at least to make some enquiries, maybe put some surveillance, wiretaps, on Vasco, and try and figure it out. Are you going to go along with that?"

Alex bent his head. Nothing had worked out quite as he planned, and what he had planned was probably flawed anyway. He sensed that Halder, despite his contradictions, and despite what Alex had earlier believed, had at least some measure of professional integrity; but could he trust him to do something counter to the interests of his own organization?

He looked across at Faymi. He was sure she had been listening intently. "*Cariño?*" he said in Spanish. "Can we trust this guy?"

"Maybe," she said, with a glance in his direction. "I think he'll try and find out the truth. And if he tries a double-cross, we'll take him down."

He nodded. He said to Halder, "The deal has to be that you tell nobody about me, about what we're doing. You may be putting your career in my hands, but I'm putting my life in yours."

"Understood." Halder got to his feet.

Alex said, "I want to add something important. Given that this is a man-made virus, with bioweapon intentions, there's probably a development process going on. They probably tried several versions before they got one going in Peru. Then we had the virus here in Miami and a couple of other particularly receptive environments like Atlanta, but that has stalled. It's a fair bet that Vasco and whoever is sponsoring him are now working on one that will spread more effectively and create a proper pandemic among cocaine users everywhere."

Halder was staring at him intently. "My God, Alex, are you saying these guys are going to release a new version? A more infectious version?"

"Doesn't that make sense? They've put a lot into this so far. Why give up now?"

"Any idea when?"

"A week? A month? Who knows. Whenever they're ready."

Halder absorbed that. "So we're under some pressure."

"I would say that's putting it mildly."

"You know, Alex, whatever this crazy organization is, it's secret, effective, well-funded, and probably ruthless. So what you said about your life being at stake isn't just true for you, it's true for all of us. So be very careful about who you talk to. Mention nothing in emails except how we're going to meet."

"Sure. I agree."

Faymi said, "And *Señor*, when you speak with Veronica, I would be happy if you told her I was a very good little girl. Who gave you a very good time. I can promise you she had no idea what we were planning."

Halder looked at her blankly for a moment, then gave a faint smile: "Faymi, that will be the easiest part of the whole deal."

CHAPTER TWENTY-TWO

Antonio Cárdenas got out of a cab and went through a high arched doorway into the restored hacienda beyond. He didn't much enjoy his visits to Mexico City, but his mood this evening was even more grim than usual. The routine in the restaurant was much what he was expecting: an affable maître d offering his apologies that Señor Aguilar hadn't yet arrived, his associates will look after you, please have a cocktail while you wait; and the minions, only two of them in this instance, explaining that the restaurant had a strict no-weapons policy, and would he mind if they just patted him down before making him comfortable; and his own light-hearted response, saying how much he appreciated being in such a safe place; which he hoped concealed his intense hatred of everything these people stood for.

He counted, in fact, on his pleasant, but not memorable, features; his lack of height; his unaggressive manner; his unfashionable spectacles; to soften the resolve and undeclared intentions which hovered like a self-willed homunculus in the corner of his brain; the part of him that managed his secret enterprise, now a few years old and deeply embedded in the structure of his life.

The minions put him in one of the smaller dining rooms, where the tables were artfully screened by sculptures and floor lamps. He waited twenty minutes, drinking a mint julep and using his smart phone to make calls. Then his host strode in, too important a man to offer explanations or excuses, but sociable enough to express a hope that his guest had been well looked after.

Antonio wasn't fooled by the small talk that followed. he thought he could see his predictions about Mexico's future clearly foreshadowed in Aguilar's remarks about political developments: the more the state and the army intervened in the fight against the cartels, the more the corruption, the bribery and the assassinations would spread through those institutions; with ultimately disastrous results.

They got down to business, appropriately enough, with the main course.

"Antonio, *amigo*, we're going to need a little more help from you." This was spoken in an offhand way, with a dismissive wave, as though what was to be asked for was trivial, not something to which he could have objections.

Antonio kept his voice respectful, but neutral. "Tell mc, *Señor.*"

"It's the usual issue, of course. The border game. I've learned that you send vehicles across the border on a regular basis, to supply your restaurant business in Texas."

"Yes, *Señor*, that's correct. I supply certain specialized products, like spices, from this side of the border. I do that not because these things can't be bought in Texas, everything can be bought in Texas, but I do it so that my country, Mexico, can benefit a little bit from what I do."

"Come on, Antonio, you run your business to make profits, just like the rest of us, and what I'm going to suggest would enable you to increase your profits. A lot." His tone was impatient.

"And also increase my risks. A lot."

"That really depends on where you see your risks as coming from."

"*Señor Aguilar...*" Antonio chose his words carefully. "My vehicles carry the *Mucho Gusto* brand name. They are clearly identifiable with me. I have spent a great deal of time and effort building a reputation for trust and reliability in the United States. I even managed to forge a relationship with the President, when he was Governor of Texas. I would lose everything if any improper use of these vehicles was detected. That's a risk I'm not prepared to take."

"Please, Antonio, don't waste my time. We both know you have no choice in the matter. The border is ours."

"But there *is* a choice here, *Señor*. You can cease and desist from making this request. For the sake of Mexico. Otherwise I will source what I need from inside Texas, and my trucks will no longer need to cross the border."

The other man lost patience. "*Madre de Dios*,what has got into you, you stupid cunt." He put down his knife and fork and leaned forward. "You can't take this attitude with me. This isn't courage, this is a man who has lost his mind. Do you think we'll let you carry on running your business in defiance of our wishes, even if you're fucking the goddamned President of the United States on a daily basis? Have you forgotten where you are? Where your family is?"

Antonio remained still, his face non-reactive, the homunculus in the corner of his brain keeping his pulsing anger safely contained. If proof were needed that these people were expanding their reach, their ambition, it was here not just in the nature of this man's request, but in his over-confident attitude, his assumption of power. it made Antonio scream out to himself that his plans weren't big enough, weren't pervasive enough. Attacking cocaine wasn't enough. He was going to have to extend that attack to meth and heroin if he was going to knock these people down, and he was going to have to do that soon.

"I'm sorry, *Señor*," he said, blinking several times behind his glasses, "if you mistake the arguments I am making for disrespect. No one could dispute the dominance of your position, even though I like to think that in my humble way I control quite a large and efficient organization, employing over a thousand men and women, most of them Mexicans." He paused very briefly to let this point sink in, and took a sip of wine. "But neither of us will benefit if I get in trouble with American law enforcement. They can be uncompromising, and it would be much harder for me to carry on doing business."

"That's a load of bullshit, and you know it. If one of your guys gets caught, you apologize, fire him, say you had no idea, and carry on as before. They can't pin it on you."

"And what happens when the next one gets caught? And the next one?"

"You're pissing me off, you know that?" Aguilar brought his fist down on the table. "You're digging yourself into a big fucking hole, Cárdenas, and I don't think I can be bothered talking to you any longer. It's like talking to a dead man." He stood up and threw his napkin on the table. "I'll give you a week to think about it. And you can pick up the fucking check." He strode out, followed by his two minions.

Antonio slowly went back to eating his dinner. He knew more about Geraldo Aguilar than Aguilar probably realized. He was a big man in *Los Zetas*, but he wasn't at the top. He wasn't the boss. They'd send someone else to talk with him before they started on a serious program of intimidation. All the same, it was a nuisance. The kind of thing that epitomized the decline of Mexico, the expansion of cartel power, and exactly what drove him crazy.

He drank some more wine and waved at the maître d.

CHAPTER TWENTY-THREE

The bar, a converted row house, had bare brick walls and African-style wooden carvings. There was a small stage on which a juggler was performing.

Alex was a few minutes early, and he sat nursing a beer, watching the entrance, tension gnawing at his stomach. Halder arrived a couple of minutes after ten, almost unrecognizable in jeans and check shirt: a construction worker in search of local color. He ordered a tonic water and reached into the pocket of his shirt.

"Here's your new documentation. Passport in the name of Guillermo Blanco, credit card, and two thousand dollars cash."

Alex checked them quickly and put them in the side pocket of his work pants. "Thanks. What did you find out?"

"As you know, I couldn't do any investigating myself, sadly it would have been too risky. My face is known. So I got an old Navy buddy who was in the NCIS, and who now runs a private security agency, to do the legwork. And he found out a lot." He paused. "The first thing he did was check out Vasco's phone records, particularly his home landline. Pretty innocuous stuff, his mother, local restaurants, some gay friends. But Pete found that there's another landline installed at Vasco's place under a different subscriber name. This produced a much more interesting set of outgoing numbers, the most important of them in

Houston. It's an unlisted number, but Pete tracked the location of the phone to a small industrial unit near the medical district. The unit is leased to a company called Clinimex, which seems to be in the business of laboratory testing. Company records show the owner as a Mexican company, and turnover is less than half a million. So I thought it was worth sending Pete to Houston to take a closer look."

"And?"

"He pulled in a couple of local investigators and did some surveillance of this Clinimex place. They identified four people involved in the business, of which two women and one man were there mostly during ordinary working hours. Pete's guys are working on getting names and backgrounds, but they look Hispanic. There was one other guy who came late, middle-aged, well-dressed, let himself in and stayed a couple of hours. It was dark when he came out and the team decided they could risk putting a tail on him. They followed him back to what Pete describes as a mid-scale apartment building in a Hispanic area. They didn't go in to the building, but they spotted lights going on in an apartment on the sixth floor. More leg work today, and they've got the apartment number and the name of the occupant. Raúl Mendoza. Social Security records identify him as a divorced male, 53 years of age, Mexican born, but currently an American citizen. No criminal record. And this is where it gets interesting. Current employment, virologist with a Houston biotech company called GeneSolve. And what do you think he's working on for the company? A vaccine against cocaine addiction."

"You're kidding."

"No."

Alex frowned and thought about where this led. He knew cocaine vaccines had been researched and even tested. Anyone involved in such work would obviously have a good understanding of the biochemistry of cocaine; and that knowledge could be a key factor in creating the

Paloma-Blow virus.

"They're a team," he said, looking up. "Him and Vasco. Vasco has the synthetic biology skills, and this guy has the cocaine skills."

"And this industrial unit conveniently houses a lab and gives them a place to work. Right? Mostly Mendoza, presumably, with Vasco making occasional visits. And there's a clincher." Halder paused. "You want another beer?"

Alex shook his head.

"Online archives of the Houston Chronicle turned up a story about Mendoza. It's a pretty sad story, as a matter of fact. Goes to motive, as they say in court. Mendoza had a daughter. Bright kid, nineteen, never been in trouble. This lowlife cokehead comes along and decides he'll use her to get the cash for his next fix. So he gets a gun in her back and hustles her along to a cash machine and tells her to use her card. Either she's out of credit or she says no, either way it seems he doesn't get the money, so he bundles her into her car and takes her to a piece of waste ground, where he rapes and kills her. Kind of revenge for not getting his fix. As a consequence of that, Mendoza and his wife go through hell, the marriage breaks up, and I think we can assume that Raúl is a tad pissed off with coke addicts in general."

"When did this happen?"

"About four years ago."

"Roughly when Vasco was starting with you?"

"A little before."

"You reckon they came together then?"

"Wouldn't that make sense? Maybe Vasco sees the story in the papers and gets in touch. Or maybe Mendoza, and I think this is more likely, has a patron down in Mexico who initiated the whole deal, some kind of a rich patriot who thinks he's going to save Mexico from destruction at the hands of the cartels. In which case Vasco was somehow recruited by Mendoza."

Alex picked up his glass and swirled the contents around. "I go with that idea. Like I told you, developing a virus like this needs resources, and you've got to be able to do trials. Which maybe a wealthy Latino could get done in the poorer countries of Central America."

"So you and I, Alex, have got to go to Houston."

Alex looked at him sharply.

"In fact, I've booked you on the afternoon flight from Dulles tomorrow. I'll take the evening flight and we'll meet up in Houston."

Halder took another document out of his shirt pocket and put it on the table. "That's your boarding pass," he said. "Okay?"

Alex picked up the boarding pass and glanced at it. He took a deep breath and let it out slowly. "Okay. You've figured out exactly what we're doing?"

Halder settled back. "I'll tell you more in Houston, Alex, but in essence I figure I've got to bring a Houston prosecutor in on this. I've set up an appointment with a guy I believe we can trust. A guy who works with the FDA. Our first job will be to persuade him of the facts as we know them. You on the technical side, me on the investigative side. Then we'll take it from there."

***

Back at his rental apartment, Alex found an envelope with his name on it. Inside was some money and a handwritten note from Faymi.

> Alejo:
> I didn't tell you that I stayed in touch with my dad in Texas. When I pretended to go home to the Dominican Republic, I was in Texas. Anyway, he had a stroke a couple of days ago. He's in hospital. So I've got to go to Texas to be with him. You probably don't believe all

this, but it's true.

Cariño, you should forget about me, your pobrecita Mexican hooker. Whether you loved me a little or not, I can't measure up to your love, and my life will always be surrounded by trouble. I'll send you a message some time to tell you I'm okay. I know you'll beat the burn, and I'm glad I gave you some help.

Yours truly, Faymi.

P.S. I left you some money. You don't need to pay me back anything.

He sat down on the bed and read through it again. He threw the money onto the bedcover. He fought back tears. If she didn't get in touch, he promised himself, he'd find her somehow. And for now it was better that she was removed from the dangerous world into which he had fallen. He could go off to Houston without an undertow of guilt. But he wished, at least, that he'd been able to say goodbye.

CHAPTER TWENTY-FOUR

Raul Mendoza thought about his wife every day, and at many times of the day. He had stopped thinking about his daughter in that same obsessive way because his daughter was gone and he had finally understood that no force on earth could bring her back. But his wife was alive and the cataclysm that had ripped her out of his life was something that he couldn't accept and couldn't forget. It wasn't his fault that this had happened. He had a right to get angry, a right to demand retribution. She should understand that. Wherever she was, whatever she was doing, she should understand that and come back to him. It wasn't that he needed her, or even loved her very much. But they had lost a daughter and they should be tied together in dealing with that and preserving her memory.

Raul pulled in to a parking bay in front of the Clinimex facility and sat in his car for a moment, putting the familiar resentments to one side, sensing how everything had changed. He was staring out at a one-storied block with red windowless siding. On the right, projected forward a little, was a reception annex with a glass door and a big window beside it. An iron pole rose out of the concrete forecourt and supported the illuminated Clinimex sign. Behind the glass at the base of the sign were four tiny CCTV cameras, sending data down the pole and into the building. Those cameras, he had learned yesterday, had detected activity in a formerly empty office across the street and one building along: low key activity, and not necessarily suspicious activity, but enough to put them on defensive alert; the adjustment of a blind, a shadow of movement, and once the flash of a lens.

For the tenth time, he let his mind range over the possibilities. It might be nothing, but assuming they were really under surveillance, and assuming it wasn't a mistake, where was it coming from? His wife? He couldn't take that idea seriously. He might have hinted at certain things, just to let her know he was doing something significant, but she wasn't technical, and she wasn't a talker. His colleagues at work? He never talked of personal matters, and they knew better than to ask; and his few friends had dropped away. They might think he was odd, embittered, but they knew what had happened to his daughter and had no reason to connect him with events in Peru and Miami.

Which left the news from Jon Vasco.

Jon had told him yesterday that something had changed in his relationship with the Commissioner, Greg Halder. Halder wasn't making eye contact in quite the usual way. He was distracted by other things. The teasing good humor between them seemed manufactured. The affair was over, was the way Jon had expressed it.

Jon was emotional, not always reliable, but he had good instincts about people. If Halder had become suspicious of him for some reason, it wouldn't be very difficult to uncover Jon's link with this Clinimex building in Houston. Surveillance would be the natural follow-up.

It was just a guess, a low probability guess at that, but there was no real choice: he had done the right thing yesterday in sending an immediate report through to the Chief. Today he could do nothing but watch and wait. He got out of the car and went into the Clinimex building, making sure he didn't look back across the street.

CHAPTER TWENTY-FIVE

The next morning, Alex took the metro to the end of the line at Wheaton and walked across to the Westfield Wheaton shopping mall. After eating a big breakfast, he went to Macy's and bought a lightweight suit, some shirts and a carry-on flight bag.

Back at the rundown row-house, the faint perfume left by a vacuum cleaner scented the air, and he found a couple of new tablets of soap in the bathroom. The owner liked to send in a cleaner now and again, just to keep an eye on the place. He checked his belongings as a matter of routine, but nothing was missing.

It was very hot in the room. He turned on the wheezy air conditioning unit and took off his shirt and sat down on the edge of the bed. Staring idly straight in front of him he could see the bay windows reflected in the glass top of the chest-of-drawers. The film of dust on the glass top, accumulated over the last few days, had gone. The girl had dusted it, as she had done before. He kicked off his shoes and lay back on the bed, thinking about Faymi. After a moment he sat up again and stared at the chest-of-drawers. He moved his head up and down and side to side, shifting the reflection of the window to different parts of the glass top.

He had no memory of how the glass top had looked after the girl had dusted it last time, but he wondered if it could have looked the way it looked now: which was, as though a couple of crude swipes with a damp cloth had pasted the dust into swirling grey lines. Maybe a different cleaner had done the work today. That seemed the likely explanation. He could ask the owner if necessary. Did it really matter?

He told himself that it didn't, but he continued to worry over it. After a few minutes he got up and stood in front of the chest-of-drawers and went through the motions of opening the drawers and taking things out and putting them back.

Sweat, he thought suddenly.

He didn't sweat a lot himself, and the air conditioner was kicking in, so he wasn't sweating now; but the room had been very hot earlier. If a man was prone to sweat, and had gone through the drawers in a hurry, he could easily have left a few drops of perspiration on the glass. Which he had then noticed and decided to wipe clean.

Alex checked the other surfaces in the room, the small writing desk and the bedside cupboard. Neither reflected light from a window, but when he tested them with a finger, he found dust.

Okay, he told himself, this new cleaner only bothered with the surfaces that showed. The cleaner was the one who was sweating. The cleaner was the one who went through the drawers, just out of curiosity. Kneeling on the floor by the bed, he looked underneath. No bombs. Standing up, and keeping as far as possible out of sight of anyone watching the window from the street, he checked the obvious spaces and looked behind the pictures for bugs. Nothing.

He opened the drawers of the chest and went through his belongings again. His camera drew his attention and he took it out and opened it up. With a deep sense of shock he saw that the memory card was missing. The card with the pictures he'd taken of Faymi and Halder. Gone. Faymi had taken it? She would have told him, surely.

Keeping well back in the shadows, he moved around and stared out of the window. His heart was beating fast. The street outside had broad pavements with trees, but the Victorian housing stock, some of it elegant in its day, with stucco moldings and bow or bay windows, had decayed and weathered into a pathetic remnant of its earlier prosperity. Ill-fitting shop-fronts and carry-out restaurants mingled with iron grills and boarded-up facades.

Was it possible that someone out there, on the opposite pavement perhaps, was watching, keeping track of him? If so, who? Halder's DIC people? He couldn't believe that Halder was that two-faced. But maybe someone in Halder's office had noticed something suspicious about what he was doing, and had put a tail on him. It sounded highly unlikely, but even if it wasn't Halder's people, he clearly had to take seriously the idea that someone was keeping him under surveillance and might take further action against him.

He moved from one side of the room to the other, noting the half dozen people in the street who were brought into view. None of them stopped or looked up at his window. No-one was idling in the shadows. He advanced gradually towards the bay window. It faced east and received no direct sunlight at this time of day. The slatted blinds were rolled up, but the glass was grimed and Alex thought there would be limited visibility into the room from outside. All the same, he crawled the last few feet, maneuvering around the chest of drawers and right up to the window. It was the view from the right-hand glass panel which interested him. The best surveillance point, he calculated, would be ten or twenty yards down the opposite side of the street.

He ran his eye along the buildings and parked cars, checking details. There was a little black box strapped to a traffic sign pole, about twenty yards away, which he thought was probably a surveillance camera. At first this didn't surprise him. But looking at it again, he realized suddenly that there were several things wrong with it. Only at head height above the pavement, it was too low, easily within reach of vandals. There were no power or phone cables on a traffic sign pole. And although it was hard to tell for sure, it seemed to be pointing straight at the stairs on the side of his building.

He got a pillow from the bed and hunkered down with his back against the corner of the chest-of-drawers, and watched the street. If the box was a camera, how did it work? The link had to be wireless, either a dedicated link to the receiver, like a cordless phone, or possibly a 3G connection, which could be picked up anywhere. But if someone was watching the camera feed, he or she needed to be nearby, ready to respond.

As he watched, he noticed that occasionally the traffic slowed and stalled, responding to a traffic light a couple of blocks away. And if a larger vehicle like a panel truck was caught in just the right position, then the view of the little black box was cut off. It didn't happen often, and it didn't last long, but it was possible, if he acted fast enough, to get out and down the stairs while a truck was blocking the camera's sight line.

The sensible thing, he realized, was to get out now while he was still free to do so. He could wait at Dulles for the flight that Halder had booked him on, and get in touch with Halder if he could. He crawled out of the window space and threw his belongings into the flight bag and then hunkered down again in the window space. It seemed to take forever for suitable trucks to come along. His heart rate climbed.

And then it was there: the light had just turned red, a truck was covering the camera. He rolled out of the window space and grabbed his flight bag and was out of the door. He hammered his way down the stairs, one hand on the rail, his eyes flicking up at the truck. It started to move before he reached the bottom and he nearly tripped and fell. He steadied himself, swung right on the pavement, into the empty space between the buildings. There was a wooden fence across the back of the lot, about seven feet high. He threw the flight bag over the fence and glanced back. The truck had stopped and was still covering the camera. He scrabbled his way up the fence and over the other side. A black guy cleaning his car looked up in surprise. Alex waved, found his bag, and jogged out to the street. A couple of blocks later he hit Florida Avenue and managed to flag down a cab.

PART THREE:
TEXAS HOLD'EM

CHAPTER TWENTY-SIX

Greg Halder was in his office at the DIC, pretending to work, while in reality trying to work out what he should tell Margaret about his trip to Houston, when the call from Vice President Pendleton came through to his secure line.

"Greg, we need to talk. I can be with you in ten minutes."

"I'll clear the decks, Mr. Vice President."

The line went dead.

Halder glanced at the clock and was surprised when, only fifteen minutes later, Margaret told him that the Vice President was in the building. But he only really began to worry when they were seated on couches and he saw the evasive but determined look in the Vice President's eyes. Trouble, obviously. And trouble was something he didn't need at the moment.

"I'll get to the unpleasant bit first, Greg. I'm suspending you from duty. Dan Oberlin will take over. I will ask you to brief him and then remove your things from this office. This is effective immediately."

Halder stared at the other man. He was surprised at how little impact Pendleton's words seemed to be having at the deeper levels of his being. It was almost as though some long-negotiated agreement was finally coming into effect, to the relief of all concerned. But at the same time he could see that what happened next was important, for lots of reasons, and that he would have to be very much on guard.

"I suppose this comes with the authority of the President?" he said.

"I don't need the authority of the President," Pendleton said testily, "but in fact, if it makes you happy, yes, it does."

"And is there a reason?"

"What about consorting with an escaped felon? Assignations with prostitutes?"

"We're an investigative agency, Mr. Vice President. These things might simply be in the line of duty."

Anger suddenly ripped across Pendleton's face. "For God's sake, Greg, don't give me the runaround. What the hell have you been playing at? If you're going to have a cozy meeting in a bar with Alex Morales, and then let him go his own sweet way, I'd expect there to be a damn good account of it in agency records. And I'd expect to be personally informed in advance."

Halder kept his gaze steady. "How did you find out about that?"

"It doesn't matter." Pendleton shook his head irritably. "A tipoff, in fact. To the President's staff. Fortunately the informant was also able to tell us where Morales was living. Given your clear abdication of responsibility, I sent two of your men there this morning. They were able to conduct a search in his absence. Which gave us some nice pictures of you with your arm round a call-girl."

Halder felt a stab of nausea. "So you have Morales in custody?"

Pendleton settled back with a grunt of disgust. "No. He managed to escape."

"Do you know where he is?"

"No."

Halder felt his shoulders subsiding with relief. So, Alex still had a chance. Although a damn slim chance, given that he himself had lost the ability to provide help and guidance. And what was he now going to tell this idiot? How far could he go without compromising Alex and the work they had started to do?

"So, Greg, if you've got any explanation for all this, now would be a good time to start."

"Mr. Vice President, I'm going to start by acknowledging that my career with the Commission is now over. The hook-up with the call-girl is a fair cop, and I know that that kind of thing is frowned upon in today's world, even though I never gave away any confidential information. But I've been seeing call-girls for years, so I always thought this would happen in the end. In fact I can save you the bother of suspending me by offering my resignation. That said, you want to know what I was talking with Morales about. Morales used the call-girl trap because he thought he could blackmail me into going public with what he thought was a DIC secret program. A program to produce a virus that would more or less eliminate the trade in cocaine. Yes, that's right, a virus that would induce what we refer to as the burn."

Pendleton stared at him with an intense frown. "He thought the virus that produces the burn, if it is a virus, is an artificial product? Made by us? Is he crazy?"

"No, sir, the crazy thing is that he's not crazy. He has rather persuasive proof. Proof, that is, that the virus is man-made. I told him such a virus wasn't made by us, but that I wouldn't set the cops on him. We both know, after all, that the charges against him are fake. I think he accepted my disclaimer about the virus."

"So what's he going to do now?"

"I don't know. I expect he'll try and get his story into the public arena. What I can do, Mr. Vice President, is try and put together the data and the arguments he used and brief you and the President. If this thing really is a synthetic virus, it could have important policy implications, don't you think?"

Pendleton stared at him briefly, and then stood up. "I accept your resignation, and I want you out of here immediately. A member of my Secret Service detail will stay behind to make sure you comply. After that we'll talk again."

CHAPTER TWENTY-SEVEN

Alex managed to speak with Halder, by their agreed method, from the Holiday Inn in Houston, where he'd checked in following the flight from Dulles. Halder's news depressed him deeply. He had come to rely on Halder's leadership and now, it seemed, Halder was out of the game. Not only would he not be coming to Houston, but their entire plan of action, which involved getting arrest warrants for Mendoza and Vasco, was shot to pieces. Without Halder's influence and authority, he could do nothing.

On top of that, it seemed that the Houston lab had become aware of Halder's investigation and had possessed the range and power to follow both Halder and himself in Washington, in due course tipping off the DIC. As Halder said, this probably confirmed that the lab was not what it seemed and that their investigation was on the right lines: but it meant the Houston people were now in defensive mode and would be harder to pin down.

He checked out of the Holiday Inn and took the metro to downtown Houston, where he used the new credit card to increase his reserves of cash. Halder told him that for the moment his new identity should be okay, and also that he'd revealed nothing to the Vice President about the investigation of Mendoza and Vasco, but he couldn't guarantee that the Pendleton's vassals wouldn't find ways of digging into his recent actions and coming up with some sort of giveaway. So he should lie low and think of some other way of putting the virus-makers out of action.

He found his way to Westheimer Road and got a bus headed west. Staring out of the window, he began to appreciate just how spread-out and tropical Houston really was. Downtown was a tall eruption of glass and concrete, and the medical corridor was more of the same; but here, the Starbucks and the government buildings and the industrial units looked as though they had been dumped at random along the highway by some careless tornado.

He got off at the 5000 block, where the buildings turned bigger again. Across the eight lane highway was the Galleria Mall, two stubby tower blocks and a few acres of parking lots. Inside the mall, out of the rain and the heat, a world of retail opened up. He explored and found a unisex hair salon, where he had his beard shaped and trimmed and some blonde highlights put in his hair. At a sports clothing store he bought an Astros cap, and a pair of sun-glasses.

Feeling a little more anonymous, he went back outside and started exploring the roads around the perimeter of the Galleria area. The shower was over, but the thick air clung to him like a damp cloak. There were a lot of hotels, most of them the big chains, likely to demand photo ID and a credit card. He tried one, explaining that he'd had some personal stuff stolen, but the clerk shook his head.

He worked his way south, across Highway 59, where the neighborhood took a downward slide and pedestrians thinned out. He found at last a seedy low-rise building bearing the name, 'Huntingdon Suites: for a good night's sleep,' and the woman at the desk told him that cash up front would be fine.

The linen was grey with use, and the toilet gave a high-pitched whine when he flushed it, but the Wi Fi worked and the air-conditioning quickly got the temperature and the humidity under control.

Feeling temporarily safe, he sank down on the bed and felt the energy drain out of him. Taking action against the virus-makers was all very well, but what the hell could he hope to do on his own? He was frustrated that he and Halder had been neutralized so easily, and half-convinced that he should use his passport, while it still functioned, to escape back home to Nicaragua.

He got up at last and bought a coke from the machine in the passage outside his room. At least he should keep faith with Halder a little longer and think through the options. He sat down on a worn armchair and drank from the bottle. His thoughts finally focused on Jerry Henckel. Henckel had helped before and he had useful connections. Except that those useful connections were people like Pedro Rojas, a cocaine producer and trafficker, the kind of person who kept the Mexican drug cartels in business. Who in turn were the kind of people he was proposing to keep in business by getting rid of the burn.

He slumped deeper in the armchair and finished his coke. What angered him, as he thought more about it, were the assaults on his liberty, by the over-zealous drug war people, who might not now include Halder, but who included DIC agents and others, and Pendleton and the justice system. The narco world itself wasn't evil because drug use was evil; the narco world was evil because of stupid laws criminalizing the use of hard drugs. The burn was a wrong on top of another wrong, and he had unfortunately to accept that it was the only one of the two wrongs he could hope to do anything about.

He checked Jerry's secure number and dialed. It took Jerry a few minutes to go through some routines and get back to him, but when he did, he was very keen to get Alex's story. Alex gave him most of it, Jerry asking questions from time to time.

"You continue to surprise me, Alex, you really do. You got Halder on your side? And you've actually identified the technicians behind the virus? Unbelievable. What's the next move?"

"I need help. Vasco and Mendoza have to be dealt with before they release any more viruses. Then we need to find out who their boss is. Everything points to him being Mexican, probably with business interests in the US."

"You want me to bring in Pedro, right?"

"How bad of a guy is he, really?"

"He wasn't entirely normal when I knew him, but I wouldn't have called him evil. Of course being a drug trafficker doesn't exactly qualify you as an honest citizen. I'm sure he can be fairly brutal. But nothing like those Mexican shitholes. He's focused on the money. And you know the kind of guys he employs. I told you what their function is in Florida. They're not *sicarios*. They work more like mercenaries: no drugs, no unnecessary violence, stay out of trouble. Like I told you before, you can trust him. Well, up to a point."

"The question is, will he trust me?"

"Good point. Pedro wouldn't be alive today if he wasn't a cautious son of a bitch. For all he knows, you might be in the hands of the cops right now, setting us up. I'll talk to him and see what he says."

***

Alex went out and bought some basic groceries and a couple of sandwiches. When he returned, he made some coffee and sat down with his laptop at the kitchen table and forced his way through some necessary research.

Jerry called him back a couple of hours later. "Pedro is not that worried about you setting us up. You remember I told you he sells most of his product to the Zetas?"

"I remember."

"You know who they are?"

"East coast Mexican cartel. Brutal, and I think ex-military in origin."

"That's about it. You probably also know that Houston is a Zeta town. There are lots of them there, I mean hundreds. Pedro has a few good contacts with them. They'd probably kill him if he tried to do any business inside Mexico, but as long as he doesn't, they get on pretty well. He can ask for favors. And not to put too fine a point on it, Alex, one of the favors he might ask, if it should turn out that you're not quite leveling with us, which I'm sure you are, incidentally... one of the favors he might ask would be that they, well, you know, take care of you."

Jerry's voice was relaxed, as though they were talking about the likelihood of the Red Sox making the World Series.

"Okay," Alex said, trying to keep his own voice steady, "I understand the situation. But I just hope you guys take circumstances into account, because although I have no intention of giving the cops any help on this stuff, they might still track me down. I might still end up in custody."

"Okay, understood, but if that happens, Alex, make sure you call your lawyer, Becky, right away. And don't tell them anything. Nothing. We'll understand. As long as you don't disclose anything about this operation, there'll be no problem."

Alex wasn't sure he believed that. "Okay."

"Pedro is talking with his advisers, but I think he's going to buy into this. I already told him long ago about the virus being man-made, so he's had time to adjust to that idea."

"So what happens next?"

"I expect he'll bring Carlos into the picture, but Carlos's team mostly don't like airport checks, so they have to move by car. We need you to do some advance work for us. This Mendoza guy, the one based in Houston... Find out if he's still around, whether he's gone to ground, whether he's surrounded by Mexicans... whatever you can."

"I've already done some work on Mendoza. What we really need to do is find him, right? Assuming, like you say, that he's hiding out somewhere."

"That would be great. But don't take any serious risks. We need your expertise."

"Okay. But if I'm going to get anywhere, safely, I need technical help. Someone who is really good with phones. Maybe if your friend Pedro has got all these connections in Houston, he could turn up a name."

***

The phone-guy showed up at Alex's suite at quarter to ten in the evening. He was a big, shambling youngster, dressed in tee-shirt, shorts and sandals, with a heavy-looking canvas bag slung across his shoulder. He seemed low on social skills, shaking hands with fastidious reluctance, and looking round Alex's accommodation with a frown of uncertainty.

"I didn't want to do this job, but the guys I usually work for said I had no choice."

"Understood. What do I call you?"

He got a couple of pieces of equipment out of his bag before replying. "Sam."

"Okay. Well, thanks for helping out."

Sam fitted a pair of lightweight headphones into his ears, and concentrated on a large smart phone in his hand. He gave a brief, disbelieving nod, and then began waving a small directional antenna at the walls of the room, his expression concentrated.

"What are you doing?" Alex said at last.

"Checking the wireless environment. A lot of people don't realize how easy it is to eavesdrop on their conversations."

"Anything suspicious?"

Twisting around on the couch, Sam completed his survey of the walls. "No. Just normal stuff. So tell me what I've got to do."

"I need the personal cell phone number of a guy called Raúl Mendoza."

Sam gave a perfunctory nod. "You got any phone numbers at all?"

"I've got a cell phone number which he lists on the web site of GeneSolve, the company he works for."

"Tell me."

Sam took off his headset and put his antenna back in his bag. Alex crossed to the desk where he'd left his laptop and read off the phone number he'd noted earlier. Sam picked up his chunky smart phone and entered the number.

"No," he said after a moment. "Not active. It's either switched off, or retired, or somewhere outside the continental United States."

Alex sighed, his disappointment acute. "Okay... In that case..."

"That's all you got?"

"That's all I've got upfront. But my gut feeling is he's using a cell phone to keep in touch with his associates. So he's using a clean phone. The question is, if I can get you close to him, can you get the number?"

Sam looked up and held his gaze for a moment. "You know where to find him?"

"I figured we'd stake out his place of work. As far as I could find out safely, he still shows up for work. But he's not living at his normal apartment address. He's hiding out somewhere. I need to find that hideout. Which means, I think you'd agree, finding the number of his clean phone. So, what I figure is, maybe he switches on his work phone during office hours."

***

At nine-twenty the next morning he was sitting at the wheel of Sam's Ford Focus, a mattress dealership to his right, a gas station and a KFC further down the road, and the GeneSolve glass-and-concrete block just visible through some trees. Mendoza's listed work phone had indeed come live and Sam, using his antenna, had confirmed that he was in the building.

The lunch hour came and went, with no sign that Mendoza was taking a break. He and Sam took turns to visit the KFC and pick up some chicken and fries and visit the restroom. Alex was concerned lest Sam lose concentration, fall asleep, or finally lose patience and quit: but he seemed to retain his interest in what his equipment was telling him, and he filled in time reading technical manuals.

It was after three when Sam suddenly focused and put his technical manual aside. He adjusted his directional antenna and checked the readings on his instruments.

"He's on the move."

"Okay."

They had determined from Sam's reconnoitering of the GeneSolve car park that the vehicle most likely in use by Raúl Mendoza was a chauffeur-driven black Impala. The chauffeur, Alex theorized, was in reality a bodyguard, and the switch away from driving his own car was part of the new defensive setup. To Alex's relief, as he swung into the light traffic and coasted down towards GeneSolve, this was the vehicle that pulled out of the GeneSolve lot and joined the traffic in front of them.

It was hard to tell whether the Impala was deliberately making evasive maneuvers, but they lost visual contact several times, and only managed to keep track of it with the help of Sam's directional antenna. The last of these maneuvers confused them for several minutes, but circling round they spotted an access road to a restaurant court. Alex eased the Ford up the access road, and they saw the black Impala at the same time, slotted into a space alongside a truck and a blue compact.

"Park facing away but with line-of-sight contact," Sam said.

Alex hesitated then swung around the edge of the lot and into a suitable space. "Okay?"

"Yeah."

"Did you see who was in the car?"

"Two guys. The one in the passenger seat was on the phone."

"Maybe the phone we're looking for?"

Sam began playing with the position of his antenna, keeping it below window level. "I can probably grab some of the conversation and get the number of the guy he's calling, as well as the number of the phone he's using. Then we'll know."

Alex looked around. To allay suspicion, he ought to go and get some coffee. He took a deep breath and got out of the car. There was a faint chance that the chauffeur driving Mendoza was someone who had followed him in Washington, but he figured his disguise would hold. He had to wait a couple of moments for service. He felt the arrival of somebody behind him in the line. When he turned around with his change and his lattes, he kept his eyes moving, as though his only thought was to steer his way out of the restaurant. Nobody in the line paid him any attention.

"Anything?" Alex said, when he got back to the Ford.

Sam didn't look up. "I'm recording a conversation. I didn't listen to it, but I'm ninety percent sure it's from the Impala."

"And it's a different number? Not the work phone number we've been following?"

"Right."

"What do you need to be a hundred percent sure it's from the Impala?"

"Another angle. When you drive out of here, pause a little before you go out on the street. I'll get another reading on it."

Alex followed Sam's instructions, coasting down the alley and pausing at the road junction until Sam said he was done.

"So, what's the verdict?" Alex said as he picked up speed and joined the traffic.

Sam didn't reply. Alex glanced over at him. He was pursing his lips and nodding his head up and down in what looked like annoyance. "The verdict is," said slowly, "that I frigging well got it… right." A thin smile broke out suddenly on his features.

Alex reached over and gave him a light punch on the arm. "So we've got the number of Mendoza's unregistered phone, right? And as long as he leaves it switched on tonight, you can tell me where he lives."

"Let's wait and see what happens. But I think so, yes."

CHAPTER TWENTY-EIGHT

Raúl Mendoza came awake for the fourth time since the start of a restless night. He opened his eyes. A faint wash of moonlight bathed the room. The window behind him, thinly covered by a sheer drape, was reflected in the full-length mirror on the door of the wardrobe. He watched and listened intently, trying to identify any sounds that might have woken him. He slept with the window open and the air-conditioning off, in spite of the heat, preferring to hear what was happening in the park around him: an occasional vehicle passing, a drunk neighbor singing. When the wind got up, the big tree close to his trailer-home might give an arthritic creak. Hurricane Martina was tracking its way across the Caribbean, and was predicted to make landfall on the Louisiana or Texas coasts, but that wasn't affecting the local weather as yet; the drape across his window was barely moving.

Raúl shifted his position on the bed and closed his eyes again. In reality, the risk of attack out here in the boondocks was surely low. He and José had worked a trick or two to avoid being tailed, and his phone was new and clean. What was Morales going to do, even if he was still in Houston?

He was beginning to relax when he thought he heard the swish of a tree branch swinging back into place. He sat up, holding his watch up to the moonlight: it was shortly after two o'clock. He wondered whether to take a look outside. His cell phone began to ring. He grabbed it from the bedside cabinet and checked the incoming number: Jon's landline. He jabbed the button and put the phone to his ear.

An automated voice said, "Motion sensor alarm at 1236 Portland Place, Bethesda, Maryland, activated this morning at 3.07 am." The message was repeated.

Raúl swung his feet to the floor as his heart beat a tattoo inside his chest. What the hell was happening now? The address was Vasco's, and it had been Jon's over-wrought idea to put him on the notification list when his alarm went off. He checked his watch again. Washington was an hour later, of course, so the message was in real time: Jon was at this moment responding, or panicking, or, like himself, trying to figure out what had triggered his alarm.

Raúl stood up and went to the window and peered out cautiously. A couple of the trailer-homes had porch-lights or night-lights still on, but it was mostly a world of dark shadows, impossible to penetrate. He retreated back to the bed and opened the drawer of the bedside cabinet and took out the inhaler. He held it in his hand and stared at it, the tension in him growing by the second. He hadn't anticipated such an acute dilemma: a situation that seemed menacing, but that was also ambiguous, uncertain. He wouldn't get a second go at infecting himself: once he'd done it, and gone through the infection cycle, he'd be immune. On the other hand, if he missed his chance, and everything slipped out of his control, he might never have another safe opportunity.

He put down the inhaler abruptly and picked up his phone and clicked on Vasco's number. Maybe Jon had already discovered that the alarm had been triggered by a bird or a cat. There was no answer. Raúl let it ring, the seconds ticking by, but nothing happened. Jon was taking care of the alarm, too busy to answer the phone. Or worse, the alarm was real and he was under attack.

Raúl canceled the call and tried to think. If Jon was going down, the latest virus was never going to get fixed and improved. He might as well release it now. But Jon might not be going down. And he himself was probably imagining the noises out there in the dark, the sense of menace.

He stood in a state of shock and uncertainty, unable to breathe. Should he call the Chief? José? He reached down suddenly and picked up the inhaler, his decision mandated by deeper layers of his brain. With skittering haste, he went into the bathroom and locked the door. At almost the same moment there was a crash and the trailer rocked on its moorings. Heavy footsteps vibrated along the floor.

Fingers shaking, he pushed at the buttons on the inhaler, felt the give of the capsule inside. He forced the air out of his lungs and put the inhaler in his mouth and drew a long steady breath. It was working: he could feel powder at the back of his throat. He held his breath for a few seconds, coughed and swallowed.

The footsteps, two or three pairs, he judged, had ranged through the trailer, to the sounds of shouts and banging doors. Now a fist banged on the door of the bathroom.

"Mendoza? You've got no chance. We're all around you. Come out quietly, hands raised."

He dropped the inhaler in the toilet and flushed. He felt his whole body trembling, a sickness in his gut. He cursed his failing heart, the accumulated ailments of the last few years. He had to stay tough. He had to stay alive. It was all winding down now towards a final payoff, and he needed a couple of days to see it through.

He reached out and unlocked the door.

CHAPTER TWENTY-NINE

The ranch-house base, to which Alex was taken by Rojas's team, was west of Houston and a couple of miles off route 59. It stood in the midst of 35 acres of flat meadow-land, with no other homes in sight. It had originally hosted a horse-breeding business, and the stables and paddocks and a covered display area were still in place; but the house itself, a confection of brick and wood and fabrics straight out of a catalogue, had taken a lot of wear and tear, perhaps from its recent narco-connected occupiers. An unpleasant smell lingered like stale incense.

It was the middle of the night, but to give himself something to do while he waited for the team to return with Mendoza, he found some cleaning materials and tried to make his room a little less repellent. When at last he picked up the sound of men entering the house, he went out to the hall. The newcomer among the four men wore only a sweatshirt, shorts and sandals, and he was restrained by handcuffs. Felipe, the only team member whom Alex knew from Miami, had a hold of his arm, but the newcomer seemed passive, his expression somewhere between watchful and resigned.

Alex recognized him both from the pictures he had found on the internet, and also as the man in the car which he and Sam had followed the previous day. In person, he looked older and browner, the long face showing firmness of character, the mouth stubborn. Alex found it hard to summon up the hatred and resentment he had briefly harbored for Greg Halder: this man wasn't a personal enemy; he was more of a deranged, tragic figure to be regarded with pity and distaste.

"Any problems?" he said in Spanish.

Alberto, the team-leader, didn't answer. He was a stocky, bullish man, with quick, impatient eyes. He was staring at Mendoza in disgust. He reached out suddenly and grabbed the man's sweatshirt and twisted it in his fist. "*Idiota! Cabron!*" he said, "You miserable piece of goat shit! You had better change your ideas by tomorrow, or I will stuff your balls up your ass and pull them out of your ears! You understand me?"

Mendoza stiffened, and his eyelids fluttered for a moment, but his expression remained firm. He said nothing.

Alberto pushed him away. "Take him to the basement," he said to the other two. "Watch him even when he pees."

As the three men passed Alex, Mendoza gave him a look, but showed no sign of interest or recognition.

"What happened?" Alex said.

"I need a beer," Alberto said and headed for the kitchen.

Alex followed.

Alberto took a can of Budweiser from the fridge and popped the tab. "The son of a bitch has a story." He swigged from the can. "Like he was just a pawn in the hands of others, didn't know what was going on, had to lend out his lab, all kinds of crazy stuff."

Alex thought about that. "No. It doesn't work. Mendoza is the guy who talks to Vasco. We've recorded a couple of calls. Mendoza is the cocaine expert."

Alberto took another swig of beer. "We'll get it out of him. He'll cut the crap tomorrow."

"Did Carlos get Vasco?"

"Yes. Vasco fell nicely into the pot. I just hope the prick is less of an idiot than this one."

* * *

Alex stayed within reach of the sitting room, where the interrogation the next morning took place, but he decided he would not contribute to the process unless he was asked. He heard Mendoza cry out a couple of times, when, Felipe told him later, an enraged Alberto had struck him across the face; but the news reported to him during the day was depressingly negative; the son of a bitch refused to understand that the game was over and that his best hope of survival was to give up the basic facts about the virus program, and the details of the organization behind it.

Alex spent most of his time working away at Mendoza's laptop, which the team had found at his hideout, but the cipher protecting the important files was a professional piece of work, and he couldn't break it. He began to wonder whether they should consider forcing their way into the Clinimex lab and looking for evidence there, but here again, these were professionals, and they would surely have dispersed the staff and removed any evidence of the virus from the lab.

Carlos arrived with Jon Vasco and a couple of other gang members in the early hours of the following morning. There was no sign of them when Alex got up. An hour after breakfast, he was sitting at the dining table with Mendoza's laptop open in front of him, having another go at the cipher, when he suddenly felt the cold barrel of a gun against the back of his neck. A voice said in Spanish:

"The long journey is over, Alex Morales. You're finally back in my custody. Turn round slowly."

Shocked, Alex half-raised his hands and twisted around in his chair. Carlos was grinning at him, the gun, if it was a gun, no longer visible.

Alex stood up in relief. Carlos gave him a hug and a pat on the back and fingered Alex's new beard.

"Not as good as mine, but okay."

Alex stared at him for a moment, uncertain of his feelings. He recognized that during his brief time as this man's prisoner, he had been affected by Stockholm syndrome: a switch of loyalty in his favor, caused in part by the escape from jail, and in part by the fair and good-humored treatment for which Carlos was responsible. He was, in fact, a man whom it was difficult not to like and admire. No doubt he'd done bad things, operated under a different moral code from his own; but he was a natural leader, and Alex's main feeling, as he squared up to the other man, was guilt at the way he had cut and run.

"You've forgiven me?" he said at last.

"For landing me in the shit? What can I say, now that you've returned to the fold? Life moves on. Let's have coffee and talk with Alberto."

Alex warmed up some muffins in the microwave and Alberto joined them and they sat at the dining table, eating the muffins and drinking black coffee. Carlos gave a colorful account of the journey from Washington with Vasco.

"The guy couldn't wait to talk. He was shitting himself. No, I mean literally. We had to stop at a gas station and march him into the rest room and get him changed and cleaned up, he was stinking up the SUV. So now he's dressed in tangerine shorts and a sort of Indian thing and he's complaining, or apologizing, that he brought the wrong wardrobe and we rushed him too much.

"Anyway, I figure I should keep the pressure on, keep hitting him with questions, which I do, as we drive, and he's all over the show. He's got half a dozen answers for everything, and some of them are off the wall. He thinks if he doesn't keep talking we're going to murder him and dump him by the roadside. I may have suggested something of the kind, mind you, and my English is not always as good as it should be, but all the same, this guy is freaked out. He sees what a lousy idea it was to create a virus that would upset a lot of people, and he's very sorry about that. But what he comes back to, over and over, is that a new version of the virus–which yes, they were working on–never got done, never got the bugs ironed out, so everything's okay, nothing was released, the planet is safe, and on and on."

"What about the Mexican end of things?" Alberto asked.

"First of all, he confirms that there is a high-profile Mexican providing funding and some logistical backup, but from the way he talks, you'd think it was him, Vasco, who was calling the shots, and this Mexican guy was just a useful backer, although he swears he doesn't know who this guy is. I pushed him, but he stuck to that, and I'm inclined to believe him. First, it makes sense for the Mexican, who is playing a very dangerous game. Second, the state Vasco is in, he's ready to tell us anything. He thinks we're the ones who are going to kill him, not the Mexican. However, he says that Mendoza knows who he is, that they go way back. Also that Mendoza once let slip that although he spends a lot of time in Mexico City, he has a base or a business in Monterrey. Zeta territory, of course. Maybe the guy has a beef with the Zetas."

"We can use that as leverage on Mendoza, but this Mendoza is a–" Alberto used a very uncomplimentary Latino word. "He denies everything. I'm glad you're here, *compadre*. Maybe you will stop me from killing the bastard."

Carlos laughed. "Maybe I'll have to stop you killing both of them. This new one is a lunatic. He wouldn't even eat a hamburger without a long spiel about all the crap in modern beef products. And this is a guy who wants to pass viruses around."

"Let me talk to him alone," Alex said. "Maybe I can get through to him on a technical level."

***

Jon Vasco was still wearing the tangerine shorts when Carlos brought him into the kitchen an hour later, but he had discovered something more conventional in the way of a shirt. Alex studied him with curiosity. He had the college kid look, the sense of entitlement, the good features, the wavy hair; but this was a college kid who'd been kicked out of school, dumped by his partner, disowned by his family; all kinds of misery were reflected on his mobile, sensitive features. His mouth, in particular, was in constant movement, perhaps to stop his lips trembling. His eyes were sharp with wounded pride.

Alex realized that this was someone very close to his own world: too old to be one of his students, but akin to his younger colleagues; someone, however, who'd gone so badly off the rails that he seemed less human, less sympathetic, than the mercenary gang-leader standing beside him.

"Shout if he does anything stupid," Carlos said. "We've got guys around, inside and out."

Alex nodded and Carlos disappeared through the arch.

"No, I won't shake hands," Vasco said, holding up his hands defensively.

"Okay, fine," Alex said. "Would you like some coffee? Muffins?"

Vasco stood still, his expression confused, as though these questions required thought. Then he said quickly, "Coffee only, Colombian if you have it."

"Would we have anything else?" Alex said as he went to the counter and poured coffee from the flask. He motioned Vasco to the breakfast alcove and they sat opposite each other, Vasco still twitching in nervous expectation.

"I want to start with the basics," Alex said. "Peru, where I first came across this thing. I presume you'd done a fair amount of preliminary development and testing, and you thought you had the right product, and you released it in Peru to make it seem as though it had evolved in that environment, a coca-rich environment."

Vasco jumped in almost before he had finished: "The virus you came across in Peru was the second to be released there, yes, for the reasons you say, the first having failed to take hold and spread. It was actually number five in a development series. We did a lot of work to make sure that it was broadly-speaking safe."

"It was never going to be safe, though, was it? It could have mutated in unpleasant ways."

"No, no, that's not true, Professor, if I may say so, there are clever ways in which you can ensure a degree of stability, genetic loops, fail-safe devices, that will weaken the infectivity of the virus if it mutates away from the original template. Of course you will have found my coded messages in the genome, but those precautionary elements might have given away the artificial origins of the virus anyway. Was it you who did the analytical work, Mr. Morales?"

"No. I showed it to a friend."

"Well, he was quite clever, but I expect he mainly believed the virus was man-made because of my messages. My little bit of vanity. Of course I didn't expect it to come out so soon. That was bad luck."

"So what were you planning to do? When events finally revealed that people like you were behind it?"

Vasco steadied his trembling hands by clasping them around his coffee mug. His eyes became more agitated. "I thought that when the virus was working, and there was a great improvement in the cocaine problem, and drug traffickers were caught, everybody would see what a good idea it was. Yes, perhaps I'd have to hide out for a little while, depend on influential protectors, but I didn't really think..."

Vasco released his coffee mug and sat back and threw up his hands. "Okay, I see the world on my own terms, but, but, *I am smart enough to do that, I should be able to do that!*" He slumped back in his chair, trembling.

Alex watched him for a few seconds, trying to understand the character he was dealing with. It seemed clear to him that Vasco believed himself to be the originator and creator of the whole project, which, at the intellectual level, might even be true: but it was also true, as far as he could see, that Mendoza was the local organizer, the paymaster, and perhaps in some measure the motivator, the one who, under the guidance of the Mexican patron, pushed the technical work forward. How the two of them had come to pool ideas and resources was something he might untangle later, but for now it didn't seem important.

"Okay," he said, "let's go back to the basics. You released the virus, version number five, in Peru. Did it spread naturally to Miami, or did you help it along?"

"We let it spread naturally. Oh, how frustrating that was!" Vasco now grabbed his hair instead of the coffee mug. "Watching it push forward a little here or there, and then fade and peter out, like a hurricane that looks good approaching the Gulf and then fails to accumulate energy and dies away. Pretending to the Commissioner that I was a dispassionate researcher, when I was seething inside! It took a brief shine to Miami, and Phoenix, and Atlanta, and we think there were probably outbreaks in Mexico that simply didn't get reported, and then it lay down and died. Back to the drawing board."

"So we were right. You were working on a version with increased infectivity."

"A new viral coat, so that those who got the old version would get the new version as well, and, as you say, greater infectivity. I produced version six, and version seven, but there were problems."

"What kind of problems?"

Here Vasco began to get technical, and excited, going into details which Alex had insufficient knowledge of the subject to follow. He backed him up, and asked questions, but Vasco chose at times to be obscure. He understood that in essence Vasco wanted a virus that would be transmitted between all members of the population, not just between those that were using cocaine. When Alex had been studying Paloma and her friends, it had been clear that only those using cocaine had fallen victim to the virus; none of the others had shown the signs of primary infection, and he was certain that neither he nor Faymi had picked up the virus themselves. This hadn't much inhibited the transmission of the virus in Peru, where the use of coca was widespread, but it seemed there wasn't enough continuity between cocaine users in the United States to take the virus reliably from one population group to another.

So Vasco had worked on a virus that would carry the genetic profile of cocaine along with it, but would not need to find cocaine itself in the blood of its victims. Non-users of cocaine would experience only the very mild, primary symptoms and would probably never know that they had been infected. There would be the advantage, however, from Vasco's point of view, that these people, the population at large, would henceforth carry the secondary sensitivity in their immune systems, and if at some stage they decided to sample cocaine, they would suffer the allergic response.

Alex was able to extract these essentials from Vasco's frenetic account, but the reasons for the failure of versions six and seven was harder to tease out of him: Vasco admitted that his prototypes were trialed somewhere in, he thought, Central America, but he seemed uneasy about providing details of the results; whether because he couldn't fully explain what was happening, or because he was hiding something, Alex wasn't sure.

"So the versions you trialed were not viable? End of story?"

"They were not viable. I failed. I failed! And then everything else begins to go wrong. I worried about the Commissioner, I worried about Mendoza, I worried about this fussy Mexican patron, and I couldn't concentrate. Raúl asks me how long do I need, how long till I can fix it, and I tell him one week, two weeks, but who knows? *Quién sabe*, as you people say. It might have taken me months! Even if I was thinking straight! Everything was collapsing and I was so angry, so angry that my..." Vasco broke off, stared fixedly at the table and then grabbed his coffee mug.

"Here's the important question," Alex said slowly. "Does this Mexican guy, whoever he is, the one who's funding you, have the resources, the bio-engineers... to finish off your work? To make this new virus viable?"

"Oh please," Vasco said with a distracted frown. "Finish off my work? Mexicans?"

"It wouldn't have to be Mexicans. Couldn't he find Indians, or Russians?"

Vasco put down his coffee cup, suddenly agitated. "Nobody can finish off my work! They'd get it wrong! They wouldn't understand the subtleties, the care you have to take. I'm not completely without morals. I care what gets out there! Believe it or not, I want to benefit the world, not dump bio-garbage into the environment."

"But does the Mexican share those feelings?"

"I don't know! Maybe not! You must get Raúl to give you his name."

CHAPTER THIRTY

Raúl Mendoza lay on his bed in the basement, struggling to stay calm. So Jon Vasco had been hauled all the way from Washington and was talking freely to Morales and the others. That was infuriating but also, probably, irrelevant. He should concentrate on his own priorities.

Raúl felt a galvanic kick in his calf muscle, followed by one in a bicep. He sat up and swung his legs to the floor. His limbs, like his heart, had acquired a life of their own, signs of increasing tension, and of the blows he had taken yesterday from the narco-shits. He was fiercely proud of his resistance, but he knew he wouldn't survive their escalating anger for long: never mind, he told himself, he wouldn't need long; an hour ago he'd begun to feel the tingling at the back of the throat that told him that the virus had taken, and that he was reaching the infectious stage. All he had to do was pass it on to the people in the house, and they, surely, would disperse it to the wider world.

He was glad when one of the men came and took him up to the sitting room. Morales was there, and the loud-mouthed one, Alberto; also a new one with a beard who seemed now to be in charge. The loathsomely familiar one was standing a little apart, weak and silly in orange shorts. How had he ever managed to cooperate with such an egotistical, self-deluding maniac? He let his eyes pass on, as though this man was just another statue, of no significance, stirring no memories.

The newly-arrived bearded one pointed to one of the high-backed chairs planted in a ring around the sitting room. Raúl sat down.

He heard Vasco say in his high, overbearing voice, "Yes, yes, that's Mendoza. No, no, Raúl. There's no point hiding like that. It's over. You're just going to hurt yourself. Please, for God's sake, don't be *stupid*."

Mendoza looked at the new leader, whose name, the gang members guarding him had told him, was Carlos. "Who is this man?" he said in Spanish.

He expected abuse of some kind to follow, and he clenched his jaw in anticipation, but Carlos grinned, as though witnessing an amusing game. "You're still going that route, huh?" he said in English. "Yeah, Alberto told me. The problem is, *Señor*, that we need to know about this *Mexicano... El Jefe...* We think you know who he is."

"I don't know about any Mexican."

"Our new friend Mr. Vasco says different."

"Okay, you think you're being *courageous*, Raúl," Vasco said, his voice sounding to Raúl like the screeching of a tomcat. "You want to do the decent thing, not betray your friends, become a HERO. Which is great, but did you stop to think that your friend, the Chief, is at this moment busting a gut to find you so that he can KILL you? Those Mexicans who a couple of days ago were looking after you and chauffeuring you around are right now hoping they can blow you up or cut your head off. *Because that's the way they do things down there!* You've become a liability."

Raúl kept his eyes down and clenched his jaw. He wanted to say, *And you think these people who kidnapped us won't do exactly the same? After they find out what they want to know? You're a fool!* But he kept his mouth shut.

"Anyway," Vasco continued, his voice full of that hectoring

superiority that set Raúl's teeth on edge, "our Mexican colleagues can look after themselves. They'll assume we've talked and they'll be in full defensive mode. Forget them. It's over, Raúl. You've got to grasp that. It's a new ballgame. As scientists, we've got to accommodate ourselves to that and behave rationally, which means in our own self-interest. You know what I think?"

Raúl didn't want to raise his eyes, but the words hung in the air and in the end he looked up, allowing his gaze to linger on Vasco for a few seconds. He was startled and vengefully pleased by what he saw: the familiar swooping of Jon's voice had concealed the wreck of his physical demeanor; Vasco looked crushed by fatigue and fear. His eyes, darting now and then in Raúl's direction, were pleading.

"Whoever you are," Raúl said, "I don't care what you think."

"No, no, Raúl, this matters! You have to consider what I'm saying!" The hectoring voice was suddenly desperate. "We have some bargaining power here. There are agencies, like the FBI, who might use us in ways that would benefit these people." Vasco waved at Carlos and the others. "Especially if we recant and give up the Chief. We'd be like hackers who attack the government and then get recruited by the government. We can improve the country's defenses against man-made viruses of all kinds. We can hand over versions six and seven. We can maybe embarrass the Vice President. We've got stuff to sell, Raúl! This is the way we have to go! There's no point dying for a dead cause!"

Raúl sat head down, mired in disgust at Vasco's abject weakness. It would be nice to pass the virus on to the FBI, have them be the carriers to the outside world, but how quickly would a handover be negotiated? How much would he have to divulge first?

Carlos was talking to him again in Spanish: "My boss wants us to take you to Laredo and hand you over to the Zetas. That's the other option. As you know, the Zetas are very good at interrogation. And torture. They'll get the name of this Chief of yours out of you, and then they'll kill him. And you. Maybe you want to think about it."

Raúl felt a chill in his stomach, but also a bleak satisfaction. This, of course, was the solution. Give the virus straight to the Zetas, the focus of the drug trade, and let them spread it around. It was the perfect retribution. He raised his eyes.

"You may do what you want, *Señor*. I have nothing to tell you."

"You don't mind being tortured by the Zetas?"

"Someone is going to torture me and kill me. It may as well be them. You may take me to Laredo as soon as you like."

"What's he saying about Laredo?" Jon said.

Carlos said, "He's saying he doesn't care if we turn him over to the Zetas."

"Raúl, Raúl, you're crazy! Give up the Chief and save your life!"

Raúl caught the look of renewed anguish on Jon's face, but he kept his gaze on the floor and said nothing. He was aware of someone else crossing into his field of vision.

"Raúl? Do you know who I am?"

The man's voice was quiet, free of the bullying sharpness characterizing the others. He spoke in Spanish. Raúl looked up briefly. It was the man he'd glimpsed on arrival yesterday, the man behind the whole disaster: Morales. He dropped his gaze and felt his heart start to kick.

"I'm Alex Morales."

Raúl waited.

At length the quiet voice went on: "So you don't care about being tortured by the Zetas. Your courage is admirable, Raúl, but I don't quite understand. You don't care about dying a horrible death? You're ready to go? Just like that? Why?"

Raúl decided to speak. "Because it's all the same to me. Death now or later. What does it matter?"

"Are you ill, maybe?"

Raúl blinked, startled by the perceptiveness of this remark, but he kept his head down and didn't reply.

"Heart disease?"

"As a matter of fact," he said slowly, grudgingly, "my heart is weak." Would that satisfy this devil?

"So you think you'll die suddenly, and it doesn't matter how or where?"

Raúl hunkered down a little more tightly and stayed silent. Morales hovered a moment longer and then moved away to talk with Carlos.

God give me strength in what I am doing, Raúl thought, and forgive me for my sins.

CHAPTER THIRTY-ONE

They left early in the morning for Laredo, in the SUV with Florida plates. Carlos was in charge, and the other team members were Felipe and Chico, a short mustachioed Cuban whom Alex remembered from the Miami safe house. Alberto and the others stayed behind at the ranch to look after Vasco. Southeast Texas unrolled past the window like a loop of tape, flat cropland or grassland, an occasional small town or trucking depot or gas station. The sky was a bronze plate, and the shadows thrown by the passing signage were shapeless blurs. Hurricane Martina, Alex had heard on a morning newscast, was now a category three, and tracking towards the Louisiana-Texas coast looking for a landing site. The upcoming weather for any particular part of the state was a crap shoot, but likely to include rain and high winds.

Mendoza started asking for a rest room break when they were barely two hours into the trip. Carlos told him to tie a string around it, but he persisted, and after twenty minutes, Carlos told Chico, who was now driving, to turn off at a rest area. There were half a dozen cars parked at the central lodge, and Carlos changed his mind. Ten minutes later they passed a row of abandoned concrete shells at the side of the road, and Carlos got Chico to pull off onto the old access road. As Carlos and Felipe bundled Mendoza into one of the old buildings, Alex got out and stretched his legs. A hot breeze was blowing and there was fine dust in the air. Mendoza came back head bowed, frowning, as though the rest room facilities had not been to his liking. He gave Alex a mechanical look, devoid of expression, as he was forced back into the SUV. It made Alex wonder again what was going on in Mendoza's mind, what was giving him this steely courage and detachment.

They passed through San Antonio and continued south on Interstate 35. They stopped at a drive-through and picked up burgers and soft drinks. The landscape was once again grassland and fencing. Dark clouds turned the bronze light at ground level into an ethereal glow. Heavy rigs pulling containers pounded the road in both directions, giving Alex the feeling that they were being sucked along a roadway corridor by a centripetal force. According to Carlos, they were a couple of hours from Laredo.

Alex was taking a turn in the back seat, Mendoza beside him, and Chico flanking Mendoza on the other side. Felipe was driving, with Carlos, in the other front seat, studying maps and the car's navigation system.

Perhaps out of boredom, Chico turned to the task of demoralizing and terrifying Mendoza.

"Looking forward to the handover, Raúl? Not long to go now. And those guys down there are really excited about getting their hands on the guy who created the burn."

Mendoza licked his lips, but didn't move his head or betray any emotion. The stubbornness was still there, but also a profound tiredness, as though he had already relinquished his hold on day-to-day living.

Something else about his face awoke in Alex a faint echo of recognition, which for the moment he couldn't place.

Carlos turned and said, "The word is the Zetas have put a six man team on to this. Jesus, Raúl, I'm used to bad people, but even I get scared when I think about what's going to happen to you. These guys are animals."

Chico gave Mendoza an irritable punch on the arm. "So give us the name of your boss and save us all a few nightmares."

Alex turned and stared out of the window. Something continued to nag at the back of his mind.

He felt Mendoza stir beside him and he heard him give a weak cough. "I am ready for these Zetas," he said in a dead voice.

Alex swung around suddenly and studied Mendoza's face. What was it that had drawn his attention a moment ago? A sheen in the eyes, a faint waxiness in the skin tone of Mendoza's brown cheeks. Why did that seem familiar? And how did it connect up with the conversation he had had with Jon Vasco, also now nagging at the back of his mind? Reviewing the previous day, he suddenly remembered the startled look in Mendoza's eyes when he had asked him if he was sick.

Alex faced forward again, different ideas coalescing. The flash of realization came from nowhere, kicking at him like a live electric current. He saw with sudden clarity the friends of Paloma whom he had tested in Miami, the filmy brightness in the eyes, the faint reddening of the cheeks. "Oh my God," he said in a strangled voice.

Chico leaned forward to look at him. Carlos said, "You okay?"

Alex spoke to Felipe. "When you picked this lunatic up from the trailer park, how did it play out?"

"What do you mean?"

"What was he doing when you grabbed him?"

"He'd locked himself in the bathroom. We told him to come out and he did."

"Did you search the bathroom?"

"We searched the whole goddamn trailer." After a second he added, "But he flushed the toilet when he was in there."

"Shit." Alex turned aside, withdrawing from Mendoza, suddenly nauseous.

"What's the problem?" Carlos said.

Alex remembered now what Vasco had told him: the new strain of the virus could be acquired by anyone, cocaine user or not. That was why it would spread so well. He took a couple of breaths and leaned forwards towards Carlos. "The problem is that I think this son of a bitch infected himself when he realized he was going down. Right now, he's probably giving all of us the latest version of the virus."

***

They took a minor exit off the highway and parked on a stretch of dirt and gravel. Alex said he needed to have a look inside Mendoza's mouth, but Mendoza refused, clenching his teeth. Chico and Felipe hauled him out of the SUV and splayed him out on the ground. Carlos put one knee on his chest and raised the butt of his gun.

"Open your mouth, you treacherous cocksucker, or I'll break your teeth. Top set then bottom set. Just to make sure you don't bite us when we go in there to prize your jaw apart."

Mendoza's eyes flickered and he opened his mouth.

"Anyone got a flashlight?" Alex said.

Chico pulled out a phone and switched on the light and handed it to Alex.

Alex dropped to his knees and lined up the light on Mendoza's mouth. "Wider," he said.

Carlos raised the gun butt. Mendoza enlarged the opening, the corners of his mouth twitching.

"Say ah."

Mendoza obliged.

Alex recognized the roseate patterning at the back of the throat. He stood up and gave the phone back to Chico. "Okay. That's it. We've got ourselves a situation. Jesus Christ I really could murder this guy."

"It's nothing," Mendoza mumbled. "I've got a bit of a cold."

"No you haven't. You know damn well what you've got. And you're looking to pass it around. That's why you didn't mind being handed on to the Zetas. That's why you wanted a rest room break this morning. You were hoping to leave some viral particles behind in a public toilet. We're just lucky that the only things you've contaminated so far are us and the vehicle."

"What do we do?" Carlos said.

"We need to talk to the guys back at the ranch, to make sure they decontaminate everything and don't go anywhere, and I need to get some more information out of Vasco."

Carlos nodded to the others and they pulled Mendoza to his feet and got him back in the SUV. Carlos spoke first with Alberto. When he put the phone down he reported good news: one of them had done some shopping, but he was not one who had been much in contact with Mendoza or the room in which Mendoza had stayed.

Alex then spoke with Jon Vasco, who had picked up the essence of the situation from Alberto, and who sounded enraged, hysterical. "What version of the virus did he use? Ask him! Ask him!"

"He's not talking."

"None of those versions was ready, there were serious problems, they weren't *meant* to be released! I can't take any responsibility for this!"

"What sort of problems?"

"Serious problems."

"Tell me."

Vasco hesitated and then spoke suddenly and quickly. "Because we broadened the transmission process away from cocaine, we found that other substances could trigger the allergic response. Tobacco, for example."

"For God's sake, are you telling me that smokers may get the burn?"

"Only if the virus spreads. You have to quarantine Mendoza! And you guys as well!"

"Okay, listen, to do that I need accurate data about the virus. Are you going to level with me?"

"Of course I'm going to level with you! I'm not some idiot fanatic like Mendoza!"

Alex talked with Vasco for a quarter of an hour, absorbing technical information, evaluating it, trying to spot inconsistencies or hesitations. When he had finished, he turned in his seat and gave Mendoza a long look. Was it his imagination, or was there finally some hint of contrition?

"What possessed you?" Alex said. "What the hell possessed you? You're willing to risk giving every smoker in the world an allergic response? The possibility of serious lung complications? For the rest of their lives? Are you completely insane?"

Mendoza's mouth tightened and he drew a ragged breath; but he didn't raise his eyes.

Alex turned to Carlos. "Vasco agrees that Mendoza might be crazy enough to do this, and he confirms that the symptoms are much what we've observed. So there you have it. We're up shit creek, with a very small paddle, which is, that we go into quarantine, all of us, and wait it out."

Carlos stayed calm. "When are we going to get it?"

"Incubation is about thirty-six hours. We can assume that Mendoza didn't infect himself until he was called out from his home by you guys, which was about two in the morning, three nights ago. So he became infectious at about two in the afternoon yesterday. So in theory, if all of us got the virus immediately, which is unlikely but just conceivable, we will become infectious at two o'clock tonight. In practice, of course, we've got to have our quarantine arrangements all laid out a few hours before that, say by nine."

"We're going to be shut away?" Chico said. "Can't go anywhere?"

"I'm afraid so. That's the way it works."

"For how long?" Felipe said.

"According to Vasco, we could remain infectious for up to three days."

"And if we killed this Mendoza guy right now, would that help?"

"Sadly, no."

"So I guess we go back to Houston," Carlos said. "Should we stock up with food on the way?"

Alex thought for a moment. "No," he said at last. "We're not infectious, but we've built up viral particles in the car from Mendoza, and we could carry those with us when we shop. You'd better tell the guys in Houston to go for the food. They should shower and put on clean clothes. Also, they should get Vasco to tell them what disinfectants would be effective against virus particles. We'll have to clean the place thoroughly before we leave it."

Carlos nodded and took out his phone.

***

They were an hour and a half from the Houston horse ranch when it began to rain. Hurricane Martina, Alex discovered, had made landfall somewhere near Corpus Christi and was tracking up towards Austin. The rain and wind gathered strength. Chico, who was driving, had the wipers going at full speed. With half an hour still to go, Carlos took a call which seemed to freeze him, for a moment, into a state of motionless shock. Then he began swearing and asking urgent questions, not all of which made sense to Alex.

"What?" he said, when Carlos finally took the phone from his ear.

Carlos closed his eyes, gave vent to a couple more expletives, and said, "You must have got the gist of that. Vasco. The son of a bitch outsmarted Tonio. Or he got very lucky."

"He's gone?"

Carlos nodded. "Into this fucking maelstrom." He waved at the window.

"What happened?"

"Good question. First, Alberto took Rico with him to shop. Okay, fair enough. But that left Tonio to look after Vasco on his own. Vasco was hobbled at the ankles with a rope, the usual drill, but Alberto had decided to let him cook, because they all thought, hey, this guy is gay, he wears fancy clothes, he's probably good in the kitchen, and probably he *is* good in the kitchen, but shit, is that enough to let him... Anyway, it started to rain, which was another distraction, and suddenly Vasco throws some molten fat at Tonio, grabs a knife and cuts the rope at his ankles, and gets in a swipe at Tonio, which draws a lot of blood. And then he's gone. Tonio is in shock, trying to stop the bleeding. He takes off after Vasco a moment later, but nothing. The guy has disappeared in the rain. Fuck. Big-time fuck. We've got to go into quarantine, but our safe house just turned into an unsafe house. Plus we've lost Vasco. Any thoughts, Professor?"

While Alex tried to analyze the situation, Felipe and Chico chipped in with their opinions of Tonio. Carlos silenced them after a moment. "I'm going to have to tell Pedro we fucked up. This is a call I do not want to make. Alex?"

Alex glanced across at Mendoza, sitting the other side of Carlos and handcuffed to him. Mendoza had clearly understood the significance of Vasco's escape: an element of hope had appeared on his weary face.

"Even if Vasco is lucky," Alex said, "and gets a ride into Houston, he's still got to find a way to get a message to his boss, whose identity, apparently, he doesn't know. So that'll take him a while, although I guess we can assume he has some way of communicating. And then this boss, whom we believe to be Mexican, maybe based in Monterrey, has got to organize some response, either by tipping off the cops, which we think he did in my case, or by getting together people of his own.

He'll prefer people of his own, I think, because he still needs to grab Mendoza, or at least silence him. But we'd better assume the cops, because that could happen much faster. The problem is, we need to clean the house as much as we possibly can, especially the room where Mendoza was living, before we get out of it. And then, of course, we need somewhere else to go, to get us through quarantine."

Carlos gave him a long frustrated look. Alex could see the anger burning deep in his eyes. At last he muttered a few more curses and began to jab at the keys on his phone.

CHAPTER THIRTY-TWO

Raul Mendoza began to understand, as the long empty days of quarantine unfolded, that his main problem was not the threats from the narco-shits, whom he despised, but the friendliness of Morales, whom he didn't.

It was a trap, of course, he could see that clearly. A version of the good cop, bad cop, routine, a mixture of implicit violence and benevolent kindness, designed to make him bond with his intellectual equal and listen to his theories of social behavior, which pretended to show that the burn was damaging innocent people. Were drug addicts innocent people? Not really, of course, they should be responsible for their lives like anyone else. But Morales managed to turn that around, arguing that if people were responsible for their lives, they ought to be able to buy what drugs they wanted, from safe and monitored government sources, thus bringing the vicious and illegal trade in drugs to an end. And thus making sure that someone like the crazed addict who killed his daughter Cynthia could get his fix easily and cheaply and wouldn't need to turn to a life of crime and violence.

Of course he could refuse to talk about Cynthia, refuse to talk about anything at all, but Morales seemed to understand his vulnerability, told him stories of other daughters, other deaths, this time from the burn, and dredged up thoughts and emotions that he had long since managed to suppress.

It didn't help that they were now in surroundings of tasteless luxury, an isolated vacation property used, they told him, by the upper-level leaders of the Zetas cartel. There was an indoor pool, an outdoor pool surrounded by palm trees, a gym, recreation rooms, movie theaters, every sort of luxury add-on, including gold-plated bathroom fixtures, a vile accumulation of thoughtless wealth that set his teeth on edge. It was an ever-present reminder of what his boss had gone to war against, risking everything to do so, and as such it strengthened his resolve to protect his identity and keep the war going; but the comfort and ease of living seemed also to increase his vulnerability to the friendliness of the snake-like Morales.

One of the last things they were clever enough to buy before the quarantine cut in was a long piece of chain and a couple of padlocks, so that despite being always tethered to some immovable object, he could adjust his posture, move limited distances, even go to the washroom in relative comfort. And although Carlos gave him a grin from time to time, the other gang members stayed out of his way and left him to the company of Morales. Morales would open a bottle of excellent wine, and pour him a glass, and chat about the science of the burn, and the cases he was familiar with, and to his shame he, Mendoza, would end up drinking the wine, and talking about Cynthia and the faithlessness of his wife, while persuading himself that his underlying convictions could not be shaken.

Morales even showed him pictures of a Miami hooker he said he had fallen in love with, a very beautiful girl whom he claimed had also been damaged by the narco world. Not losing her life, as Cynthia had, but losing her ability to relate normally to men because of being raped constantly by her Mexican husband. Mendoza was inclined to see this story as another ploy by the wily Nicaraguan to soften him up, generate sympathy where none was due; but something in his voice, a slight trembling of his fingers as he brought up pictures on his laptop of Faymi, as he called her, in Washington, persuaded Mendoza in the end that Morales might be expressing his genuine feelings.

"Given the problems," he said, sipping his wine and unable to kill a certain interest, "why did you fall in love with her?"

"Is it ever rational?" Morales said, his expression turned inward. "The beauty helped, I guess, but mainly I think it was because she has a deep and indestructible kind of integrity, and despite everything she suffered, an ability to care for others. Including me, when I was on the run from these guys and the cops."

Morales paused. "Of course she lives a peculiar life, going to bed with assorted scumbags, and half the time she's in a fantasy world, making stuff up, but beyond all that, she has a quality… I'm not sure how to define it… She remains true to herself. She goes her own way. I came to respect her, a lot, and then, before or after, I don't know when, I fell in love. She doesn't believe me, of course, but one day, maybe, I'll convince her."

Mendoza sighed and said nothing.

"Anyway, it was Faymi who made it possible for me to study the burn virus as it was passing through Miami, and I told you already about the friend of hers who died. A girl with parents, maybe, just like you. Was your daughter attractive, Raúl? I'm sure, as a parent, you must have thought so."

Another unfair question, best put aside. But with that painful, and somehow inexplicable, series of events now awakened in his mind, he was drawn on, deeper into the web, as though the suffering must be relived to be understood.

"My daughter wasn't beautiful, like your friend Faymi, but yes, she was attractive. She had a natural appeal. People liked her. She was good with them. She…"

And suddenly, he found himself crying. The worst thing he could do, lose control of his emotions in front of this man, and yet he knew, at the same time, that the defenses he had put in place for these many years had finally to go. He was a dead man, probably, and maybe it was time to face his god and face himself.

Morales waited quietly for his tears to run their course.

Mendoza took a deep draft of wine and gathered himself. "I didn't trust her," he said. "That was the crime I committed. That's the truth that I think you want to get out of me. I didn't trust her. That's what my wife blames me for. And it was unfair. I didn't want to admit it at the time, but I was unfair to her. Like I told you, she was a good person. I thought she was at risk, I thought she was mixing with the wrong people, I thought she was having too much fun, but it was me. I thought I was going to lose her. I tried to be too controlling. I gave her deadlines and rules, and she was just a kid trying to find..." He broke off.

At last Morales said quietly, "Are you telling me, Raúl, that you think you're to blame for what happened to her?"

"Of course I'm to blame."

"Why? Just for being controlling?"

"Her credit card. I didn't trust her with money. So I insisted she had a card with parental oversight. With my oversight, in fact. This wasn't in the news reports. Only my wife knew. So when this bastard..." His voice caught, and he had to struggle for control. "When this bastard held a gun on her and told her to get some money for him, she couldn't. She had to call me for a pin update. And my phone was switched off. I was busy doing an audit. This deadbeat never mentioned all that, when they caught up with him the same evening. He just said the girl refused to give him the money. But there's a record of that call to me, and I know what she was calling me about, even though it's maybe surprising that he allowed her to make the call. She called me for the pin update. It's obvious. That's why she couldn't give him the money for a fix. That's why he raped her and killed her. And it's my fault. For not trusting her with money. For not trusting her, period."

He gave a shuddering sigh and stopped. He couldn't understand why he'd told all this to Morales, but he didn't regret telling somebody. He'd unblocked a deep sense of guilt, and maybe there was still time to come to terms with that.

Morales stared at him for a long time. "Did you ever think, Raúl, that you were trying to control your daughter in a way that didn't allow for her personal circumstances and character? And that, on a larger scale, you've been doing exactly the same thing with the burn?"

CHAPTER THIRTY-THREE

Alex kept a check on disease symptoms twice a day: after breakfast and after supper. All of them except Felipe had acquired the virus, but now, on their third day in their new safe house, relaxing in the pool or working out in the gym, their symptoms had started to abate. Alex told Carlos that in another day or two they could probably regard their quarantine confinement as over.

"So where do we stand with Mendoza?" Carlos said. He was pouring out coffee. "You said you might be getting through to him. Is the son of a bitch going to give up *el jefe*? Not that I'm sure that's going to be a lot of use any more. If Vasco hooked up with him and told him about Mendoza, they're both of them long gone."

Alex took the mug that Carlos handed him and sat down at the onyx-topped kitchen table. "But it's the only hope we've got, isn't it? Creating these viruses is a large-scale project, and if we know who's behind it, maybe your guys, and the law enforcement guys, can find some way of shutting it down, even if the guy himself has gone to ground."

"I hope you're right, Alex. Anyway, as you say, it's our only hope, so clearly we're going to go on trying. And that means Mendoza."

"No promises, but I think he's opening up to what he was really trying to do with the burn. Apparently, he thought he was personally to blame for his daughter's death, because he wouldn't let her have her own independent credit card, and when she got killed because of that, he tried to shift that blame onto a whole class of person, drug addicts. The burn was kind of his revenge writ large, and I think he begins to understand that. I think he also understands that the burn is going to kill a lot of basically innocent people. The problem as I see it is that *el jefe* is someone whom he admires and whom he doesn't want to betray."

"Talk to him some more. Tell him your ruthless compadres are getting ready to turn him over to the Zetas. Tell him if he does the right thing, he'll save a lot of lives, and he'll be free to start over."

"Is that true?"

Carlos shrugged his shoulders and drank some coffee. "It's true if he starts over in, say, Patagonia, and doesn't set foot in the United States. Or I think it is. I'd have to check with Pedro."

"Okay. I'll talk to him. Is it safe, by the way, to take him back to Laredo? Or anywhere, for that matter. Vasco might have been smart enough to make a note of the registration plate numbers of your vehicles."

"Yeah, we thought about that. Pedro is getting us a new vehicle. Should be with us later today."

"Okay. I'll do what I can. I'd like to keep him out of the hands of the Zetas."

"Me too, Alex, believe me."

***

Alex spent most of the afternoon with Mendoza. Mendoza seemed to have given way to his fundamental loneliness, and to want to spend time in discussion. But Alex couldn't locate any sense of regeneration or self-forgiveness in the other man's weary acceptance of personal error. Instead he seemed to feel that he had driven his life into a corner from which there was no honorable recovery. The tenacity of will which had supported his vision of a transformable, controllable, world for so long had now turned in another direction.

He sat with Carlos by the pool after supper and gave him a summary of Mendoza's state of mind.

"You know what? He doesn't care if you threaten to torture him and kill him and deliver him to the Zetas. He thinks his life is over anyway, and he doesn't really want to give up the name of his friend. So what he wants, in fact, is more or less the reverse: he wants you to guarantee that you *will* kill him, if he gives up the name of his friend. He sees it as a sort of just outcome."

Carlos stared at him. " He *wants* us to kill him? He wants to die?"

"That's what he's saying."

"Is he serious? I don't like it, but could we in fact do some kind of a deal?"

"I don't like it either. He's in a pretty depressed state. Also there's a catch. Part of any deal would have to include having a a priest hear his confession. He doesn't want to die in a state of sin."

Carlos shook his head. "Pedro is never going to allow us to bring a priest here, to this place. So we'd have to go and find a catholic church with an attendant priest. Even that's risky. He could try all kinds of stuff. He'd certainly have to give us the name first and then trust us."

"Trust us to kill him afterwards."

"Yes."

"And could he trust us to kill him afterwards?"

"Why not? I'd let you take care of it, Alex."

"Thanks." He was silent for a moment. "You know, it makes me sick to my stomach, but it might be the only way. I think he'd give us the correct name, because he wants to die at peace with the world, and that means untying himself from the burn."

"Okay. Talk with him again. See if he really understands what he's saying. I'll have a word with Pedro."

***

Alex had trouble sleeping that night, despite the comfort of his king-size bed. His further conversations with Mendoza had confirmed that Mendoza was ready to die, preferred to die, after betraying his friend, *el jefe*. But that mindset, Alex believed, arose out of severe stress and was temporary: which made the act of killing him more like murder than assisted suicide.

Carlos had been joking, of course, when he said that he, Alex, could undertake the merciful act, but he, Alex, was the one who had taken Mendoza on his journey of self-examination, who had helped him uncover the repressed guilt, and he couldn't therefore deny responsibility for Mendoza's present state of mind. But even if he was going to feel permanent guilt over Mendoza's death, he still couldn't escape the bottom line: it seemed to be the only way of stopping the burn.

He wished he could talk to Greg Halder, but under the circumstances that looked too risky. Halder was a marked man. And he, Alex, was in a place that it would be very unwise to reveal through some failure of communications security. He remembered that Halder was going to make an effort to prove to Pendleton, and even the President himself, that the burn virus was man-made, and therefore something to be resisted; something that much more politically toxic. He would like to know the result of that effort. But in his heart he knew that it didn't change the situation in a fundamental way: the new burn virus would be developed and released by Mendoza's Mexican boss, and with or without the assistance of the drug warriors, it would spread around the world. The only possible counter-attack they could enable involved knowing the identity of this Mexican project leader, and the only way they could discover that involved guaranteeing Mendoza's death.

***

Alex checked symptoms after breakfast the next morning, his brain fuzzy from a headache and lack of sleep. All of them seemed clear, but he decided it would be safer to wait another day and then begin the final cleanup and disinfection process. Meanwhile they could give Mendoza a final chance to recant, if not from his decision to give up his boss, at least from the decision to end his life.

He was lying down, half way through the morning, trying to catch up on some rest, when Carlos burst into his room.

"Raúl's had a heart attack. Or something. Can you come?"

He rolled off the bed, stumbled, and followed Carlos outside to the sun deck. The heat was palpable, but some of the moisture had gone from the air following the heavy rains. The sky was blue. Mendoza, he learned later, had asked to spend some time, time which he probably thought was his last on this earth, outside, enjoying the palms and the bougainvillea. He'd got hot, the compadres said, and had tried to cool off by dipping his legs in the pool. The weight of the chain around his ankles had caused him to fall in. He could swim, apparently, but the chain had hampered his movements, and he nearly drowned. The compadres hauled him out onto the deck, but they were aware that something was wrong. He was lightheaded, not in control. They laid him out on the deck.

Alex saw that the chain was still attached to Mendoza's ankle. Carlos waved at Chico, who came forward with the key and undid the padlock. The chain fell away. Alex knelt beside Mendoza and put a hand on his bare chest. Mendoza's skin was pale, his eyes tracking back and forth, not focusing on Alex. His heart was pumping, but the rhythm was erratic.

"Raúl? Can you hear me? What do you feel?"

Mendoza glanced at him briefly. He made a slight movement of his shoulders, half opened his mouth.

"Arms kind of funny," he said at last, in despairing tones. "Anyway... it's the heart... always known..."

Alex looked up at Carlos, who was hovering beside him. "You know what I'm going to tell you. We need to get him to hospital."

"And we both that isn't going to happen. What are his chances?"

Alex concentrated on the heart rhythm. "Not so good," he said quietly.

Mendoza started breathing more quickly, his expression growing agitated. He spoke in short gasps. "We can still trade... not hospital... a priest... find me a priest."

Alex glanced at Carlos and then leaned towards Mendoza. "You're saying you'll give us *el jefe* if we promise to get you to a priest?"

"Yes... please... before I die."

"Shit," Carlos said. "We have the new vehicle, but we didn't yet locate the priest. Felipe!" he called out. "Get the Yellow Pages and find us the nearest catholic church." He dropped down on one knee beside Mendoza. "Raúl, I swear to you in God's name that if you give us *el jefe* I will do my damnedest to find you a priest. It's risky for us, and we're still in quarantine, but I'm a man of my word. We'll do it even if we have to carry you into the church."

Alex thought that Mendoza's face had turned greyer, and his breathing was shorter. But his mouth seemed to relax, as though some decision point had passed.

"The man you want is..." A couple of quicker breaths. "Antonio Cárdenas. He lives in Monterrey." Mendoza settled back, as though absorbing what he'd done. "He owns the..." More breaths. "Mucho Gusto chain... of restaurants."

Carlos had pulled a pen from his pocket and was writing on his hand. "Antonio Cárdenas," he repeated.

"You should know..." Mendoza said, barely audible.

"Yes?"

"He's a personal friend... of the President."

"Cárdenas?"

A mumble from Mendoza.

"The President of the United States?" Alex said.

"When he was Governor," Mendoza breathed, "of Texas."

"Jesus, that's dynamite," Carlos said, springing to his feet.

Felipe reappeared on the sun deck, clutching the Yellow Pages.

"Bring that with you, Seminary Boy," Carlos said. "You didn't get the virus anyway. You can go into the church and find the priest. Come on, Alex. Let's get this guy into the car. We'll carry him on a sun lounger."

With the other compadres helping, they got Mendoza onto a sun lounger and carried him through the house to the front driveway. Carlos trotted over to the new vehicle, another big SUV, and drove it out around to where they were standing. They swung Mendoza onto the back seat. He fell over sideways and lay still. Carlos leaned into the vehicle and put a hand on his face. After a moment, he stepped back.

"Your call, Alex."

Alex leaned in and felt for a pulse on Mendoza's neck. He didn't have much hope. Mendoza's eyes were closed and the muscles of his face were slack, as though he was sleeping peacefully. He pulled back out of the vehicle and shook his head.

Carlos said, "The poor sucker never could catch a break. Whereas I'm beginning to think that God is on our side. Come on, let's get him back inside."

PART FOUR: MEXICAN STANDOFF

CHAPTER THIRTY-FOUR

Antonio Cárdenas glanced once at the sky and walked quickly across the ancient plaza towards the Mayan pyramid that occupied the western side. The howler monkeys, in their usual place on the upper branches of the tall mahogany tree, challenged him with raucous baritone grunts; but he paid them no attention. Neither they, nor the bats that flew around at twilight, nor the jaguars that occasionally wandered past in the jungle, were intruders he cared to acknowledge. The pyramid, its excavated face rising a dozen steep steps above him, a ruined temple on top, had cost him so much time and effort over the years that he thought of it as his personal sanctuary, his own creation, and only secondarily as part of the historic heritage of the country.

He paused to look up again into the clotted sky. Surveillance drones were hard to see, but his intelligence was that the Americans could deploy them in Guatemala if required; and that would be a game-changer. There was no surfaced roadway within fifteen miles, and in the old days, with nearly five thousand archeological sites dotted around the country, it would have been hard to collect information on a modest group of half-buried monuments like his. Now, potentially, it was different. He had to keep activity low by day, and move supplies on the jungle pathways at night. And still they might work it out. That is, if Mendoza had talked; and he still had no intelligence on that.

Mendoza, of course, had no knowledge of his installation here. But the President of the United States, say, with the facilities at his disposal, might put a few things together and make a stab at finding it. In which case, and assuming he was successful, what would he decide to do? Would he give his old friend some leeway, and let him finish the job? Or would he send in the CIA and shut him down?

He turned abruptly and swung back the heavy steel door in the base of the pyramid. The corridor beyond led down some stairs and into a large natural cave. The floor had been leveled with stone and cement, and the space was divided up by walls of painted concrete blocks. It was cool. He nodded at several occupants and made his way through to the lab occupied by Jon Vasco. Jon was slumped forward with his head on his desk, apparently asleep. Cárdenas watched him with mixed feelings. Discussions with Jon were always difficult. Jon hated any decisions or opinions that were not his own. He also hated Guatemala, the climate, the barbarities of Mayan culture, and anyone who couldn't speak English. But he was terrified of the surrounding jungle, recoiled when the howler monkeys howled, or when bats flew close, and he saw snakes everywhere; so he mostly behaved himself and got on with his work.

Vasco raised his head suddenly and gave a little shudder as he saw Cárdenas watching him. He waved his hands defensively, as though defending his territory, his right to sleep when he wanted. Cárdenas hadn't known him in the flesh before his escape from the narco-gang in Houston, but whatever charm he might once have possessed was now buried beneath anxious facial tics and a thin frown of complaint.

Cárdenas pushed an office chair close to Vasco and sat down and leaned towards him. "Listen, I need to know the truth. How good is this new version of yours? Did you really make the breakthrough? Are you sure?"

Jon raised his head and compressed his lips. "You've asked me that a dozen times. What's the matter with you? Has something happened?"

"Just tell me."

"I don't know. How can I know?" His mouth twitched. "I don't even know what you're asking. We have to finish the trial and then, probably, we'll find out."

Cárdenas stared at Vasco, trying to evaluate his expression. "And how long will that take?"

"You keep asking me that as well. What's wrong with you? Can't you count?"

"I lose track. I assume things can change. How long?"

"On past indications, another seven or eight days."

"That includes data from all the trialists?"

"Ninety percent."

Cárdenas let the air out of his lungs. "That may be too long."

Alarm appeared in the other man's eyes. "What do you mean? What's happening? You have news of some kind?"

Cárdenas pushed his chair back a little. "You must be aware, Jon, that if Mendoza talked there will be people trying to find us. I'm sure they won't be successful, but all the same, we should assume our time is limited."

"Tony, I'm telling you, we need seven or eight days. To be sure that we're clean, that we're back to a pure play on cocaine, seven or eight days. Seven or eight days, Tony!"

Cárdenas waited a second, gave his words extra weight. "Jon, in five days we're going to have everything ready, down to the last detail. The virus bulked up to more than a sufficient quantity, the delivery medium absolutely right, not too fluid, not too sticky, an aerosol with the right powers of penetration, a detonator that triggers at the right moment. I know the work is mostly done, but I want it all thoroughly checked. I want a demonstration. I want at least six release canisters ready to use. Okay? Work with Kerim. He's here because he knows this stuff. He has CBW experience."

Vasco slumped forward on his desk, his fingers looking for things to touch and move around. "I suppose when they get here, whoever these people are, they'll just kill us. Is that right? Like human sacrifices up on top of this thing, back in the days of Kukulkan. In their eyes, we're just some kind of a liability."

"Don't think about it. Just get the job done. Then we can go somewhere else. Believe me, Jon, I'll look after you."

"Yeah. Because I'll be the liability."

CHAPTER THIRTY-FIVE

By the time Alex Morales had made his way to a student apartment close to the University of Texas campus in San Antonio, found for him by a friend of Dennis Carver's, the emotional ups and downs, the struggle with Mendoza, had left him stupefied with fatigue. He slept for half a day. Then he was hungry. He went out and bought a couple of shopping bags full of food, and cooked himself a big steak.

His new home was a neat studio, with student life reflected in the possessions left behind by the absent tenant. When he finally settled down to review his situation, the familiar context seemed to emphasize the extreme disconnect in his life and circumstances. What the hell was he going to do now? He was still a fugitive, wanted on a drug charge: and his brief membership of a narco gang wasn't going to help his claims of innocence.

He'd bought a clean new phone on a previous shopping expedition, and replaced his laptop. He judged the apartment's internet connection safe to use. He started with a call to Jerry Henckel, who was in touch with Carlos's Colombian boss, Pedro Rojas, and who told him that, as they had feared, Antonio Cardenas had made a clean getaway several days ago. His estate near Monterrey was more or less deserted, in the care of a small caretaker staff. The investigators comprised not only members of the Zetas cartel, but also the local police. They searched through everything but found no clues, except that his Cessna light aircraft had gone. His family, it seemed, had sought refuge in Spain, but of the man himself, and of Jon Vasco, there was no trace.

He got to his feet and slowly made himself some coffee. They had foreseen the early escape of Cardenas, but the absence of leads from anyone connected with him was a disappointment. At last he decided to risk calling Greg Halder. He went through the routine they had set up and was surprised to hear his voice at the end of the line.

"Is this connection still safe?" Alex said.

"Hey, Alex. Great to hear from you. Yeah, we should be okay to talk for a bit. I'm still *persona non grata*, but so far they're leaving my personal life alone."

Alex gave Halder a quick update on his Houston adventures without mentioning names or places.

"My God, Alex, you make me think I've got it easy, just sparring with the Vice President. But that's a bummer, this burn guy getting away. What's the next move?"

"Good question. For the moment, wait around and hope for a breakthrough. Listen, you told me you were going to try and force Pendleton to look at my evidence showing the burn virus is man-made. How did that go?"

"As a matter of fact, not too bad. I don't know whether he really wanted to understand the origins of the burn, or whether he just wanted to know what we had, so that he could deal with it, discredit it, whatever, but he finally agreed to look at it. I should tell you that since Vasco disappeared, your laptop has disappeared as well, straight out of DIC safekeeping."

"Shit. The bastards. What did you do?"

"I knew your connections, of course, so I got what I needed from someone whose name I won't mention."

"And Pendleton understood the implications?"

"Oh yeah. I think so. The bad news is that his on-the-record response was that you had concocted the whole thing, faked the DNA, because everyone knows you're mixed up with drug traffickers, and you want to get everyone fighting the burn."

"So he's sticking to that nonsense."

"Publicly, yes. Privately, my guess is he knows this stuff is real, because he knows you were set up, or he damn well ought to know that, he knows your record, he knows you were doing the work at the Miller, so why wouldn't he believe you? So the good news is that he sees the policy implications, and will want to inform his patron, the President."

Alex paused for thought. "Listen, Greg, there's something important I didn't tell you yet. When Mendoza gave us the name of the Mexican virus-maker, he also told us that this guy was a friend of the President. Apparently he owns a chain of restaurants in Texas, and he got to know the President when he was Governor of Texas. So if you can think of a way of letting the President know that the man behind the virus is his friend, Antonio Cárdenas, he might finally understand that the risks are personal. And if anyone can find Cárdenas and deal with him, it's got to be the President of the United States."

"Okay. Antonio Cárdenas. I'm writing that down. Count on it, I'll get the message through to the President somehow. Where do we stand with the Senator at this moment?"

"Camilleri? Yeah, I've been thinking about him. I think if you told him the full story he might want to help. But first I'd better call him so he knows we're bona fide."

"Let me know, Alex. And watch your back."

Alex sat still and finished his coffee. Fatigue was overpowering him again: after doing some dishes, he crawled into bed and slept.

***

In the morning, he managed to make direct contact with David Van Hoyle and they arranged a callback from the Senator. His phone rang just after lunch.

"Alex?" Camilleri's voice was warm. "You don't know how glad I was to get David's message. Can I assume you're okay? Safe somewhere?"

"I'm okay. I won't go into the details, but I'm okay."

"Thank God. Ever since the arrest, and then the kidnap, I've been realizing how stupid I was, how I completely failed to look after you after sending you off to Peru. In the end I leant on your uncle, and he told me that you'd escaped the kidnappers. But he didn't know what had happened to you since. So hearing your voice like this, it's a big relief."

"Senator, I'm not blaming you for anything, in fact I need your help, but I'd better get something straight first. According to Greg Halder–who as you probably know has been suspended from office–according to Halder, the Vice President was blackmailing you with photos of a young woman, and that's why you pulled back on investigating the burn."

The Senator was silent for a moment. "Maybe I shouldn't have said I was stupid. Maybe I should have said I was a coward. The kind of miserable, self-serving coward I despise. The fact that half of Congress is cut from the same pathetic cloth is no excuse. I know that very well. But at first, Alex, when that over-entitled son of a bitch waved those pictures at me, I thought maybe it could be better for you to get out of the risky world I'd put you in. I thought you probably weren't going to get any answers out of those hookers. I thought we might re-group and put together a better-protected team. And like everyone else in Congress I was too busy raising campaign finance and trying to do at least a few of my senatorial duties to stop and think it through. So I didn't respond as I should have done. I realized that the moment you got arrested."

"I'm happy to let all that go, Senator. I realize it wasn't easy for you. The question is whether the fix is still in. Are you going to be able to help me now? Specifically in relation to Jack Pendleton and the President?"

"You know the really stupid thing, Alex? Those pictures weren't as threatening to me as Jack wanted to believe. I told Bea about the relationship with Lydia a few years ago. I always regretted it, and I selfishly wanted her forgiveness. She was upset for a while, but she got over it and we've been stronger ever since. So the pictures getting published would have been a huge embarrassment, to her and to me, and might have upset my career a bit, but the big thing, the main thing, is that it wouldn't have destroyed my marriage. So I could have called Jack's bluff. And if he brings the issue up again, it would give me a perverse satisfaction to tell him to go to hell. Believe me, I don't intend to be a coward a second time around. So what can I do to help?"

***

He had to wait two more days to hear back from Halder. Alex sensed the frustration in his voice.

"Yeah, the Senator came through for us, Alex. He could get the attention of the President where I couldn't. And of course I didn't trust Pendleton. So we know for sure that POTUS is aware of the fact that the burn virus is man-made, and that his friend Antonio Cárdenas made it. That is, if he believes either of those things, but he didn't in fact deny that he knew Cárdenas. And what Camilleri told him about you would probably have swung him around on the man-made virus issue. So he's probably on board for the whole package, depending on exactly what his knowledge and assessment of Cárdenas might be. What we don't know, however, and it wouldn't surprise me if we never know, is what he plans to do about it. It'll be a matter of a presidential finding, not on the public record, and a secret action by the CIA or other paramilitaries."

Alex was silent for a moment. He realized there were possibilities here he hadn't considered. "You mean he might send a task force off to find Cárdenas, assuming he knows him well enough to guess where he might be, or he might do nothing?"

"Right. Or if he sends a lone operative or two to find him, there are two possibilities, aren't there? One, they eliminate him. Two, they tell him to make sure that any virus he releases looks clean and natural, and certainly doesn't contain any messages from Vasco."

Alex felt a chill go through him. Why had he not seen that? "You mean all I will have done is warn these guys that they've got to clean up their act?"

"What do you think? If Vasco takes out his messages and tinkers a bit, can he make the virus look natural?"

Alex swore to himself and thought hard. "I don't know. I've kind of assumed that people like Dennis would spot it for man-made even without the messages, but could that be fudged? Could you produce experts to take the other side? I suppose you could."

"We live in a corrupt world, Alex. One thing's for sure: if the President decides to go that route, he and Pendleton are going to have you and I and a couple of others firmly out in the cold, firmly discredited. Or worse."

"You mean?"

"I mean, watch your back."

CHAPTER THIRTY-SIX

Alex spent an hour in intense thought, and then put through a call to Pedro Rojas in Colombia. Rojas was quick to follow his analysis of events in Washington, and quick to offer help. Alex gave a half-smile as he closed the call. The enemy of his enemy really did seem to be his friend.

Rojas somehow mobilized a car and a driver within three hours of getting his call. Alex was back in Houston by the evening. He checked into a familiar-looking room at the Huntingdon Suites and managed to get some fitful sleep. In the morning he shopped for clothes at the Galleria Mall, and changed into tan dress pants and a monogrammed shirt. His new driver came for him at lunch time and presented him with a new passport, credit card, and driving license in the name of José Estévez, and ten thousand dollars in cash.

He was, he realized, on a crazy mission that might go nowhere, but at some point, he kept telling himself, he would encounter some kind of clue, some indication of where Antonio Cárdenas had dug himself in. People who knew him were the best bet, and Raúl Mendoza, from several things he had said during their time in quarantine, had known him a long time. He caught his first break when Mendoza's friends at GeneSolve put him in touch with Mendoza's estranged wife.

He found himself being uncharacteristically swift and pressing with

Mrs. Mendoza, especially after waiting twenty minutes for her to get free of her duties as an assistant counsellor at a cancer clinic. He flashed her a smile of reassurance, shook her hand quickly, and then hustled her through the spacious hallways to the building's café area.

It wasn't until they were sitting at a table, coffee and pastries ordered, that he took a close look at her. Like Mendoza himself, she seemed nearly at retirement age, and her face spoke not just of the passage of time, but also of suffering and endurance.

Alex suddenly leaned forward and put his hand, palm down, on the table. "I won't waste your time, Mrs. Mendoza, in circling around things. You're not Hispanic, of course?"

"No," she said. "I am originally Dutch. And my name is Margriet. You will please call me Margriet."

He dipped his head. "I'd be glad to. Margriet, I came to know your husband under very unusual circumstances, just a couple of weeks ago. I'm very sorry to have to tell you that those circumstances led, ultimately, to his death."

She blinked a couple of times and drew breath, her grey eyes fixed on his. "Raúl is dead?"

"Yes. What perhaps makes it worse is that I can't tell you where he is buried. But I know that he's dead. I was present when he died."

"Which was, please, in what manner?" She remained still and watchful, emotions contained.

"A heart attack."

She dropped her gaze and studied the table in dignified silence. "Yes. He had heart problems. Was he under a great deal of stress?"

"Why do you ask that?"

She sighed and laced her hands together. "Raúl was involved in something that... made him obsessive. Ever since our daughter died. He lost all perspective. He wanted to strike back at the drug traffickers. I don't know exactly how..." She raised her eyes suddenly and gave him a piercing, anxious look. "Do you know how, Mr. Estévez?"

"Yes, I know how, Margriet, and I'll try and explain it to you."

He plunged in, telling her who he was, and the full story of the burn virus. At the end, after describing Mendoza's death, he leaned forward slightly, watching her, hoping he hadn't given her too much, too fast.

Her upper lip was trembling slightly, but she controlled herself. "As I told you, I'm not completely surprised. He never gave up telling me I should support him, that he was doing something important." She took a quick, unsteady breath. "But something like this… Oh, Raúl." Tears appeared on her cheeks.

"He wasn't a bad man, Margriet. Just misguided to the point of obsession. And he redeemed himself by giving up Tony Cárdenas. Raúl may have had the original idea, but Tony was the guy who forced it through. And Tony is the reason I'm here. I'm hoping that you knew Tony and remember him and can tell me something about him."

***

Mendoza's apartment block was a downscale building on a corner with traffic lights. There was no tree cover or landscaping, just some parking spaces back from the street, and a garage entrance ramp down the side. Nico, Alex's driver, swung in to the far end of the lot and drove back past the cars. None of them were occupied. Nico backed into a slot. "I'll call you if anything gets suspicious," he said.

Alex jumped out and headed for the entrance porch, Margriet close behind him. The entrance doors were locked, but one of the buzzers was marked 'Superintendent'. Alex pushed it and held it down for a few seconds. As they waited, he stepped back out of the porch and looked around for cameras. He couldn't see any. He glanced at his watch. It was close to two o-clock. He pushed the buzzer again. A minute later an overweight man in overalls approached from behind them.

"Hello," Margriet said brightly. "I am Margriet Mendoza. Do you remember me?"

The man stared at her for a moment, not showing much interest. "You're Raúl's wife, right? Sure, I remember. He used to talk about you." His expression suggested this wasn't a pleasant memory. "Ain't seen Raúl in a while."

"Well, that's the problem," Margriet said. "Neither has anyone. Not for several weeks. I'm hoping you can let us into his apartment so we can find out what's happened."

"Somethin' for the cops, wouldn't you say?"

Alex lost patience. "Of course we'd make it worth your while." He took a wad of notes from his pocket and began peeling off hundred dollar denominations. The man glanced behind him and then turned back to watch Alex, his expression mildly surprised, mildly interested.

Alex got to five notes and stopped. He raised his eyes and waited.

"You just want to look around, right?" the man said.

"Right."

"Should be okay. As long as you don't take anything."

The man took out some keys and let them into the building. He came with them to the fifth floor and opened the door of an apartment. Alex handed over the money. The man took the notes with a bemused shake of the head and retreated towards the elevator.

Mendoza's apartment was a living space about twenty-five feet square, furnished with cheap knockdowns. There was as study area in one corner, with a desk and a filing cabinet and some cartons containing papers.

Margriet said, "I'll probably recognize some of the paperwork. Why don't I go through everything and separate any connected with Tony?"

"Great. Just dump them on the floor and I'll read them later. Meanwhile I'll go through the other stuff."

He went into the bedroom and pulled out the drawers of the vanity and opened the door of the walk-in closet. Clothes, but nothing that seemed important. In the kitchen, he looked in cupboards and drawers and examined the fridge-freezer, which was still running, still cold. There wasn't much inside the fridge: an old carton of milk, some dried out vegetables; some candy. And a couple of plastic food containers.

In the bathroom there were quite a few bottles in the medicine cabinet, but nothing he could relate in any way to Cárdenas. He shook his head and went back to the main room. Margriet had already found a couple of items of correspondence and he spread them out on the floor and began reading through them.

"By the way," Margriet said, "a couple of these cartons contain stuff from the lab that Raúl ran in his spare time. Didn't that have some connection with Tony?"

He looked at her sharply. "The Clinimex lab?"

"Yes." She pointed. "Those cartons at the end."

He jumped to his feet and found the cartons she was pointing at. Labels on top indeed showed Clinimex as the addressee. Opening the first, he found books, articles, hand-written notes, DNA printouts: highly technical stuff, but recognizable to him as broadly within the sphere of molecular genetics, with several titles specifically mentioning synthetic organisms. The second box was much the same. Alex saw immediately what Mendoza had done: in cleaning compromising evidence out of his Clinimex operation, where he and Vasco had worked on the virus, he'd brought stuff here, to his home; and before he could figure out what to do with it next, he'd been forced to abandon his home and hide out in the rented trailer; where Rojas's men had grabbed him.

So there might be other things here in the apartment besides the lab notes: maybe even samples from the secret lab where the trials had been done; because the Clinimex lab was where those trials samples would have been analyzed. He half ran back to the kitchen and pulled open the fridge door. He grabbed the plastic food containers and opened them one after the other. The second one contained a dozen or more dark red tubes.

He pulled one out of the container and tried to read the label. It said, "V5.2, S17," and there was a date a little over a month old. For an instant he froze, the tube in his hand, trying to see all the implications. Yes, there'd be some degradation in a domestic fridge, but DNA should still be viable. Nothing else was essential. It was his second lucky break.

He put the tube and the container back in the fridge and returned to the main room, newly energized. He settled down to work carefully through all the documents that Margriet was putting aside.

They worked for an hour and a half. The item that absorbed his repeated attention was a large photograph of a half-cleared patch of jungle, a biggish vegetation-covered mound in the foreground, and a handwritten caption in Spanish: *Believe it or not, there's a temple under this, and an underground river below that!*

There was nothing else to identify the place depicted, or the purpose of sending the photograph, but he was convinced that it had come from Cárdenas, and Margriet agreed. She remembered Tony, many years ago, expressing an interest in archeology.

"What kind? Where?"

She frowned. "I don't know. Mexico, I suppose. Isn't this a Mayan or Toltec site?"

"Possibly. But where? Is there anything distinctive about this patch of jungle? Never mind. That needs an expert. Did you get the impression that Tony was interested enough to conduct an excavation? Was he that serious?"

"Maybe. Tony was a serious man. And rich, of course."

"Margriet, I bet you this is where he's got his secret lab. It's the perfect cover."

***

Lisa's name had come into his head within minutes of finding the blood samples. He got her number and called her as soon as they were back in the car. She told him he could walk to her offices from the Comfort Inn in Palo Alto. They dropped Margriet back at her building. He thanked her profusely and promised to let her know the outcome. At his hotel, he picked up his bags and some ice to pack around the samples, and Nico drove him north to the airport. He bought a thermos container at the airport, repacked the samples and the ice, and got a flight to San Francisco. He rented a car, and drove down Highway 101, checking in to the Comfort Inn in the middle of the night, local time. He slept deeply and felt energized when he got up at six. Lisa said she was always at work by seven.

After breakfast, he took the samples from the mini-fridge and walked out to the roadway, El Camino Real. He headed west. It was a clean fresh morning, a lot cooler than Houston. He'd once visited Stanford, a few miles away, but this, he realized as he took in his surroundings, was a little different. This was low budget Silicon Valley, well-kept but undistinguished, lube joints mixed with Starbucks mixed with factory outlets in a long straight line, everything fed by wires on poles.

He turned right after a couple of blocks and found his way to a second floor office unit half-hidden by leafy trees. A small sign on the deck at the top of the stairs said, DNA ATLAS. He went up the stairs and turned the handle of the door facing the deck. It opened. The big office beyond was decorated in pale, washed-out colors, with lots of potted plants. Lisa herself was the only occupant. She looked up from a screen and gave a little scream and jumped up. She ran over and gave him a hug.

She was a big girl, and Alex felt as though he'd been hit by a large and friendly dog.

"Hey! You meant it! You're in Palo Alto. Wow. This is so cool." She backed away. "Come on, sit down, tell me everything. I can't believe this." She waved at a pale-wood couch.

Alex remembered the huge enthusiasm and energy she brought to everything. She was one of the brightest students he'd ever had, not always easy to keep up with, liable to question everything, and finally seduced away, like many high-flyers, by the lure of business, leaving her studies incomplete. He wasn't surprised when she successfully negotiated a start-up and got her business going, although he knew she'd had problems.

He put the thermos on a low table and sat on the couch. Lisa drew an office chair close.

"Lisa, this is great. You look terrific."

"I feel terrific. At least when I'm not fighting with the banks. But come on, what's this all about?"

"That could take a long time. Lisa, I'd love to tell you the whole story, but I'm going to have to be selective. Let me start with some bad stuff. Like the fact that the police, and certain federal agencies, the DIC in particular, really want to know where I am, so they can put me back in jail on drugs charges. And the fact that in spite of being an escaped felon, I desperately need your help immediately, as a matter of high priority. That is if you can do what I think you can do."

"You know me, I can do everything. And why wouldn't I want to help my favorite professor? But shit, Alex, are you serious? You were in *jail*, for Christ's sake?"

"Jail and a few other things. I'll tell you the whole story one day, but for now let me cut to the chase. I need to find someone, a Mexican, before the President of the United States finds him. If I don't, he may release more of the virus that causes the burn. Do you know about the burn?"

"The burn, the burn..." Lisa jumped up and went to her desk and began tapping on her keyboard.

"Try Peru and cocaine or coca."

"Okay." Lisa tapped away, studying her screen.

Alex stayed quiet. Lisa seemed to get some results, because she stayed intent on her screen, reading.

"Okay," she said at last. "Got it. Response to coca or cocaine, burning in the throat, et cetera, started in Peru, apparently some spread to United States, although not well documented. No cause yet established."

"The cause is a virus. In fact, a man-made virus."

Lisa stared at him. "Holy shit. Alex, what the hell have you got yourself into?"

"I ask myself the same question. If it's any reassurance, I change my phone often, and I don't think the cops know I'm in Palo Alto. One of the benefits of opposing the DIC on this issue is that the Drug Trafficking Organizations fall over backwards to give me their support. Fake ID and stuff." He reached into his back pocket and took a new wad of hundreds. "And while I think of it, here's my contribution to your business." He put the money on the table. "Five thousand bucks, give or take. It's clean, you can spend it, but you'd better not ask where it came from."

Lisa was still staring at him, mouth half open.

He said, "And I don't think I've ever seen you at a loss for words before."

She gave a brief cackle of laughter. "Listen, I'm in full-blown shock. Jesus Christ, bro, you were always, like, a normal guy!" She stood up and came back to sit close to him. "So go on, widen the conspiracy, tell me what I've got to do to earn my drug money."

"I've got to find this guy, right? Antonio Cárdenas. The DTOs, and probably the CIA, have been trying to find him, but he's gone to ground, we think somewhere in Central America. Somewhere, presumably, that's pretty remote. This is just my guess, but the trials he conducted to assess this virus were done by enlisting local indigenous people and paying them well. And this is probably in the same place that he's now gone to ground. What I've got in that thermos are, I think and hope, blood samples from those trial volunteers. If you can tell me what indigenous group they belong to, and where that group is located, then I'm a big leap further on."

"Boy oh boy, is that ever a challenge for my database." Lisa jumped up and swung around in circles, pumping her fist. "I tell you frankly, Alex, we need some luck. Central America is good, because I've put a hell of a lot of work into that region, and I've got some great people down there scouting DNA. And you're right, there are regional variations, tribal variations, that are quite subtle, so in theory we might pin it down to within a few square miles, but still... How many samples have you got?"

"Thirteen."

"That helps. We can do some cross analysis between the samples and pick out key features. Normally, of course, we've got one sample only, our typical customer just wants to know who his ancestors are and where they came from, and that's a lot more tricky. Yours are the indigenous people themselves, or very close relatives, and you've got thirteen, which is great. But still, like I say, we've got a ways to go before we've really got a complete map. I'll do my best and hope we get lucky."

"How long do you need?"

"I'll call you. We do all the sequencing here in house and I'll put your job top of the pile. Maybe late afternoon."

"I really appreciate it."

"How's Angie taking all this?"

"Angie moved on."

"Thank God. Shall I tell you something? You never looked happy with that woman. You always looked as though you thought she was screwing somebody else."

"Yet when she really was screwing somebody else," he said, looking at Lisa with a faint smile, surprised that he felt no pain, "I didn't see it. There you go. Another dumb Hispanic, surprised by infidelity."

"Come to supper tonight."

He stood up and went across to her and put his arm around her. "You're taking this so well, you know that? I appreciate it a lot. But if we get lucky, I'm afraid I'll be on my way to wherever you find those samples came from. This really is a hell of a big deal." He stepped away towards the door.

"And if we don't get lucky?"

"I'll be wracking my brains for the next big idea. Probably head back to Houston."

"Whatever happens, come back and see me sometime."

He held her gaze. "Love to," he said and headed out the door.

CHAPTER THIRTY-SEVEN

It wasn't the backpacking season, and Alex and his companions, posing as part-time archeologists with an interest in underground rivers, had their choice of guides. The first of these grew alarmed by the machine pistols and other weaponry which Carlos and his men failed to conceal, and which he must have judged as inappropriate equipment for archeologists. The second they fired after a couple of days of trekking north through the jungle, because his knowledge seemed less extensive than he had pretended, and because he showed too much interest in the origins of their Spanish accents. The third they picked up in a small village: his Spanish wasn't fluent, but it was okay, and he wasn't interested in their weaponry, or their accents; he was interested in something they were able to supply freely; American dollars.

He was an Amerindian with a pock-marked face, a pony-tail, and a dour and forbidding manner. He called himself Pancho to conceal his real name, or because he had grown impatient with non-native efforts at pronouncing it. He didn't try and sell his skills, so they were lucky that chance recommendations of other villagers had led them to him. After a day advancing north under his guidance, it became apparent that he was the real deal: he knew everything about the land and its secrets.

Alex was driven by an increasing sense of intensity and impatience. He knew they had a chance: a wild and crazy chance, but a chance; a chance of being right about Cárdenas and getting to him in time; and in spite of the swampy heat, the mosquitoes, the rain, the thunder, and their heavy backpacks, he was constantly urging them forward, unhappy when they stopped to eat or sleep.

Carlos, whose arm had almost completely healed, had already begun calling him *El Comandante*, but in a good-humored, playful way, not, it seemed, put out by his assumption of authority. Alex took the lead in part because he felt surprisingly at home: the warm jungle, with its monkeys and bats, its wealth of dripping fronds and dramatic hardwoods, its sinkholes and rocky screeds, was like the Nicaragua he had known as a boy.

His immediate goal was to find the Mayan site depicted in Mendoza's photograph. Lisa had been slightly less lucky than she had hoped in pinning down the DNA in the blood samples, but she was fairly sure she had narrowed it down to about 600 square miles in northern Petén, Guatemala. It was a big area, no doubt with a lot of Mayan sites within it, but Alex made himself see the positives: it was an area you could cross on foot in a couple of days, and they had some other significant clues to work with.

The President was meant to have a team out looking as well: but the President, and his duplicitous crony Jack Pendleton, would do whatever they believed was in their best interests. There might even be some paramilitary types hanging out with Cárdenas right now, giving him protection. That could represent a hell of a problem, but they'd deal with that when they found the site.

***

The gradual ascent along the river valley offered the constant temptation of a refreshing plunge; but they were not dressed for swimming, and Alex urged them to keep going until dusk. At last they stripped and swam in a darkening pool, a sluggish current tugging at them, and then Pancho moved them back to higher ground to sleep, grunting sourly that the nocturnal wildlife drawn to the river included snakes and jaguars.

After eating, when they were all sitting round a citronella candle, Pancho lit up a cigarette. Chico stood up and moved away from him, muttering darkly. Alex himself felt a faint rawness at the back of his throat, something he'd begun to notice over the last couple of days, whenever cigarette smoke was close enough for the smell to linger in his nostrils. It had come as a shock to him to realize that he was suffering from an attenuated form of the burn; and that this sensitivity might be with him for the rest of his life. Suddenly, as Carlos said, it was personal. For Chico, prevented from smoking by the pain, and driven to distraction by the sight of other people enjoying a cigarette, it was a lot worse, it was infuriating. "I'm going to kill that son of a bitch," he said on several occasions, "just for doing this to us."

They started early in the morning and pushed on to a point where the tree cover was less intense, and the soil gave way to rocky protrusions. At the base of a low escarpment they came at last to the place where the river emerged from the face of the rock. They followed a track around a broad pool, and climbed onto a shelf of rock that took them inside a cave, where another pool glinted in the darkness. The cave narrowed down after ten or fifteen yards to the point where the water emerged from a tunnel.

Alex shone his flashlight quickly around and went back outside. He took out his tablet and brought up the maps he had loaded into memory. He went over to Pancho, who was standing apart, looking back down the river valley.

"You think this is it? The underground river we're looking for?"

Pancho shrugged. "I cannot know that, *Señor*. But there are certainly Mayan ruins." He indicated with movements of his arm the area beyond the escarpment. "Several of them."

"How long does the river stay underground?"

"Nobody knows. Probably there is more than one river, connecting."

"You told us that one of these Mayan ruins is probably standing directly above this river."

Pancho looked into the distance, nodding his head slowly, neither agreeing nor disagreeing.

"Can you take us there?"

Pancho thought about that. "Maybe there is a better idea. I will go by myself."

"Why?"

"Your safety. My safety. I can see, *Señor*, that you have business to settle here. Perhaps dangerous business. On my own I can ask questions, find people I know. If you are seen…" He shrugged. "I don't know."

"And these questions you want to ask?"

Pancho frowned. He held up one hand with the fingers outstretched, and grasped his index finger with the fingers of his other hand, as though making his points clear to a child. "One. You say this is a Mexican who owns these ruins. So that is one question. Two." He moved to his middle finger. "He has foreigners, at least one American, living there, so that is another question. Three." The next finger. "He keeps or pays local people for security. Four. He spends a lot of money." He threw up his hands. "Lot of questions."

Alex restrained a smile. "You'll need more money."

Pancho nodded. "Yes, yes, more money. To give to the people I talk to."

Pancho's pleas for more money, *más dinero*, while not unreasonable, were common enough for Carlos and the others to call him *Señor Más Dinero* behind his back. Alex glanced around. The others were coming out of the cave.

"Pancho," he said, looking hard at the other man, "you understand that we are not people it would be wise to betray?"

Pancho held his gaze. "Very well I understand that, *Señor*."

"How long do you need?"

"One full day is enough."

Alex hated the prospect of delay, but he understood that Pancho was talking sense: on his own, he would move quicker, find out more. He took out a wad of American currency and peeled off ten hundreds. "Take us with you as far as you can. Then we'll wait for you."

CHAPTER THIRTY-EIGHT

Too many ambiguities, Antonio Cárdenas thought, as he stopped at the edge of the excavation trench and stared down at the water left by the afternoon's downpour. Usually there was somebody here doing maintenance, now it was empty. He turned back towards the lab. The atmosphere in the village had changed in the last few days, everyone a little cautious, withdrawn. The guards, provided by the government nominally to deter looters, in practice on his own payroll and with broader responsibilities, hadn't always shown up for their shift. He heard distant aircraft more often than usual. Looking up, he realized that it was a while since he had heard the angry shout of the howler monkeys. The branches of the mahogany tree were empty. You too? he thought.

He stared at the pyramid, wet stone steps shining in the sun, cloaked around its shoulders and sides by over a thousand years of accumulated debris. Flourish and die, he thought; that was the fate of the Mayans. And maybe there's nothing we can we do to stop these grand cycles. Maybe the Mexico of today is dying, but the next Mexico will be great. And my efforts will mean nothing.

He went through the door and down to the lab. Vasco was sitting glumly at his desk staring at a screen showing data accumulated from the trial. Cárdenas motioned to the man standing in the shadows to leave them alone and sat down beside Vasco. Vasco gave him only the briefest of glances.

"You're not religious, are you, Jon?" Cárdenas said.

Vasco turned his head. "No. Religion is for dupes."

"Okay. That makes life simpler, I suppose."

Vasco stared at him. "How can you live next to a temple where the priests tore out the hearts of living victims and believe in a religion? Tony, for God's sake… for Kukulkán's sake… Be *logical.* Be *reasonable.*"

"Yes. Exactly. So what do you make of it? This fourth result?"

"I don't know. It looks contaminated. You failed to isolate the subjects from the previous trial."

"What do you mean? They were all in secure quarantine. I wasn't here, but I'm sure the procedures were followed."

"I'm talking about later. I'm talking about *mental* contamination. What procedures did you use to ensure against that? You should have locked those guys up."

"So you're saying this fourth subject heard about tobacco producing the burn and he invented the same result."

"No, I'm not saying he invented it, I'm saying he *imagined* it. That's what happens when your subjects are not properly naïve. They conjure things up because they're expecting it. Or they think you're expecting it.

"So you're saying we can ignore this particular result?"

"No. I'm not saying that. I'm saying this trial is crap."

Cárdenas took a deep breath. "Jon, you know what's riding on this. We have three subjects who produced a clean result. The burn from cocaine and nothing else. And it's not as though we rely on oral testimony. We can see and measure the inflammation from the burn. And there's nothing there after exposure to tobacco smoke. Doesn't that look as though you've done the job? Fixed the virus?"

Vasco fiddled with his mouse, stared at the screen. "This fourth guy also shows physical evidence of the burn with tobacco and coffee. Coffee, Tony!"

"But only in very attenuated form. Surely he could induce that level of response just because he wanted to?"

"Of course he could. But maybe he didn't. What I'm saying is the trial is crap."

"To my mind, it's good enough." He paused, watching the other man. Vasco didn't turn, as though absorbed in the minutiae of the data. "Anyway, I've made a decision. We should get a couple more results tomorrow. If they're okay, that's it. I'm sending out the couriers to do the release as planned. And we should evacuate this place as well."

Cárdenas had expected objections, but instead Vasco gave him an alarmed glance, and then sat still, taking shallow breaths. "Where are we going?" he said at last.

"I've got a couple of ideas. There's a monastery that will give us sanctuary for a while."

"A monastery?"

"Some dupes, as you call them, who believe in helping others."

Vasco lowered his head and sighed. "Okay. But there's no future for us, Tony, you know that. I don't know why you bother."

***

Cárdenas slept well, but at one-twenty in the morning he sat up in bed, awake and listening. Howler monkeys back? No. The quiet but unfriendly beeping of his warning system. He pulled out a tablet-sized device from the cupboard in his bedside chest and studied the screen, which showed a skeletal plan of the site. A blue ring surrounding the monument-symbols represented the cable pair he had buried in the early days of excavation. The electrical field generated between the cables enabled his system to assess the size and position of anything crossing the ring. A point on the north side of the ring was flashing white, code for a human-sized intruder. Even as he watched, a second white point appeared: another intruder about 100 yards away from the first.

It was as his intuition had told him: they were here. The Americans. A mile away. He had five or ten minutes, perhaps more. They wouldn't realize they had been detected, and might not be in a hurry. For a moment he closed his eyes and gave way to a feeling of intense frustration. Talbert, my friend, could you not have given us one more day? Then he put the screen back in the cupboard and reached up and turned on the room light.

As he slipped on his sandals, he found himself staring at the green jade carving that sat on top of his bedside chest. He would never see it again. It was the final dispossession. He picked up a flashlight and went quickly through the hanging-string doorway and into the next cubicle. Jon Vasco was lying on his bed, but the light or the warning beeps had woken him up. He raised his head and stared wild-eyed into the beam from the flashlight.

"Intruders," Cárdenas said quietly, "probably the special forces we've been expecting."

"I knew it." Vasco said, his voice high and unsteady. "They're coming for me again, Tony. It's like Houston. But this time it's not your guys. This time they'll kill me."

"If you're quick, you can come with me."

"No. I can't do that." He gave an involuntary shudder. "I'll drown."

"Then stay with the others and go outside. They're not going to kill all of you.."

Vasco suddenly sat up and began struggling with his shoes. "I knew it would come to this. I knew it."

Cárdenas spun away and went into several other cubicles, turning on lights. The occupants were stirring. The beeping was almost inaudible here, but a sense of alarm was spreading, He settled on a local man called Tibo as his spokesman.

"We're under siege. Get everyone up and go outside. It's safer that way. But stay as a group. The important thing is to cooperate with these people. Give them what they want. Good luck."

He touched the arms of a couple of the men and then moved quickly out through the main door of the building, directing his flashlight into the darkness outside. As he ran across the uneven plaza he was struck by the silence, the absence of anything unusual in the black surroundings. When he reached the door in the base of the pyramid he stopped and looked back. Could he be mistaken? Could this intrusion have a benevolent purpose?

A bright white light suddenly illuminated the plaza. He looked up. Flares were exploding. For a moment he was blinded. A few seconds later, another burst of light showered down from the black sky. Again he caught a snapshot of the plaza, the jungle setting behind. Several people had emerged from the services building. Vasco didn't seem to be one of them. Was he crazy enough to try and escape, into the jungle he hated?

As the light died again, he turned and caught a glimpse of a camouflaged figure, rifle in hand, breaking free of the jungle cover to his right. Stung into action, he flung the heavy door back and jumped through into the cave. The lights came on. He pushed the door closed and rammed home the heavy iron bolts.

He'd been thinking about this emergency procedure for days, what exactly he'd do if hostile forces arrived. He ran down the corridor to the lab, grabbed a travel bag from the floor by his desk, and opened the refrigerator. He took a plastic tray from the middle shelf and emptied the contents, the dozen brightly packaged candy bars he'd specified, into the bag. He ran back to the stairs.

He thought he heard the distant sound of a voice filtering through the air system. An amplified voice out in the plaza? Demanding surrender? He picked up a portable lamp and started down the tunnel. The air turned colder. There was a pounding on the main door behind him. My God, they'd been quick. And they knew where the lab was.

He hurried onwards. He came to a stone wall across the tunnel and another steel door with a digital lock. He dropped the bag and punched in the combination. Just as the door swung inwards, the whole tunnel seemed to crack like a whip, as though a wrecking ball had struck the door at the top. He grabbed the bag and stumbled forwards, ears ringing. He put down the bag and the lamp and pushed the door back until it closed. He swung an iron grill into place and shot the bolts. He picked up the lamp and raised it above his head. Below him and to his right, the cave was half-filled with dark water, moving silently and sluggishly towards a tunnel at the far end. A rocky path to his left ran down to the water's edge.

He grabbed the bag and hurried on down the path, watching his footing. At the platform by the water's edge, he put down the bag and the lamp and pulled open the doors of the steel cupboard. He took a wetsuit from a hanger and kicked off his sandals. He climbed into the bottom part of the suit, grabbed bootees from a shelf. He began wrestling with the top part of the suit, pulling it on over his shirt, struck suddenly by a paralyzing sense of weakness, as though at this final hurdle his energy and competence would disappear. With a furious effort he forced the top into place and strapped on a weight belt and a waterproof pouch and guidance electronics. He bent stiffly and opened his bag and took out three of the candy bar packages and put them in the waterproof pouch. Then he threw the bag into the water. He watched for a second as it caught the dark current. He turned to the tanks of air. They were harnessed and ready to go. He swung them onto his back and strapped them in place.

A thunderclap of sound echoed around the cave. He staggered to keep his balance. Looking back up the path, he saw the iron grill clanging end over end into the water. There was a big hole where the door had been. Drops of water splattered into his face. He kept moving on pure instinct, putting on fins, reaching for the mouthpiece, slotting it into place, grabbing for a mask. Beams of light appeared on the walls of the cave, swung round, half-blinded him. For a moment he thought he wouldn't be able to see the last piece of equipment he needed, the underwater lamp. Then he felt the handle under his hand. He lumbered backwards and fell into the water.

Another torrent of sound set the cave vibrating like a giant combustion engine, but as his weight took him downwards, it was muffled, reminding him of when he was a child and he had shut the world out by sinking below the waters of the bath. He twisted round, holding the lamp in his hands but not switching it on, letting himself move with the current. By some miracle, the bullets had missed him. He tried not to breathe. But already the faint luminescence above him was fading out as he slid into the tunnel. He heard in the distance another echoing blast of gunfire. Too late, my friends, your bird has flown the nest. He switched on the lamp and took in a deep draught of air.

CHAPTER THIRTY-NINE

Alex and his companions were weary, their nerves on edge. The jungle, black as pitch except where the beams of their flashlights penetrated, pushed against them, roofed them in. Their clothes were dirty as well as damp and their footing was often in puddles. There were constant surprises: clusters of bats, scuttling lizards, angry macaws. Pancho seemed to know where they were, and assured them they were closing in on their target. Alex used GPS to find their location on his tablet's maps, but he wasn't sure about the accuracy of the result. His biggest concern was how they would know, when they got to Pancho's chosen site, that they had found the right place; let alone where the people were, where the lab was, how it was defended.

A splintered glow of light, penetrating the jungle foliage, and lasting for seconds, changed their mood in an instant. They froze, pointed their flashlights down, and listened intently. Alex believed that the light could only have come from the place they were looking for, Cárdenas's site. Interpreting the light was harder: was there any reason why he would illuminate his surroundings in the middle of the night?

They began edging forward again, and saw the next sustained burst of light with greater clarity. Flares, Alex thought.

He pointed his flashlight at Pancho. His pockmarked face was raised towards the sky, his mouth pulled in to a tight frown. "That's it?" Alex said. “The site we’re looking for?”

Pancho turned his head and nodded. “Yes. I think so, Señor.”

So it looked like Talbert Austin’s paramilitaries had finally arrived. The question was: were they here to help or to hinder the President’s friend?

He pointed his flashlight at Carlos, who was standing on the balls of his feet, a faint smile on his face. “I say we leave Pancho and the backpacks here, grab some weaponry and move on as fast as we can.”

Carlos said nothing, but waved at Chico and Felipe with a gesture that said: do it. Alex shrugged out of his backpack and delved into it for the Beretta machine pistol that Carlos had given him. It slotted nicely into the pocket on the flank of his camouflage pants.

He turned again to Pancho and said, “How far is the site?”

“Two or three kilometers.”

“Okay. Stay here.”

“*Señor*... The equipment will not go away. I should follow behind you... In case you need something.”

Alex stared at him and then made the connection. There was a lot of money in his back pocket. Also in Carlos’s back pocket. If they were wounded or killed...

“Okay,” he said. “But don’t get too close.”

He had another thought and returned to his backpack. “We’d better take the NVDs. Flashlights will be risky.”

Carlos nodded and went back and burrowed in his backpack. Alex found the bulky-looking binoculars and tied the straps of the head harness around his neck, letting the device hang against his chest. The equipment he had sourced for himself and Carlos weighed almost two pounds with the harness, but it would amplify light into the low infrared about 40,000 times. He had a feeling it would turn out to be worth the effort of carrying it this far.

When Carlos and the others were ready, he said, “Let’s go,” and led the way forward at a rapid walking pace. The meagre path they were on threw up obstacles in the shape of rocky outcrops, muddy hollows, branches and fronds swinging at them out of the dark, and fallen trees. Alex kept his flashlight pointed low. According to Pancho, the path would open up a little after a mile, and the final approach would be slightly easier.

They saw the flash from the first explosion as a reflection off the clouds, lighting up the jungle in a momentary glow. They stopped and listened. The thump came a few seconds later, sharp and loud. These guys were blowing things up already? In which case, he thought, this was definitely not a friendly operation. And his own efforts, the mad scramble of the last few days, were for nothing.

"Let's keep moving," he said, trying not to dwell on the negative.

The next explosion was muffled, weak, and there was no preceding glow. They stopped and doused their lights.

"That was inside a building. Or underground," Alex said. "What the hell is going on?"

"They're blowing up the lab?" Carlos said.

"Maybe. But they haven't had time to set that up. Anyway, we should use the NVDs. We should be able to get in close if we're not showing any light. Chico, Felipe, stay here and don't use the flashlights unless you really have to. Keep Pancho here as well."

Carlos was already strapping the head harness on so that the night vision device was held in place over his eyes. Alex did the same. The world suddenly changed from black to a landscape of objects and colors. The colors weren't right, and the objects were a little fuzzy, but after a moment of adaptation to the sensory flood, and some adjustments to the device, he could make out stands of vegetation, a mound of some kind, and a tract of rocky land moving gently upwards with thicker jungle on the left.

"We should split up," Alex said. "I'm going to cross to that mound and work up under cover of those trees. Carlos, you should keep to the left and use the jungle."

"What are we going to do when we get there?"

"We watch and see what's going on. If these guys are doing a responsible job of destroying the whole show, we can leave them to it. If they're treating a guy we believe to be Tony Cárdenas like royalty, then we get suspicious. If we find Jon Vasco anywhere, we grab him, because he'll tell us everything."

"Got it." Carlos made a final adjustment to his NVD and set off quickly along the jungle fringe.

Alex put his flashlight in his left thigh pocket and started across the rocky terrain. The landscape bobbed up and down as his NVD tugged at the head harness. He put up a hand to steady it. Instinctively he concentrated on the objects on which he was about to place his booted feet. At the mound, covered by grass and creepers that were more brown than green, he adjusted his course and headed into a small stand of trees and bushes. He could just see Carlos about fifteen yards up to his left.

After what he guessed was two hundred yards, Carlos in and out of view, he seemed still to be walled in by jungle, nothing else visible ahead. He was getting used to the NVD version of reality, and was more confident about maneuvering through the trees, but uncertain what to expect next. A blur of light obscured his vision for a moment, and the surroundings seemed to darken. Moving his head backwards and forwards, he calculated that some kind of fixed lamp had been deployed, probably in the central area they were headed for. Not much light was getting through the trees, but the NVD had compensated by reducing the light amplification. Turning around, he found that the normal rendering of the landscape returned.

He looked across at Carlos, and could just make him out between the trees. He waved, and then pushed on carefully, debating whether to remove the NVD and get a better sense of the new light source.

A human voice, amplified in some way, penetrated through the trees. He stopped and listened. The words were thin and muddied, and he couldn't hear the words or even what language it was. Someone, he guessed, was using a loudhailer to address the inhabitants of the site. It sounded as though it was about two football fields away. He moved on, carefully but quickly.

Then he saw another light, and this one was moving, probably fifty yards away up the rocky open area to his left. He froze again and then dropped to one knee. The light was a beam, and the beam wasn't pointed at him, so his NVD was not badly affected. The image darkened, but he could make out a human form. The human form wore a helmet and had a machine rifle slung over his shoulder. He wasn't attempting to hide. He walked confidently in the middle of the open space, swinging his flashlight, on a route that would take him between Carlos and himself.

Alex cautiously extracted the machine pistol from his pocket and slithered all the way down so that he was flat on the jungle floor. He realized then, as the man drew closer, that he was also talking in a loud voice. Alex could just make out the words:

"Jon? Jon? If you're hereabouts let's hear from you, buddy. I'm an American and we'd like to get you home, safe and sound. Listen, it's tough out here. Without help, on the run, you're going to die. Do yourself a favor, give us a shout, and all is forgiven. Jon?"

So they were out looking for Vasco. As the man came closer, swinging his powerful flashlight into the jungle on each side of him, Alex realized that he and Carlos were in danger. He worked his gun arm into a support position on his left hand. He put the Beretta into single shot mode. The paramilitary was about ten yards away, the sweep of his flashlight a lot closer than that. Where exactly was Carlos? Was there a crossfire risk? And anyway, was he going to wound or kill a man who was merely following orders?

As the beam of the flashlight came closer, making the image of the man more fuzzy because of bleed-through glare, Alex stopped breathing, everything suspended in a slow-moving instant of time.

The man stopped. Alex went cold, desperately computing how the situation could evolve. Then he saw that the beam of the flashlight had fallen away. The guy was just standing there, looking up into space. Then Alex understood. The guy was *listening*. His helmet was wired, and unlike Cárdenas, these guys would have no inhibitions about using wireless coms.

"You got tracking intel from the drone?" the paramilitary said, his voice aggrieved. "Why the hell didn't they say so sooner?" He listened again. "Sure it's difficult through the clouds, but Jesus..." He waited some more, turning his head. "And what makes us think they've got it right?" A short pause. "Okay, okay. Give me a bearing and corrections as I go. How fast is he moving?" The man listened. "Okay." He swung the flashlight up and into the jungle to his left, a point about two yards from where Alex was lying. "I'm under way. Keep me posted" He lumbered forward in a half-run, his boots crunching on the rain-wet vegetation.

Alex waited a couple of seconds and then got quickly to his feet and put the gun back in his pants pocket. He listened to the sounds of the man receding through the jungle. He went half a dozen paces forward to the point where the man had been standing and waved across the open space towards where he hoped that Carlos was hiding. Carlos jumped almost immediately into view and headed across the open space. Alex turned away and began tracking the path of the paramilitary agent. He couldn't see him, but his NVD picked up the glow of his flashlight through the trees. He had to keep moving quickly and it took Carlos a few minutes to catch up with him.

"You hear any of that?" Alex said quietly over his shoulder, as they continued to jog carefully forward.

"He's looking for Vasco, right?"

"Right. And it seems they've got drone surveillance, presumably using active infrared. So they could pick us up as well."

"*Comandante*, you certainly have a nose for trouble."

"Glad to be of service, *amigo*."

They kept going, Alex using one hand to steady the NVD and the other hand to fend off branches. They slowed a couple of times when the glow up ahead seemed to get nearer; the guy was probably doing some course corrections, Alex thought. His sense of direction told him that they were circling around the Mayan site, but also moving away from it. The fixed source of light he had picked up before had gone, although he could detect a faint glow coming off the clouds.

Up ahead the glow from the flashlight disappeared. He stopped. Carlos came up beside him. They exchanged a glance and then moved on slowly. A wash of light appeared ahead, obscuring the surrounding features of the jungle, telling them that the flashlight was now pointed back in their direction. They dropped flat.

Carlos said in his ear, "I'm going to circle round to the right."

"Agreed."

He watched Carlos crawl away with lizard-like twists of his body. The flashlight had moved on again as though the holder was going in a circle. Alex crawled forward. As the picture in his NVD returned to normal, he caught a glimpse of something up ahead, the outline of a small mound. He was startled by the sound of a raised voice.

"Jon? We know you're in there, buddy, and we know you've got to be pretty scared, and we understand that, but we're Americans, and we're on your side, so now is the time to act sensible. Come on out and we can save your life and get you home."

Alex judged the owner of the voice was the same man he had heard before, and that he was about fifteen yards away through the trees. All he could see was the glow of his flashlight on one side of the mound. The man had referred to himself in the plural, but Alex couldn't see any other source of light. Maybe another agent was on his way.

Alex pulled out the Beretta and began to inch his way forward. The damp twigs and branches on the jungle floor were not likely to make much noise, and small sounds were common; but he knew that anything above background level would get the man's attention, possibly prove disastrous. The man started speaking again, repeating his message, and Alex used the opportunity to gain a few feet. And there, along one particular sightline through the trees, the man became visible.

It was the same helmeted figure, standing, Alex now saw, close to a cave-like hole in the mound. Alex could make out a few more details of the mound itself, a couple of places on the sloping sides where rough agglomerations of masonry showed through the vegetation, as though at some point in the recent past it had been partially excavated.

"Jon," the man said, "we don't have a lot of time, so if you're not coming out, then I'm coming in. Just remember we're not going to harm you, we're going to get you home."

The man put his flashlight on the ground, pointing at the hole in the mound, and turned on a light on his helmet. He took hold of his rifle in both hands, raised the butt to his shoulder, sighted down it. He looked like he'd be using that rifle very soon, assuming he found someone inside the mound. Which meant, Alex thought, his chest tight, that he ought to shoot this guy in order to save Vasco. He raised his gun.

He heard the crash of a falling object to his left, and felt his heart kick in startled alarm. The man swung around, the light on his helmet strong enough to penetrate the trees and blind Alex's NVD for a split second. The image steadied and he saw the agent moving cautiously through the trees towards a point a few feet to his left. Alex tried to slither backwards and keep his gun in play. The agent shouted something, but hadn't seen him yet. Shoot him now, Alex thought.

A swift-moving shadow with black tubes sticking out of his eyes appeared behind the agent and leapt towards him and did something which Alex couldn't see. The agent fell without a sound. Alex felt a wave of nausea and then forced himself into action. He got up and stumbled forward through the trees.

"I'm going for Vasco," he said to Carlos as he went by.

"Okay. I'll watch for the others."

Alex pulled his flashlight out of his pocket and closed in on the dark hole in the mound. Please don't tell me we killed a man for nothing, he thought. He slackened the head harness and pulled off the NVD. No need to frighten the guy unduly. He turned on the flashlight and went through what he now saw was a stone-framed doorway. There was a short tunnel ahead with blackened walls.

"Jon, this is Alex Morales. We met in Houston." His voice echoed back at him from the darkness. "We dealt with the guys who were chasing you. So let's have a talk."

He went down the tunnel, which opened up into an empty space, dripping with damp. A fetid smell hit his nostrils. The floor seemed to consist of mounds of garbage. He swung his flashlight around. One of the mounds of garbage made a moaning sound and pointed a gun at him. He felt an incongruous sense of relief. A man hadn't died in vain.

He turned the flashlight around and held it out in front of him so that it illuminated his face. "Alex Morales, Jon. Remember? I can help you if you give me a chance."

He turned the flashlight again. Now he could see that he was looking at a very disturbed Jon Vasco. His eyes were wild and he was jabbing towards him with the gun.

"Back off!" he screamed. "You're like the others. Maybe you want to kill me too!"

Alex realized he was still holding his own gun in his right hand. He put it carefully in his pocket. "No. I want you to tell me what's happened to the virus. And to Cárdenas. And then I want you back in the United States to give evidence."

Vasco stared. "What's the point?" he wailed, shaking the gun backwards and forwards. "What's the point? They'll still kill me. They'll kill me before I can open my mouth!"

"No. We'll make sure that doesn't happen. There are a lot of people, including members of Congress, who will want to hear what you have to say."

Vasco let the gun drop as though it had become too heavy to keep aloft. "I'll never make it. I'll never make it out of this hellhole of a country."

"We'll get you out. That can be done." Alex took a careful step forward and squatted down on his haunches. "Jon, your only hope is with me. I think you know I'll give you a fair break. What I need to know right away is what's happened to the virus. Did you release it? A new version? Or did these cowboys destroy it? And what happened to Cárdenas?"

Vasco's agonies had turned inward. His head slumped. "Oh God oh God oh God."

"Jon. We're got zero spare time. These guys are still out there. I need to know now."

Vasco raised his eyes at last, looked at him for a moment, and then suddenly began talking very fast.

CHAPTER FORTY

When Antonio Cárdenas finally dragged himself from the water and tried to stand up, he fell over backwards with a clang as his air tanks hit the rocky shelf. He lay helpless for a moment, like a tortoise turned over on its shell. At last he freed himself from the harness and slid off the tanks. He lay stretched out, breathing pure air, for a time he couldn't quantify. It felt like five minutes, but when he raised his arm and looked at his watch in the light of the lamp it was already after half-past-three.

He sat up, momentarily confused. Had he gone to sleep? He turned to get up and felt the weight of the fins on his feet. He reached down and pulled them off, remembering the long underwater journey, the Americans shooting at him. What was happening now, back at the site? The Americans would have talked to people, trying to find out where he'd gone. But not even Vasco knew where the underground river surfaced, so how were they going to find that out in a hurry?

Antonio released the weight belt and hauled himself to his feet. He picked up the lamp. Drone surveillance wouldn't do much good, he thought. Even with infrared to get through the clouds, the drone had to know where to look. So it was surely as he had foreseen: once he'd escaped, they'd have a hard time picking up his trail.

He worked his way round the wall of the cavern, looking for the piece of rock, about nine inches across, that was bordered by a thin groove. He began to think he was on the wrong side of the cavern, but at last he found it, convincingly camouflaged by the surrounding creases in the limestone. He took a knife from his belt and worked the piece of rock loose. In the excavated space behind, he found the cache of things he had stored there ten days before: clothes, boots, a couple of good flashlights, an automatic pistol, and a lightweight backpack.

He sat down and peeled off his wetsuit. Only then, black and ominous in the light of the lamp, did he discover the blood low down on his right leg. He grabbed the wetsuit trousers and searched for the bullet hole. He found two bullet holes, close together: entry and exit. He put the lamp close to his leg: there it was, redder now in the light, an inch-and-a-half-long surface wound on the back of his calf. Wet with blood. And painful, he now realized.

He cursed. He hadn't thought of a first aid kit. He used his knife to cut a strip off the bottom of the shirt he was due to put on, and tied it tightly around the wound. It was a nuisance; but a minor nuisance; it wouldn't stop him doing what he had to do.

He got dressed in the shirt, camouflage pants, and boots. He flexed his leg: the pain was slight, easy to ignore. He put the flashlights and the gun in the pockets of his pants. Then he reached down and picked up the waterproof pouch and took out the three sealed packets. He examined them in the light from the underwater lamp. They looked in good condition; the release tab ready to be pulled. Kerim had done well. If he had the good luck to activate one in a confined and crowded space, there was nothing alarming in the packaging left behind; just the remains of a candy bar. He opened the backpack and put them inside and sealed it up.

He didn't feel any need to rethink his decision. Whatever Vasco said, three good test results were enough. The new virus was good to go. And before he died, God willing, he would find a way to launch it on the world.

CHAPTER FORTY-ONE

Alex was exhausted and in low spirits by the time he and Carlos hauled themselves up the rocky screed beside the river and into the cavern. He wasn't sure he believed Jon Vasco's story of Cárdenas's escape plan: Jon could get over-excited when explaining things, and traveling miles underwater seemed an unlikely feat for a middle-aged man; but he felt there was no choice but to take it at face valuc. After leaving Vasco with the others, they mollified Pancho with *más dinero* and set off with him at the fastest rate they could sustain. They reached the outflow cavern in just over two hours.

Too late, Alex thought, to catch Cárdenas, even if Vasco was telling the truth: the Mexican had started before them, and unless there were obstacles on the way, he would have done the trip in an hour or so. All the same, he was able to banish some of his intense fatigue when they found air tanks and a discarded wetsuit.

"Blood, *Señor,*" Pancho said behind them, his flashlight directed at a point on the rocky shelf close to the discarded wetsuit.

Alex picked up the wetsuit and began examining it carefully in the light of his flashlight. He found the pair of holes in the trouser leg and handed it over to Carlos.

"Well, well," Carlos said after a quick inspection, "it seems your American friends tried to kill him after all."

"A small wound, I believe," Pancho said, bent over and studying the rock shelf further along. "Blood in two places, no more."

"Pancho," Alex said, his tone facetious, "if you can find us a tracker dog in the next ten minutes, there's lots of *más dinero* for you." He looked at his watch, his mind already moving on. It was four-thirty-five. About half an hour to first light, according to Pancho. Their chances of catching their man were slipping rapidly away. If Cárdenas had some way of summoning help, a local man with a truck, he was already gone.

"I need maybe an hour," Pancho said.

Alex looked up. "What?"

"To find a dog."

"Is this true?"

"Maybe a little less. Dogs are common in our country."

Alex felt the exhaustion creeping over him, eroding the hope he knew he must sustain. Come on, *El Comandante*, he told himself; this is your show; only you can keep this going.

He took a one hundred dollar bill out of his pocket and handed it to Pancho. "I don't know whether you're serious, *amigo*, but anyway, go for the dog."

"And can the dog attack this man, *Señor*?"

"Yes. Of course. And you can stand on him as well. Carlos, let's you and I follow the script."

They went back outside the cavern. Pancho disappeared silently into the darkness. Alex and Carlos hurried along the river bank until they came to a place where a track emerged from the jungle. Alex pointed his flashlight at the river. The black water was moving quickly, but spread out in separate channels. He took his tablet out from under his shirt, and his gun from his pants pocket, and gave them to Carlos. Holding up his flashlight, he waded into the water. The current tugged at him, but his footing felt secure. He crossed and then crossed back again for his gun and his tablet.

"Remember," he said: "take the dirt road to the paved road and turn right."

"Got it. Last to Santa Elena buys the beer. And good luck, *Comandante*."

***

Alex struck his own course with the aid of his tablet and GPS. Alone, he felt that the near-hopeless challenge of finding Cárdenas was his personal responsibility, something that required faith, and he battered against the weariness of his body to push himself on more quickly through the resisting jungle. Cárdenas, they were assuming, had taken the direct route to the only paved road in the region, in search of transportation. Carlos, with luck, should end up two or three miles east of Cárdenas on that road; and he should end up two or three miles west of him. They should get him in a pincer movement. Except that the Mexican, probably, would be long gone.

Or maybe not. He had to keep the faith. It was early, even by local standards, and there would be hardly any traffic. Pancho didn't know when the first chicken bus would come along; but he also said that no one knew when the first chicken bus would come along; it was a variable schedule. People went down to the road and waited. And in spite of all that, they were always crowded.

He stopped, his flashlight pointing at a large colony of ants busy beneath the spines of a small palm tree. He should have made the connection earlier. A crowded bus: a lot of people in a confined space. If Tony had the idea of releasing the virus, instead of just escaping to fight another day, he would like the idea of a crowded bus.

He pulled out his tablet and checked his location and then blundered onwards, kicking out at recalcitrant tree-limbs, batting at leafy fronds.

He noticed at last that a faint light was accumulating overhead, and it seemed to him like the first favorable omen of the whole expedition. But also a reminder of passing time. Dawn was not far off. And chicken buses, like a lot of other things, would no doubt be more common in daylight.

He was able to put away his flashlight after a few minutes and concentrate on making good time. He broke clear of the jungle just as the light in the east stabilized behind the cloud cover and returned the world to normal. Beyond the drainage ditch was a paved road, winding away in both directions. After so many miles of jungle, it seemed like a miraculous manifestation of civilized life. He crossed the ditch and stood on the edge of the road looking in one direction and then the other. There was no traffic in sight.

He began walking east. A patch or two of pale blue sky appeared overhead. His clothes felt as though they were beginning to dry. His fatigue receded and his senses sharpened. There was still a chance; he should still take this seriously. He became aware of a small clearing up ahead; and back against the jungle, some kind of building. This was unexpected: there was no village marked on the map. He quickened his pace. As he came closer, he heard the hum of a generator in the background, and saw a sign attached to the wall of the shack. And two people sitting on a bench outside.

He slowed his pace, trying to assess this new situation. Number one, these people could give him information. Number two, if one of them was Tony Cárdenas he wouldn't know, because he didn't know what Cárdenas looked like. A very stupid omission.

But these two, he now saw, were a man and a woman, dressed in clothing typical of the local peasants, and younger, yes, definitely younger than Cárdenas. They were drinking something black from worn-looking mugs.

He went straight up to them. "*Hola*, *Señor*, *Señora*, how are you? I am a tourist from Nicaragua, as you see, walking…" He waved back the way he had come. "…but hoping perhaps to get a bus soon. Are you expecting one?"

They stared at him as though he had arrived from Mars. Alex wondered if the bulge in the thigh of his pants revealed itself too clearly as a gun, even though the butt was not visible. Or whether they didn't speak Spanish.

At last the man said, "Yes. A bus will come." The Spanish was slow, and accented, but understandable.

"Did a bus come by already? In either direction?" Alex pointed both ways along the road.

"No, *Señor*. Not since daylight."

"Thank you."

He hesitated after that. Ask about a Mexican stranger? Wait here for the bus? Or keep walking?

One thing he knew. Cárdenas would want to get on a bus. So the best way to find him was to be on the bus himself.

He waved goodbye to the couple, crossed to the south side of the road, and walked until the shack was obscured by trees. He hunkered down in the drainage ditch and listened for sounds of a bus. Slowly the sun appeared above the trees. He had to stand up several times and shake the fatigue out of his legs. A couple of heavy trucks went by, one in each direction. A pickup. A Land Rover. A tourist bus, sealed up and air-conditioned. A vintage Ford with fins. And then he heard the laboring grunt of an engine and he stood up to see a colorful old bus, hood sticking out at the front, luggage strapped to the railed roof, coming at him out of the west.

He flagged it down. There was no door at the front, just an opening and a couple of stairs. He got aboard, told the driver he wasn't going far, and gave him a five dollar bill. The driver gave him a look, an indifferent nod, and struggled with the gear lever. It went in place with a thump, and the bus gradually got going. Alex looked around. The worn seating was packed with native people, a few exhibiting flashes of woven color in their clothing, and baskets that possibly contained the chickens after which the buses were named. Several of the women were chatting to each other, but most of the rest were watching him silently. He decided to hang on to the pole near the front and watch the roadway. His heart was banging in his chest. Either they drove for a few miles and nothing happened, in which case that was it: failure; or they stopped.

They stopped. Alex got down off the bus and stared at the person boarding; it was a woman.

A couple of miles more and they stopped again. This time the person waiting to board was a man. A middle-aged man, slightly below average height. He wore rough cotton pants and shirt, stained by damp, and carried a small pack on his back. There was a look of wary intelligence in his eyes.

Alex used his prepared approach. "I am a government official, *Señor*, and I am required to search you before you get on the bus."

The other man weighed this up thoughtfully. He seemed calm. Alex had a sudden sense that all was known: this man was Tony Cárdenas; and this man knew that he was Alex Morales.

"For what reason?" the man said.

"The usual reason. Drugs. Please empty your pockets and hand over the backpack." As he spoke, he undid the button holding his gun in place in his pants pocket.

"I have no drugs, *Señor*. Perhaps you'd like some chocolate." The man took something that looked like a candy bar out of his shirt pocket and waved it in front of him.

"Put it on the ground," Alex said. "And everything else in your pockets." His attention was distracted by movement in the distance, further along the roadway: somebody and some kind of animal was crossing the road to the southern side. Carlos?

He looked back to see that the object the man was taking out of his pocket was a gun. He kicked out instinctively with his boot. Cárdenas, whom he was no longer in doubt that this was, was caught unawares. He got his gun out of range of the boot, but in doing so he skittered a few feet back down the slope of the ditch.

"Driver!" Alex yelled, turning towards the open platform of the bus. "Go! Go! This man is dangerous! Drive off!"

The driver was watching the encounter and he seemed to agree. He revved the engine and began working at his gear lever. Alex heard the sound of barking in the distance.

Cárdenas steadied himself and pointed the gun at Alex. Alex felt a ferocious kick in the ribs on his right side and fell over. The sound of a gunshot hung in the air as an afterthought. He was aware of the bus behind him beginning to move. He struggled to sit up and regain control. Cárdenas was approaching, totally focused, gun raised. Alex understood that his intention was to finish him off, permanently cancel the threat. He felt numb, nothing in his body working well enough to contrive a defense.

The barking of the dog was much closer, and it was the sound of an angry dog in full flight. Cárdenas turned towards the sound, hesitated, and suddenly ran towards the doorway of the slowly-moving bus. Alex climbed to his feet by an effort of will.

A dog the size of a Doberman was running full speed towards Cárdenas along the edge of the road, an excited bark escaping him every few yards. Just as the dog seemed about to reach him, Cárdenas leaped aboard the bus and grasped the rail and pulled himself up the step. The dog hadn't the courage to do the same. It trotted along beside the bus, barking furiously.

Alex found himself running as well. This was the last moment, the last chance. Daggers of pain shot up the side of his ribcage. The bus seemed not to be moving faster, perhaps because of the driver's uncertainty about his new passenger. He thought he could hear someone shouting. The dog was going to trip him up. He kicked out at it and it swerved. With a huge effort, he jumped for the bottom step, teetered there on unsteady feet, grabbed the side rail, fell forward up the step. He aborted the scream of pain that tore up into his mouth. He got his head up. Cárdenas was two-thirds of the way up the aisle of the bus. He had something in his hands, something brightly colored, like the candy bar he had offered him outside the bus.

The virus delivery mechanism. A perfect disguise.

Got to stop that, a voice seemed to shout in his head; got to stop that now. He twisted, maneuvered his right hand down to his thigh. Please, please, let me get this gun. Every twist of his body meant more pain. He got his hand on it at last, sneaked it out of his pocket, settled the butt into his palm. Got you, the voice inside him breathed. The driver was still driving, hoping to get god knows where, and the bumps in the road made the bus bounce gently on its hard springs. Alex got the gun out in front of him, his arm on the floor of the bus.

Cárdenas had both hands on the candy bar. His gun was somewhere else. He was trying to pull something on the candy bar.

"No, no," Alex cried out, but he wasn't sure he had made any noise. It had no effect on Cárdenas. The aisle was narrow, and Alex saw frightened faces on both sides. His Beretta swayed with every bump in the road. He had to shoot up. Cárdenas's head and part of his torso was above the level of the passengers' heads. He got his left hand under his right, levered the gun up and fired once. Cárdenas still there. Twice. Cárdenas still there. Three times. Cárdenas fell down.

The last thing Alex heard was the scream of the brakes as the driver finally decided to stop the bus.

CHAPTER FORTY-TWO

He woke up to the sound of macaws and a crushing pain in the right hand side of his chest. He was lying on his back and he could see the limbs of trees laced across a cloudy sky. The pain held him motionless, as though he was pinned down by a heavy weight, and his breathing was shallow. He tried swallowing. That worked okay, and to his relief he didn't taste any blood.

He remembered a few things after the shooting on the bus: people clustering around after he fell back out of the bus; the arrival of Carlos; Carlos and Pancho hoisting him through the jungle, one each side of him, his arms around their necks. He couldn't work out from the sky what time it was, but it was raining a little, so maybe it was afternoon. In which case, hours had gone by.

He tried raising his head. It hurt, but he got a glimpse of the surrounding jungle, and what seemed to be a river nearby. The next moment, someone was kneeling beside him. He blinked in astonishment. It was a very disheveled Jon Vasco. He rested his head back on its hard support. Vasco was still there, within sight, his face alight with anxiety and doubt.

"My God, you're awake. You're okay. Are you? Are you okay?"

Alex swallowed again. He tried speech. "What happened?" he croaked. "How did you..."

"How did I get here? The others brought me. Chico and Felipe. The guide, Pancho, showed up and brought us here. Wherever here is, I don't really know. Pancho has gone to get a doctor. How do you feel? You'll probably be okay. Do you want some water?"

"What about Carlos?"

"Gone. Also the others, Chico and Felipe, all gone. There's quite a complicated story I have to tell you about that. It's basically supposed to look like they left you to die. But you're probably not ready for all that. What can I do for you? There's a little food. Carlos said the bullet didn't puncture a lung because it hit square on to the rib. The rib is broken and probably painful but it didn't puncture a lung either. So you're very lucky. They bound it up and the bleeding isn't too bad. But of course you need drugs to stop infections. So we hope the doctor comes soon."

Alex stared up at the trees, breathing quietly. "What about the virus? What about Cárdenas?"

"Are you sure you're ready for all this?" Vasco's anxious face swung into view for a moment.

"Yes."

"Okay. Cárdenas is dead. And buried. That's what Carlos said. He gave everyone on the bus two hundred dollars and asked them not to talk about it. He told them that the dead man was a bad man who had tried to give them all a disease. Then he collected up the delivery canisters, the candy bar things, and he found one further back on the highway and one in Tony's pocket, and the one he tried to open. But it was still sealed. So nothing was released. Which was just as well, because the testing wasn't good enough. Anyway, we lit a fire and destroyed them. I promise you, believe me, I supervised it, I saw it happen. Carlos made me promise that I would work to prevent this kind of thing happening again. And I said I would. And that's the truth. He said I was supposed to get killed too. Both of us. Because his boss thought it was safer that way. You see what kind of people these are? Anything to do with drugs and people go nuts. They lose their humanity. You see what I wanted to do with this virus? But I was telling the truth, I'll help the government, I'll do my best, I can't go through this kind of thing again."

Alex concentrated on not breathing too fast, or too deeply, while he tried to evaluate what Vasco had said. Could it be true that Rojas wanted him dead? Feeling himself not too far from that condition, the simplicity of death now revealed to him, it seemed more than possible, it seemed likely. He knew too much about Pedro's organization. He had too many stories to tell. His usefulness was at an end. And these guys didn't waste much time on sentiment.

His mind drifted for a few moments. Ideas came and went. He could work it all out later. The main thing was that Carlos had deceived his boss in some way, pretended that he'd shot Morales and left him to die. Which proved something about Carlos, or humanity, that redeemed some portion of this situation. Possibly. But which still left some important things unresolved.

"Jon?"

"I'm here."

"Are you going to stay with me for a while?"

"Of course. As long as you need me. I have nowhere else to go."

"How are we going to live?"

"Pancho said he would take us to his home."

Of course, Alex thought, closing his eyes with a faint smile. *Más dinero*.

* * *

Pancho not only gave them a room in his home, and fed them, and got them a doctor, he also bought Alex a cell phone with a lot of pre-paid calls. After a few days Alex felt well enough to drive with Pancho to the outskirts of Santa Elena, where they was cell phone coverage. Alex was able to sit with only minor discomfort in the cab of Pancho's truck and make calls to the United States. He made contact with David Van Hoyle, and on his second outing in Pancho's truck he got to talk with Senator Bob Camilleri.

"My God, Alex. The first time you disappeared was bad enough, but this time... Will you believe me if I tell you I couldn't even concentrate on campaign finance? There was no clear news about anything. Not from the President, and obviously not from the scumbag who deputizes for him. I finally turned up an unconfirmed story that the cops tried to bring you in again on the drug charge. So, outright betrayal. Tell me you escaped safely and that you're okay."

"I'm okay, Senator. Yeah, the cops tried to grab me in New Brunswick, but I managed to outrun them. Sometimes it helps to know a few drug traffickers. I'm guessing that Pendleton decided to take me down while he still could."

"The son of a bitch is going down himself, Alex. This time around I'm not letting you down, I promise you that. In fact, I've got a big story to tell you. I got out there and flashed some senatorial muscle, and a couple of things fell into place. But before I get into that, tell me what you know about Cárdenas and the virus. The President isn't saying, and Jack is looking kind of nervy. I get the feeling he thinks the new virus is out there, and spreading, and that he might be heading for deep shit. Which he is, but not just because of the virus."

"I have good news on that, Senator. We got Cárdenas, and we prevented the release of the virus. Jon Vasco himself will you give his word on that. I won't tell you where we are just yet, but he's with me, and when it's safe, I'd like to bring him with me back to the United States. I think we can get him to testify."

The Senator made a noise like a rodeo cowboy bringing down a bullock. "Great news, Alex. That'll put the icing on the cake. Listen, can you give me some idea how you managed all this?"

Alex gave him a lightly censored account, and the Senator listened quietly.

"I look forward to getting the whole story from you in person, Alex, and believe it or not, that can happen as soon as you want. You're no longer a wanted man."

Alex looked out of the window of the truck and saw the jungle subtly transform itself: it was no longer a substitute for Nicaragua, but more like an unconvincing movie set. "Really? Are you sure?"

"Let me tell you about it. I talked with your lawyer, Beccy Adelstein, about your situation, determined that something positive, something outside the purview of our traitorous friend, should be done, and we decided to hit on the DIC Special Agent in Charge in Miami, Dan Meadows. It wasn't quite as much fun as our good cop, bad cop, routine with Faymi that time, but we showed him the Halder affidavit, and I also told him I would subpoena him to appear under oath before my Senate caucus, and what would happen to him then if he didn't level with us. And you know what, Alex? The fact that Halder was murdered, the fact that he respected him, the fact that the Vice President is an asshole, the fact that he's in a decent guy who felt bad about what happened to you... Well, it all added up. I didn't really need to push very hard. He gave us everything, the guy who planted the coke in your car, all the secondary details. We got it all in writing. It's solid, Alex. There's no chance a prosecutor will move against you with that kind of evidence available. And the really big thing, the hip, hip, hooray stuff, is that if you've got Vasco, and if we maybe lean on Linda a bit to pony up with what she heard at her dad's farm, and if I maybe have a word with the judge who denied you bail, well then, I think we can bring down the *real* bad guy. Anyway, bring him down enough that his political career is permanently damaged. Jack may be lucky that you stopped the release of the virus, but that's where it ends. The rest of his shenanigans are there on the record. And you know how good that makes me feel? Call it a politician's love of power. Or call it just desserts for a guy who tried to blackmail me into betraying my trusted servant, Alex Morales. Call it what you want, that cocksucker is going down."

***

A day later, his spirits revived, Alex got Pancho to take him once again to the outskirts of Santa Elena. This time he put through a call to Faymi.

"*Querida*, it's all over. I'm a free man, and I'm coming home."

"Are you sure? Are you sure it's safe?"

"Senator Camilleri says so, and I trust him. I'm coming home. And I'm coming to see you."

"Me? Your little *pobrecita*? *Alejo*, I've told you..."

"I know, I know, but I want to see you. I want to give you something. Will your father mind?"

"My dad? Why would he mind?"

"It depends what you told him about me. If anything."

"I told him the truth. I told him you were a professor at Rutgers."

"What did he say?"

"He said Harvard would be better, but if that's all I could come up with..."

His rib hurt, but for the first time in weeks, Alex began to laugh.

www.ingramcontent.com/pod-product-compliance
Lightning Source LLC
Chambersburg PA
CBHW051416170626
46809CB00006B/2181
9781914195495